SHORT STORIES
Twenty-One Stories
A Sense of Reality
May We Borrow Your Husband?

TRAVEL
Journey Without Maps
Another Mexico (The Lawless Roads) *
In Search of a Character

ESSAYS
Collected Essays

PLAYS
The Living Room
The Potting Shed
The Complaisant Lover
Carving a Statue
The Return of A. J. Raffles

AUTOBIOGRAPHY
A Sort of Life

BIOGRAPHY
Lord Rochester's Monkey

British title

Graham Greene

THE HUMAN FACTOR

Simon and Schuster · New York

Library of Congress Cataloging in Publication Data

Greene, Graham, date.
The human factor.

I. Title.

PZ3.G8319Hu   1978   [PR6013.R44]   823'.9'12   77-17169

ISBN 0-671-24085-4

A novel based on life in any Secret Service must necessarily contain a large element of fantasy, for a realistic description would almost certainly infringe some clause or other in some official secrets Act. Operation Uncle Remus is purely a product of the author's imagination (and I trust it will remain so), as are all the characters, whether English, African, Russian or Polish. All the same, to quote Hans Andersen, a wise author who also dealt in fantasy, "out of reality are our tales of imagination fashioned."

To my sister Elisabeth Dennys,
who cannot deny some responsibility

I only know that he who forms a tie is lost. The germ of corruption has entered into his soul.

—JOSEPH CONRAD

Part One

Chapter I

Castle, ever since he had joined the firm as a young recruit more than thirty years ago, had taken his lunch in a public house behind St. James's Street, not far from the office. If he had been asked why he lunched there, he would have referred to the excellent quality of the sausages; he might have preferred a different bitter from Watney's, but the quality of the sausages outweighed that. He was always prepared to account for his actions, even the most innocent, and he was always strictly on time.

So by the stroke of one he was ready to leave. Arthur Davis, his assistant, with whom he shared a room, departed for lunch punctually at twelve and returned, but often only in theory, one hour later. It was understood that, in case of an urgent telegram, Davis or himself must always be there to receive the decoding, but they both knew well that in the particular sub-division of their department nothing was ever really urgent. The difference in time between England and the various parts of Eastern

15

and Southern Africa, with which the two of them were concerned, was usually large enough—even when in the case of Johannesburg it was little more than an hour—for no one outside the department to worry about the delay in the delivery of a message: the fate of the world, Davis used to declare, would never be decided on their continent, however many embassies China or Russia might open from Addis Ababa to Conakry or however many Cubans landed. Castle wrote a memorandum for Davis: "If Zaire replies to No. 172 send copies to Treasury and FO." He looked at his watch. Davis was ten minutes late.

Castle began to pack his briefcase—he put in a note of what he had to buy for his wife at the cheese shop in Jermyn Street and of a present for his son to whom he had been disagreeable that morning (two packets of Maltesers), and a book, *Clarissa Harlowe*, in which he had never read further than Chapter LXXIX of the first volume. Directly he heard a lift door close and Davis's step in the passage he left his room. His lunchtime with the sausages had been cut by eleven minutes. Unlike Davis he always punctually returned. It was one of the virtues of age.

Arthur Davis in the staid office was conspicuous by his eccentricities. He could be seen now, approaching from the other end of the long white corridor, dressed as if he had just come from a rather horsy country weekend, or perhaps from the public enclosure of a racecourse. He wore a tweed sports jacket of a greenish overall color, and he displayed a scarlet spotted handkerchief in the breast pocket: he might have been attached in some way to a tote. But he was like an actor who has been miscast: when he tried to live up to the costume, he usually fumbled the part. If he looked in London as though he had arrived from the country, in the country when he visited Castle he was unmistakably a tourist from the city.

"Sharp on time as usual," Davis said with his habitual guilty grin.

"My watch is always a little fast," Castle said, apologizing for the criticism which he had not expressed. "An anxiety complex, I suppose."

"Smuggling out top secrets as usual?" Davis asked, making a playful pretense at seizing Castle's briefcase. His breath had a sweet smell: he was addicted to port.

"Oh, I've left all those behind for you to sell. You'll get a better price from your shady contacts."

"Kind of you, I'm sure."

"And then you're a bachelor. You need more money than a married man. I halve the cost of living . . ."

"Ah, but those awful leftovers," Davis said, "the joint remade into shepherd's pie, the dubious meatball. Is it worth it? A married man can't even afford a good port." He went into the room they shared and rang for Cynthia. Davis had been trying to make Cynthia for two years now, but the daughter of a major-general was after bigger game. All the same Davis continued to hope; it was always safer, he explained, to have an affair inside the department—it couldn't be regarded as a security risk, but Castle knew how deeply attached to Cynthia Davis really was. He had the keen desire for monogamy and the defensive humor of a lonely man. Once Castle had visited him in a flat, which he shared with two men from the Department of the Environment, over an antique shop not far from Claridge's—very central and W.1.

"You ought to come in a bit nearer," Davis had advised Castle in the overcrowded sitting-room where magazines of different tastes—the *New Statesman*, *Penthouse* and *Nature*—littered the sofa, and where the used glasses from someone else's party had been pushed into corners for the daily woman to find.

"You know very well what they pay us," Castle said, "and I'm married."

"A grave error of judgment."

"Not for me," Castle said, "I like my wife."

17

"And of course there's the little bastard," Davis went on. "I couldn't afford children and port as well."

"I happen to like the little bastard too."

Castle was on the point of descending the four stone steps into Piccadilly when the porter said to him, "Brigadier Tomlinson wants to see you, sir."

"Brigadier Tomlinson?"

"Yes. In room A.3."

Castle had only met Brigadier Tomlinson once, many years before, more years than he cared to count, on the day that he was appointed—the day he put his name to the Official Secrets Act, when the brigadier was a very junior officer, if he had been an officer at all. All he could remember of him was a small black moustache hovering like an unidentified flying object over a field of blotting paper, which was entirely white and blank, perhaps for security reasons. The stain of his signature after he had signed the Act became the only flaw on its surface, and that leaf was almost certainly torn up and sent to the incinerator. The Dreyfus case had exposed the perils of a wastepaper basket nearly a century ago.

"Down the corridor on the left, sir," the porter reminded him when he was about to take the wrong route.

"Come in, come in, Castle," Brigadier Tomlinson called. His moustache was now as white as the blotting paper, and with the years he had grown a small pot-belly under a double-breasted waistcoat—only his dubious rank remained constant. Nobody knew to what regiment he had formerly belonged, if such a regiment indeed existed, for all military titles in this building were a little suspect. Ranks might just be part of the universal cover. He said, "I don't think you know Colonel Daintry."

"No. I don't think . . . How do you do?"

Daintry, in spite of his neat dark suit and his hatchet face, gave a more genuine out-of-doors impression than Davis ever did. If Davis at his first appearance looked as though he would be at home in a bookmakers' compound, Daintry was unmistakably at home in the expensive enclosure or on a grouse moor. Castle enjoyed making lightning sketches of his colleagues: there were times when he even put them on to paper.

"I think I knew a cousin of yours at Corpus," Daintry said. He spoke agreeably, but he looked a little impatient; he probably had to catch a train north at King's Cross.

"Colonel Daintry," Brigadier Tomlinson explained, "is our new broom," and Castle noticed the way Daintry winced at the description. "He has taken over security from Meredith. But I'm not sure you ever met Meredith."

"I suppose you mean my cousin Roger," Castle said to Daintry. "I haven't seen him for years. He got a first in Greats. I believe he's in the Treasury now."

"I've been describing the setup here to Colonel Daintry," Brigadier Tomlinson prattled on, keeping strictly to his own wavelength.

"I took Law myself. A poor second," Daintry said. "You read History, I think?"

"Yes. A very poor third."

"At the House?"

"Yes."

"I've explained to Colonel Daintry," Tomlinson said, "that only you and Davis deal with the Top Secret cables as far as Section 6A is concerned."

"If you can call anything Top Secret in our section. Of course, Watson sees them too."

"Davis—he's a Reading University man, isn't he?" Daintry asked with what might have been a slight touch of disdain.

"I see you've been doing your homework."

"As a matter of fact I've just been having a talk with Davis himself."

"So that's why he was ten minutes too long over his lunch."

Daintry's smile resembled the painful reopening of a wound. He had very red lips, and they parted at the corners with difficulty. He said, "I talked to Davis about you, so now I'm talking to you about Davis. An open check. You must forgive the new broom, I have to learn the ropes," he added, getting confused among the metaphors. "One has to keep to the drill—in spite of the confidence we have in both of you, of course. By the way, *did* he warn you?"

"No. But why believe me? We may be in collusion."

The wound opened again a very little way and closed tight.

"I gather that politically he's a bit on the left. Is that so?"

"He's a member of the Labour Party. I expect he told you himself."

"Nothing wrong in that, of course," Daintry said. "And you . . .?"

"I have no politics. I expect Davis told you that too."

"But you sometimes vote, I suppose?"

"I don't think I've voted once since the war. The issues nowadays so often seem—well, a bit parish pump."

"An interesting point of view," Daintry said with disapproval. Castle could see that telling the truth this time had been an error of judgment, yet, except on really important occasions, he always preferred the truth. The truth can be double-checked. Daintry looked at his watch. "I won't keep you long. I have a train to catch at King's Cross."

"A shooting weekend?"

"Yes. How did you know?"

"Intuition," Castle said, and again he regretted his reply. It was always safer to be inconspicuous. There were times, which grew more frequent with every year, when he daydreamed of complete conformity, as a different character might have dreamt of making a dramatic century at Lord's.

"I suppose you noticed my gun-case by the door?"

"Yes," Castle said, who hadn't seen it until then, "that was the clue." He was glad to see that Daintry looked reassured.

Daintry explained, "There's nothing personal in all this, you know. Purely a routine check. There are so many rules that sometimes some of them get neglected. It's human nature. The regulation, for example, about not taking work out of the office . . ."

He looked significantly at Castle's briefcase. An officer and a gentleman would open it at once for inspection with an easy joke, but Castle was not an officer, nor had he ever classified himself as a gentleman. He wanted to see how far below the table the new broom was liable to sweep. He said, "I'm not going home. I'm only going out to lunch."

"You won't mind, will you . . .?" Daintry held out his hand for the briefcase. "I asked the same of Davis," he said.

"Davis wasn't carrying a briefcase," Castle said, "when I saw him."

Daintry flushed at his mistake. He would have felt a similar shame, Castle felt sure, if he had shot a beater. "Oh, it must have been that other chap," Daintry said. "I've forgotten his name."

"Watson?" the brigadier suggested.

"Yes, Watson."

"So you've even been checking our chief?"

"It's all part of the drill," Daintry said.

Castle opened his briefcase. He took out a copy of the *Berkhamsted Gazette*.

"What's this?" Daintry asked.

"My local paper. I was going to read it over lunch."

21

"Oh yes, of course. I'd forgotten. You live quite a long way out. Don't you find it a bit inconvenient?"

"Less than an hour by train. I need a house and a garden. I have a child, you see—and a dog. You can't keep either of them in a flat. Not with comfort."

"I notice you are reading *Clarissa Harlowe*? Like it?"

"Yes, so far. But there are four more volumes."

"What's this?"

"A list of things to remember."

"To remember?"

"My shopping list," Castle explained. He had written under the printed address of his house, 129 King's Road, "Two Maltesers. Half pound Earl Grey. Cheese—Wensleydale? or Double Gloucester? Yardley Pre-Shave Lotion."

"What on earth are Maltesers?"

"A sort of chocolate. You should try them. They're delicious. In my opinion better than Kit Kats."

Daintry said, "Do you think they would do for my hostess? I'd like to bring her something a little out of the ordinary." He looked at his watch. "Perhaps I could send the porter—there's just time. Where do you buy them?"

"He can get them at an ABC in the Strand."

"ABC?" Daintry asked.

"Aerated Bread Company."

"Aerated bread . . . what on earth . . .? Oh well, there isn't time to go into that. Are you sure those—teasers would do?"

"Of course, tastes differ."

"Fortnum's is only a step away."

"You can't get them there. They are very inexpensive."

"I don't want to seem niggardly."

"Then go for quantity. Tell him to get three pounds of them."

22

"What is the name again? Perhaps you would tell the porter as you go out."

"Is my check over then? Am I clear?"

"Oh yes. Yes. I told you it was purely formal, Castle."

"Good shooting."

"Thanks a lot."

Castle gave the porter the message. "Three pounds did 'e say?"

"Yes."

"Three pounds of Maltesers!"

"Yes."

"Can I take a pantechnicon?"

The porter summoned the assistant porter who was reading a girlie magazine. He said, "Three pounds of Maltesers for Colonel Daintry."

"That would be a hundred and twenty packets or thereabouts," the man said after a little calculation.

"No, no," Castle said, "it's not as bad as that. The weight, I think, is what he means."

He left them making their calculations. He was fifteen minutes late at the pub and his usual corner was occupied. He ate and drank quickly and calculated that he had made up three minutes. Then he bought the Yardley's at the chemist in St. James's Arcade, the Earl Grey at Jackson's, a Double Gloucester there too to save time, although he usually went to the cheese shop in Jermyn Street, but the Maltesers, which he had intended to buy at the ABC, had run out by the time he got there—the assistant told him there had been an unexpected demand, and he had to buy Kit Kats instead. He was only three minutes late when he rejoined Davis.

"You never told me they were having a check," he said.

"I was sworn to secrecy. Did they catch you with anything?"

"Not exactly."

"He did with me. Asked what I had in my macintosh pocket. I'd got that report from 59800. I wanted to read it again over my lunch."

"What did he say?"

"Oh, he let me go with a warning. He said rules were made to be kept. To think that fellow Blake (whatever did he want to escape for?) got forty years freedom from income tax, intellectual strain and responsibility, and it's we who suffer for it now."

"Colonel Daintry wasn't very difficult," Castle said. "He knew a cousin of mine at Corpus. That sort of thing makes a difference."

Chapter II

Castle was usually able to catch the six-thirty-five
train from Euston. This brought him to Berkhamsted
punctually at seven twelve. His bicycle waited for him at
the station—he had known the ticket collector for many
years and he always left it in his care. Then he rode the
longer way home, for the sake of exercise—across the
canal bridge, past the Tudor school, into the High Street,
past the gray flint parish church which contained the helmet of a crusader, then up the slope of the Chilterns toward his small semi-detached house in King's Road. He
always arrived there, if he had not telephoned a warning
from London, by half-past seven. There was just time to
say goodnight to the boy and have a whisky or two before
dinner at eight.

In a bizarre profession anything which belongs to an
everyday routine gains great value—perhaps that was one
reason why, when he came back from South Africa, he

chose to return to his birthplace: to the canal under the weeping willows, to the school and the ruins of a once-famous castle which had withstood a siege by Prince John of France and of which, so the story went, Chaucer had been a Clerk of Works and—who knows?—perhaps an ancestral Castle one of the artisans. It consisted now of only a few grass mounds and some yards of flint wall, facing the canal and the railway line. Beyond was a long road leading away from the town bordered with hawthorn hedges and Spanish chestnut trees until one reached at last the freedom of the Common. Years ago the inhabitants of the town fought for their right to graze cattle upon the Common, but in the twentieth century it was doubtful whether any animal but a rabbit or a goat could have found provender among the ferns, the gorse and the bracken.

When Castle was a child there still remained on the Common the remnants of old trenches dug in the heavy red clay during the first German war by members of the Inns of Court OTC, young lawyers who practiced there before they went to die in Belgium or France as members of more orthodox units. It was unsafe to wander there without proper knowledge, since the old trenches had been dug several feet deep, modeled on the original trenches of the Old Contemptibles around Ypres, and a stranger risked a sudden fall and a broken leg. Children who had grown up with the knowledge of their whereabouts wandered freely, until the memory began to fade. Castle for some reason had always remembered, and sometimes on his days off from the office he took Sam by the hand and introduced him to the forgotten hiding-places and the multiple dangers of the Common. How many guerrilla campaigns he had fought there as a child against overwhelming odds. Well, the days of the guerrilla had returned, daydreams had become realities. Living thus with the long familiar he felt the security that an old lag feels when he goes back to the prison he knows.

Castle pushed his bicycle up King's Road. He had bought his house with the help of a building society after his return to England. He could easily have saved money by paying cash, but he had no wish to appear different from the schoolmasters on either side—on the salary they earned there was no possibility of saving. For the same reason he kept the rather gaudy stained glass of the Laughing Cavalier over the front door. He disliked it; he associated it with dentistry—so often stained glass in provincial towns hides the agony of the chair from outsiders—but again because his neighbors bore with theirs, he preferred to leave it alone. The schoolmasters in King's Road were strong upholders of the aesthetic principles of North Oxford, where many of them had taken tea with their tutors, and there too, in the Banbury Road, his bicycle would have fitted well, in the hall, under the staircase.

He opened his door with a Yale key. He had once thought of buying a mortise lock or something very special chosen in St. James's Street from Chubb's, but he restrained himself—his neighbors were content with Yale, and there had been no burglary nearer than Boxmoor in the last three years to justify him. The hall was empty; so seemed the sitting room, which he could see through the open door: there was not a sound from the kitchen. He noticed at once that the whisky bottle was not standing ready by the siphon on the sideboard. The habit of years had been broken and Castle felt anxiety like the prick of an insect. He called, "Sarah," but there was no reply. He stood just inside the hall door, beside the umbrella stand, taking in with rapid glances the familiar scene, with the one essential missing—the whisky bottle—and he held his breath. He had always, since they came, felt certain

27

that one day a doom would catch up with them, and he knew that when that happened he must not be betrayed by panic: he must leave quickly, without an attempt to pick up any broken piece of their life together. "Those that are in Judea must take refuge in the mountains . . ." He thought for some reason of his cousin at the Treasury, as though he were an amulet, which could protect him, a lucky rabbit's foot, and then he was able to breathe again with relief, hearing voices on the floor above and the footsteps of Sarah as she came down the stairs.

"Darling, I didn't hear you. I was talking to Doctor Barker."

Doctor Barker followed her—a middle-aged man with a flaming strawberry mark on his left cheek, dressed in dusty gray, with two fountain pens in his breast pocket; or perhaps one of them was a pocket torch for peering into throats.

"Is anything wrong?"

"Sam's got measles, darling."

"He'll do all right," Doctor Barker said. "Just keep him quiet. Not too much light."

"Will you have a whisky, Doctor?"

"No, thank you. I have still two more visits to make and I'm late for dinner as it is."

"Where could he have caught it?"

"Oh, there's quite an epidemic. You needn't worry. It's only a light attack."

When the doctor had gone Castle kissed his wife. He ran his hand over her black resistant hair; he touched her high cheekbones. He felt the black contours of her face as a man might who has picked out one piece of achieved sculpture from all the hack carvings littering the steps of a hotel for white tourists; he was reassuring himself that what he valued most in life was still safe. By the end of a day he always felt as though he had been gone for years leaving her defenseless. Yet no one here minded her African blood. There was no law here to menace their life together. They were secure—or as secure as they would ever be.

"What's the matter?" she asked.

"I was worried. Everything seemed at sixes and sevens tonight when I came in. You weren't here. Not even the whisky . . ."

"What a creature of habit you are."

He began to unpack his briefcase while she prepared the whisky. "Is there really nothing to worry about?" Castle asked. "I never like the way doctors speak, especially when they are reassuring."

"Nothing."

"Can I go and see him?"

"He's asleep now. Better not wake him. I gave him an aspirin."

He put Volume One of *Clarissa Harlowe* back in the bookcase.

"Finished it?"

"No, I doubt whether I ever shall now. Life's a bit too short."

"But I thought you always liked long books."

"Perhaps I'll have a go at *War and Peace* before it's too late."

"We haven't got it."

"I'm going to buy a copy tomorrow."

She had carefully measured out a quadruple whisky by English pub standards, and now she brought it to him and closed the glass in his hand, as though it were a message no one else must read. Indeed, the degree of his drinking was known only to them: he usually drank nothing stronger than beer when he was with a colleague or even with a stranger in a bar. Any touch of alcoholism might always be regarded in his profession with suspicion. Only Davis had the indifference to knock the drinks back with a fine abandon, not caring who saw him, but

29

then he had the audacity which comes from a sense of complete innocence. Castle had lost both audacity and innocence forever in South Africa while he was waiting for the blow to fall.

"You don't mind, do you," Sarah asked, "if it's a cold meal tonight? I was busy with Sam all evening."

"Of course not."

He put his arm round her. The depth of their love was as secret as the quadruple measure of whisky. To speak of it to others would invite danger. Love was a total risk. Literature had always so proclaimed it. Tristan, Anna Karenina, even the lust of Lovelace—he had glanced at the last volume of *Clarissa*. "I like my wife" was the most he had ever said even to Davis.

"I wonder what I would do without you," Castle said.

"Much the same as you are doing now. Two doubles before dinner at eight."

"When I arrived and you weren't here with the whisky, I was scared."

"Scared of what?"

"Of being left alone. Poor Davis," he added, "going home to nothing."

"Perhaps he has a lot more fun."

"This is my fun," he said. "A sense of security."

"Is life outside as dangerous as all that?" She sipped from his glass and touched his mouth with lips which were wet with J & B. He always bought J & B because of its color—a large whisky and soda looked no stronger than a weak one of another brand.

The telephone rang from the table by the sofa. He lifted the receiver and said "Hello," but no one replied. "Hello." He silently counted four, then put the receiver down when he heard the connection break.

"Nobody?"

"I expect it was a wrong number."

"It's happened three times this month. Always when

you are late at the office. You don't think it could be a burglar checking up to see if we are at home?"

"There's nothing worth a burglary here."

"One reads such horrible stories, darling—men with stockings over their faces. I hate the time after sunset before you come home."

"That's why I bought you Buller. Where *is* Buller?"

"He's in the garden eating grass. Something has upset him. Anyway, you know what he's like with strangers. He fawns on them."

"He might object to a stocking mask all the same."

"He would think it was put on to please him. You remember at Christmas . . . with the paper hats . . ."

"I'd always thought before we got him that boxers were fierce dogs."

"They are—with cats."

The door creaked and Castle turned quickly: the square black muzzle of Buller pushed the door fully open, and then he launched his body like a sack of potatoes at Castle's fly. Castle fended him off. "Down, Buller, down." A long ribbon of spittle descended Castle's trouser leg. He said, "If that's fawning, any burglar would run a mile." Buller began to bark spasmodically and wriggle his haunches, like a dog with worms, moving backward toward the door.

"Be quiet, Buller."

"He only wants a walk."

"At this hour? I thought you said he was ill."

"He seems to have eaten enough grass."

"Be quiet, Buller, damn you. No walk."

Buller slumped heavily down and dribbled onto the parquet to comfort himself.

"The meter man was scared of him this morning, but Buller only meant to be friendly."

"But the meter man knows him."

"This one was new."

31

"New. Why?"

"Oh, our usual man has got the flu."

"You asked to see his card?"

"Of course. Darling, are *you* getting scared of burglars now? Stop it, Buller. Stop." Buller was licking his private parts with the gusto of an alderman drinking soup.

Castle stepped over him and went into the hall. He examined the meter carefully, but there seemed nothing unusual about it, and he returned.

"You *are* worried about something?"

"It's nothing really. Something happened at the office. A new security man throwing his weight about. It irritated me—I've been more than thirty years in the firm, and I ought to be trusted by this time. They'll be searching our pockets next when we leave for lunch. He *did* look in my briefcase."

"Be fair, darling. It's not their fault. It's the fault of the job."

"It's too late to change that now."

"Nothing's ever too late," she said, and he wished he could believe her. She kissed him again as she went past him to the kitchen to fetch the cold meat.

When they were sitting down and he had taken another whisky, she said, "Joking apart, you *are* drinking too much."

"Only at home. No one sees me but you."

"I didn't mean for the job. I meant for your health. I don't care a damn about the job."

"No?"

"A department of the Foreign Office. Everyone knows what that means, but you have to go around with your mouth shut like a criminal. If you told me—me, your wife—what you'd done today, they'd sack you. I wish they would sack you. What *have* you done today?"

"I've gossiped with Davis, I've made notes on a few cards, I sent off one telegram—oh, and I've been interviewed by that new security officer. He knew my cousin when he was at Corpus."

"Which cousin?"

"Roger."

"That snob in the Treasury?"

"Yes."

On the way to bed, he said, "Could I look in on Sam?"

"Of course. But he'll be fast asleep by now."

Buller followed them and laid a bit of spittle like a bonbon on the bedclothes.

"Oh, Buller."

He wagged what remained of his tail as though he had been praised. For a boxer he was not intelligent. He had cost a lot of money and perhaps his pedigree was a little too perfect.

The boy lay asleep diagonally in his teak bunk with his head on a box of lead soldiers instead of a pillow. One black foot hung out of the blankets altogether and an officer of the Tank Corps was wedged between his toes. Castle watched Sarah rearrange him, picking out the officer and digging out a parachutist from under a thigh. She handled his body with the carelessness of an expert, and the child slept solidly on.

"He looks very hot and dry," Castle said.

"So would you if you had a temperature of 103." He looked more African than his mother, and the memory of a famine photograph came to Castle's mind—a small corpse spread-eagled on desert sand, watched by a vulture.

"Surely that's very high."

"Not for a child."

He was always amazed by her confidence: she could make a new dish without referring to any cookbook, and nothing ever came to pieces in her hands. Now she rolled the boy roughly on his side and firmly tucked him in, without making an eyelid stir.

"He's a good sleeper."

"Except for nightmares."

"Has he had another?"

"Always the same one. We both of us go off by train and he's left alone. On the platform someone—he doesn't know who—grips his arm. It's nothing to worry about. He's at the age for nightmares. I read somewhere that they come when school begins to threaten. I wish he hadn't got to go to prep school. He may have trouble. Sometimes I almost wish you had apartheid here too."

"He's a good runner. In England there's no trouble if you are good at any sort of games."

In bed that night she woke from her first sleep and said, as though the thought had occurred to her in a dream, "It's strange, isn't it, your being so fond of Sam."

"Of course I am. Why not? I thought you were asleep."

"There's no 'of course' about it. A little bastard."

"That's what Davis always calls him."

"Davis? He doesn't know?" she asked with fear. "Surely he doesn't know?"

"No, don't worry. It's the word he uses for any child."

"I'm glad his father's six feet underground," she said.

"Yes. So am I, poor devil. He might have married you in the end."

"No. I was in love with you all the time. Even when I started Sam I was in love with you. He's more your child than his. I tried to think of you when he made love. He was a tepid sort of fish. At the University they called him an Uncle Tom. Sam won't be tepid, will he? Hot or cold, but not tepid."

"Why are we talking about all that ancient history?"

"Because Sam's ill. And because you are worried. When I don't feel secure I remember what it felt like when I knew I had to tell you about him. That first night across the border in Lourenço Marques. The Hotel Polana. I thought, 'He'll put on his clothes again and go

34

away forever.' But you didn't. You stayed. And we made love in spite of Sam inside."

They lay quietly together, all these years later, only a shoulder touching a shoulder. He wondered whether this was how the happiness of old age, which he had sometimes seen on a stranger's face, might come about, but he would be dead long before she reached old age. Old age was something they would never be able to share.

"Aren't you ever sad," she asked, "that we haven't made a child?"

"Sam's enough of a responsibility."

"I'm not joking. Wouldn't you have liked a child of ours?"

This time he knew that the question was one of those which couldn't be evaded.

"No," he said.

"Why not?"

"You want to look under stones too much, Sarah. I love Sam because he's yours. Because he's not mine. Because I don't have to see anything of myself there when I look at him. I see only something of you. I don't want to go on and on forever. I want the buck to stop here."

Chapter III

1

"A good morning's sport," Colonel Daintry remarked halfheartedly to Lady Hargreaves as he stamped the mud off his boots before entering the house. "The birds were going over well." His fellow guests piled out of cars behind him, with the forced joviality of a football team trying to show their keen sporting enjoyment and not how cold and muddy they really felt.

"Drinks are waiting," Lady Hargreaves said. "Help yourselves. Lunch in ten minutes."

Another car was climbing the hill through the park, a long way off. Somebody bellowed with laughter in the cold wet air, and someone cried, "Here's Buffy at last. In time for lunch, of course."

"And your famous steak-and-kidney pudding?" Daintry asked. "I've heard so much about it."

"My pie, you mean. Did you really have a good morning, Colonel?" Her voice had a faint American accent—the more agreeable for being faint, like the tang of an expensive perfume.

"Not many pheasants," Daintry said, "but otherwise very fine."

"Harry," she called over his shoulder, "Dicky" and then "Where's Dodo? Is he lost?" Nobody called Daintry by his first name because nobody knew it. With a sense of loneliness he watched the graceful elongated figure of his hostess limp down the stone steps to greet "Harry" with a kiss on both cheeks. Daintry went on alone into the dining room where the drinks stood waiting on the buffet.

A little stout rosy man in tweeds whom he thought he had seen somewhere before was mixing himself a dry martini. He wore silver-rimmed spectacles which glinted in the sunlight. "Add one for me," Daintry said, "if you are making them really dry."

"Ten to one," the little man said. "A whiff of the cork, eh? Always use a scent spray myself. You are Daintry, aren't you? You've forgotten me. I'm Percival. I took your blood pressure once."

"Oh yes. Doctor Percival. We're in the same firm more or less, aren't we?"

"That's right. C wanted us to get together quietly—no need for all that nonsense with scramblers here. I can never make mine work, can you? The trouble is, though, that I don't shoot. I only fish. This your first time here?"

"Yes. When did you arrive?"

"A bit early. Around midday. I'm a Jaguar fiend. Can't go at less than a hundred."

37

Daintry looked at the table. A bottle of beer stood by every place. He didn't like beer, but for some reason beer seemed always to be regarded as suitable for a shoot. Perhaps it went with the boyishness of the occasion like ginger beer at Lord's. Daintry was not boyish. A shoot to him was an exercise of strict competitive skill—he had once been runner-up for the King's Cup. Now down the center of the table stood small silver sweet bowls which he saw contained his Maltesers. He had been a little embarrassed the night before when he had presented almost a crate of them to Lady Hargreaves; she obviously hadn't an idea what they were or what to do with them. He felt that he had been deliberately fooled by that man Castle. He was glad to see they looked more sophisticated in silver bowls than they had done in plastic bags.

"Do you like beer?" he asked Percival.

"I like anything alcoholic," Percival said, "except Fernet-Branca," and then the boys burst boisterously in— Buffy and Dodo, Harry and Dicky and all the silver and the glasses vibrated with joviality. Daintry was glad Percival was there, for nobody seemed to know Percival's first name either.

Unfortunately he was separated from him at table. Percival had quickly finished his first bottle of beer and begun on a second. Daintry felt betrayed, for Percival seemed to be getting on with his neighbors as easily as if they had been members of the old firm too. He had begun to tell a fishing story which had made the man called Dicky laugh. Daintry was sitting between the fellow he took to be Buffy and a lean elderly man with a lawyer's face. He had introduced himself, and his surname was familiar. He was either the Attorney-General or the Solicitor-General, but Daintry couldn't remember which; his uncertainty inhibited conversation.

Buffy said suddenly, "My God, if those are not Maltesers!"

"You know Maltesers?" Daintry asked.

"Haven't tasted one for donkey's years. Always bought them at the movies when I was a kid. Taste wonderful. There's no movie house around here surely?"

"As a matter of fact I brought them from London."

"You go to the movies? Haven't been to one in ten years. So they still sell Maltesers?"

"You can buy them in shops too."

"I never knew that. Where did you find them?"

"In an ABC."

"ABC?"

Daintry repeated dubiously what Castle had said, "Aerated Bread Company."

"Extraordinary! What's aerated bread?"

"I don't know," Daintry said.

"The things they do invent nowadays. I wouldn't be surprised, would you, if their loaves were made by computers?" He leaned forward and took a Malteser and crackled it at his ear like a cigar.

Lady Hargreaves called down the table, "Buffy! Not before the steak-and-kidney pie."

"Sorry, my dear. Couldn't resist. Haven't tasted one since I was a kid." He said to Daintry, "Extraordinary things computers. I paid 'em a fiver once to find me a wife."

"You aren't married?" Daintry asked, looking at the gold ring Buffy wore.

"No. Always keep that on for protection. Wasn't really serious, you know. Like to try out new gadgets. Filled up a form as long as your arm. Qualifications, interests, profession, what have you." He took another Malteser. "Sweet tooth," he said. "Always had it."

"And did you get any applicants?"

"They sent me along a girl. Girl! Thirty-five if a day. I had to give her tea. Haven't had tea since my mum died. I said, 'My dear, do you mind if we make it a whisky? I

39

know the waiter here. He'll slip us one.' She said she didn't drink. Didn't drink!"

"The computer had slipped up?"

"She had a degree in Economics at London University. And big spectacles. Flat-chested. She said she was a good cook. I said I always took my meals at White's."

"Did you ever see her again?"

"Not to speak to, but once she waved to me from a bus as I was coming down the club steps. Embarrassing! Because I was with Dicky at the time. That's what happened when they let buses go up St. James's Street. No one was safe."

After the steak-and-kidney pie came a treacle tart and a big Stilton cheese and Sir John Hargreaves circulated the port. There was a faint feeling of unrest at the table as though the holidays had been going on too long. People began to glance through the windows at the gray sky: in a few hours the light would fail. They drank their port rapidly as if with a sense of guilt—they were not really there for idle pleasure—except Percival, who wasn't concerned. He was telling another fishing story and had four empty bottles of beer beside him.

The Solicitor-General—or was it the Attorney-General?—said heavily, "We ought to be moving. The sun's going down." He certainly was not here for enjoyment, only for execution, and Daintry sympathized with his anxiety. Hargreaves really ought to make a move, but Hargreaves was almost asleep. After years in the Colonial Service—he had once been a young District Commissioner on what was then the Gold Coast—he had acquired the knack of snatching his siesta in the most unfavorable circumstances, even surrounded by quarreling chiefs, who used to make more noise than Buffy.

"John," Lady Hargreaves called down the table, "wake up."

He opened blue serene unshockable eyes and said,

"A catnap." It was said that as a young man somewhere in Ashanti he had inadvertently eaten human flesh, but his digestion had not been impaired. According to the story he had told the Governor, "I couldn't really complain, sir. They were doing me a great honor by inviting me to take pot luck."

"Well, Daintry," he said. "I suppose it's time we got on with the massacre."

He unrolled himself from the table and yawned. "Your steak-and-kidney pie, dear, is *too* good."

Daintry watched him with envy. He envied him in the first place for his position. He was one of the very few men outside the services ever to have been appointed C. No one in the firm knew why he had been chosen—all kinds of recondite influences had been surmised, for his only experience of intelligence had been gained in Africa during the war. Daintry also envied him his wife; she was so rich, so decorative, so impeccably American. An American marriage, it seemed, could not be classified as a foreign marriage: to marry a foreigner special permission had to be obtained and it was often refused, but to marry an American was perhaps to confirm the special relationship. He wondered all the same whether Lady Hargreaves had been positively vetted by MI5 and been passed by the FBI.

"Tonight," Hargreaves said, "we'll have a chat, Daintry, won't we? You and I and Percival. When this crowd has gone home."

2

Sir John Hargreaves limped round, handing out cigars, pouring out whiskies, poking the fire. "I don't enjoy shooting much myself," he said. "Never used to shoot in Africa, except with a camera, but my wife likes all the old English customs. If you have land, she says, you must have birds. I'm afraid there weren't enough pheasants, Daintry."

"I had a very good day," Daintry said, "all in all."

"I wish you ran to a trout stream," Doctor Percival said.

"Oh yes, fishing's your game, isn't it? Well, you might say we've got a bit of fishing on hand now." He cracked a log with his poker. "Useless," he said, "but I love to see the sparks fly. There seems to be a leak somewhere in Section 6."

Percival said, "At home or in the field?"

"I'm not sure, but I have a nasty feeling that it's here at home. In one of the African sections—6A."

"I've just finished going through Section 6," Daintry said. "Only a routine run-through. So as to get to know people."

"Yes, so they told me. That's why I asked you to come here. Enjoyed having you for the shoot too, of course. Did anything strike you?"

"Security's got a bit slack. But that's true of all other sections too. I made a rough check for example of what people take out in their briefcases at lunchtime. Nothing serious, but I was surprised at the number of briefcases . . . It's a warning, that's all, of course. But a warning might scare a nervous man. We can't very well ask them to strip."

42

"They do that in the diamond fields, but I agree that in the West End stripping would seem a bit unusual."

"Anyone really out of order?" Percival asked.

"Not seriously. Davis in 6A was carrying a report—said he wanted to read it over lunch. I warned him, of course, and made him leave it behind with Brigadier Tomlinson. I've gone through all the traces too. Vetting has been done very efficiently since the Blake case broke, but we still have a few men who were with us in the bad old days. Some of them even go back as far as Burgess and Maclean. We *could* start tracing them all over again, but it's difficult to pick up a cold scent."

"It's possible, of course, just possible," C said, "that the leak came from abroad and that the evidence has been planted here. They would like to disrupt us, damage morale and hurt us with the Americans. The knowledge that there was a leak, if it became public, could be more damaging than the leak itself."

"That's what I was thinking," Percival said. "Questions in Parliament. All the old names thrown up—Vassall, the Portland affair, Philby. But if they're after publicity, there's little we can do."

"I suppose a Royal Commission would be appointed to shut the stable door," Hargreaves said. "But let's assume for a moment that they are really after information and not scandal. Section 6 seems a most unlikely department for that. There are no atomic secrets in Africa: guerrillas, tribal wars, mercenaries, petty dictators, crop failures, building scandals, gold beds, nothing very secret there. That's why I wonder whether the motive may be simply scandal, to prove they have penetrated the British Secret Service yet again."

"Is it an important leak, C?" Percival asked.

"Call it a very small drip, mainly economic, but the interesting thing is that apart from economics it concerns the Chinese. Isn't it possible—the Russians are such nov-

43

ices in Africa—that they want to make use of our service for information on the Chinese?"

"There's precious little they can learn from us," Percival said.

"But you know what it's always like at everybody's Center. One thing no one can ever stand there is a blank white card."

"Why don't we send them carbon copies, with our compliments, of what we send the Americans? There's supposed to be a *détente*, isn't there? Save everyone a lot of trouble." Percival took a little tube from his pocket and sprayed his glasses, then wiped them with a clean white handkerchief.

"Help yourself to the whisky," C said. "I'm too stiff to move after that bloody shoot. Any ideas, Daintry?"

"Most of the people in Section 6 are post-Blake. If their traces are unreliable then no one is safe."

"All the same, the source seems to be Section 6—and probably 6A. Either at home or abroad."

"The head of Section 6, Watson, is a relative newcomer," Daintry said. "He was very thoroughly vetted. Then there's Castle—he's been with us a very long time, we brought him back from Pretoria seven years ago because they needed him in 6A, and there were personal reasons too—trouble about the girl he wanted to marry. Of course he belongs to the slack vetting days, but I'd say he was clear. Dullish man, first-class, of course, with files—it's generally the brilliant and ambitious who are dangerous. Castle is safely married, second time, his first wife's dead. There's one child, a house on mortgage in Metroland. Life insurance—payments up to date. No high living. He doesn't even run to a car. I believe he bicycles every day to the station. A third class in history at the House. Careful and scrupulous. Roger Castle in the Treasury is his cousin."

"You think he's quite clear then?"

44

"He has his eccentricities, but I wouldn't say dangerous ones. For instance he suggested I bring those Maltesers to Lady Hargreaves."

"Maltesers?"

"It's a long story. I won't bother you with it now. And then there's Davis. I don't know that I'm quite so happy about Davis, in spite of the positive vetting."

"Pour me out another whisky, would you, Percival, there's a good chap. Every year I say it's my last shoot."

"But those steak-and-kidney pies of your wife's are wonderful. I wouldn't miss them," Percival said.

"I daresay we could find another excuse for them."

"You could try putting trout in that stream . . ."

Daintry again experienced a twitch of envy; once more he felt left out. He had no life in common with his companions in the world outside the borders of security. Even as a gun he felt professional. Percival was said to collect pictures, and C? A whole social existence had been opened up for him by his rich American wife. The steak-and-kidney pie was all that Daintry was permitted to share with them outside office hours—for the first and perhaps the last time.

"Tell me more about Davis," C said.

"Reading University. Mathematics and physics. Did some of his military service at Aldermaston. Never supported—anyway openly—the marchers. Labour Party, of course."

"Like forty-five percent of the population," C said.

"Yes, yes, of course, but all the same . . . He's a bachelor. Lives alone. Spends fairly freely. Fond of vintage port. Bets on the tote. That's a classic way, of course, of explaining why you can afford . . ."

"What does he afford? Besides port."

"Well, he has a Jaguar."

"So have I," Percival said. "I suppose we mustn't ask you how the leak was discovered?"

45

"I wouldn't have brought you here if I couldn't tell you that. Watson knows, but no one else in Section 6. The source of information is an unusual one—a Soviet defector who remains in place."

"Could the leak come from Section 6 abroad?" Daintry asked.

"It could, but I doubt it. It's true that one report they had seemed to come direct from Lourenço Marques. It was word for word as 69300 wrote it. Almost like a photostat of the actual report, so one might have thought that the leak was there if it weren't for a few corrections and deletions. Inaccuracies which could only have been spotted here by comparing the report with the files."

"A secretary?" Percival suggested.

"Daintry began his check with those, didn't you? They are more heavily vetted than anyone. That leaves us Watson, Castle and Davis."

"A thing that worries me," Daintry said, "is that Davis was the one who was taking a report out of the office. One from Pretoria. No apparent importance, but it did have a Chinese angle. He said he wanted to reread it over lunch. He and Castle had got to discuss it later with Watson. I checked the truth of that with Watson."

"What do you suggest we do?" C asked.

"We could put down a maximum security check with the help of 5 and Special Branch. On everyone in Section 6. Letters, telephone calls, bug flats, watch movements."

"If things were as simple as that, Daintry, I wouldn't have bothered you to come up here. This is only a second-class shoot, and I knew the pheasants would disappoint you."

Hargreaves lifted his bad leg with both hands and eased it toward the fire. "Suppose we did prove Davis to be the culprit—or Castle or Watson. What should we do then?"

"Surely that would be up to the courts," Daintry said.

46

"Headlines in the papers. Another trial *in camera*. No one outside would know how small and unimportant the leaks were. Whoever he is he won't rate forty years like Blake. Perhaps he'll serve ten if the prison's secure."

"That's not our concern surely."

"No, Daintry, but I don't enjoy the thought of that trial one little bit. What cooperation can we expect from the Americans afterwards? And then there's our source. I told you, he's still in place. We don't want to blow him as long as he proves useful."

"In a way," Percival said, "it would be better to close our eyes like a complaisant husband. Draft whoever it is to some innocuous department. Forget things."

"And abet a crime?" Daintry protested.

"Oh, crime," Percival said and smiled at C like a fellow conspirator. "We are all committing crimes somewhere, aren't we? It's our job."

"The trouble is," C said, "that the situation *is* a bit like a rocky marriage. In a marriage, if the lover begins to be bored by the complaisant husband, he can always provoke a scandal. He holds the strong suit. He can choose his own time. I don't want any scandal provoked."

Daintry hated flippancy. Flippancy was like a secret code of which he didn't possess the book. He had the right to read cables and reports marked Top Secret, but flippancy like this was so secret that he hadn't a clue to its understanding. He said, "Personally I would resign rather than cover up." He put down his glass of whisky so hard that he chipped the crystal. Lady Hargreaves again, he thought. She must have insisted on crystal. He said, "I'm sorry."

"Of course you are right, Daintry," Hargreaves said. "Never mind the glass. Please don't think I've brought you all the way up here to persuade you to let things drop, if we have sufficient proof . . . But a trial isn't necessarily the right answer. The Russians don't usually bring

things to a trial with their own people. The trial of Penkovsky gave all of us a great boost in morale, they even
exaggerated his importance, just as the CIA did. I still
wonder why they held it. I wish I were a chess player. Do
you play chess, Daintry?"

"No, bridge is my game."

"The Russians don't play bridge, or so I understand."

"Is that important?"

"We are playing games, Daintry, games, all of us. It's
important not to take a game too seriously or we may lose
it. We have to keep flexible, but it's important, naturally,
to play the same game."

"I'm sorry, sir," Daintry said, "I don't understand
what you are talking about."

He was aware that he had drunk too much whisky,
and he was aware that C and Percival were deliberately
looking away from each other—they didn't want to humil-
iate him. They had heads of stone, he thought, stone.

"Shall we just have one more whisky," C said, "or
perhaps not. It's been a long wet day. Percival . . .?"

Daintry said, "I'd like another."

Percival poured out the drinks. Daintry said, "I'm
sorry to be difficult, but I'd like to get things a little
clearer before bed, or I won't sleep."

"It's really very simple," C said. "Put on your maximum security check if you like. It may flush the bird without more trouble. He'll soon realize what's going on—if
he's guilty, that is. You might think up some kind of test—
the old marked fiver technique seldom fails. When we are
quite certain he's our man, then it seems to me we will
just have to eliminate him. No trial, no publicity. If we
can get information about his contacts first, so much the
better, but we mustn't risk a public flight and then a press
conference in Moscow. An arrest too is out of the question. Granted that he's in Section 6, there's no information

48

he can possibly give which would do as much harm as the scandal of a court case."

"Elimination? You mean . . ."

"I know that elimination is rather a new thing for us. More in the KGB line or the CIA's. That's why I wanted Percival here to meet you. We may need the help of his science boys. Nothing spectacular. Doctor's certificate. No inquest if it can be avoided. A suicide's only too easy, but then a suicide always means an inquest, and that might lead to a question in the House. Everyone knows now what a 'department of the Foreign Office' means. 'Was any question of security involved?' You know the kind of thing some back-bencher is sure to ask. And no one ever believes the official answer. Certainly not the Americans."

"Yes," Percival said, "I quite understand. He should die quietly, peacefully, without pain too, poor chap. Pain sometimes shows on the face, and there may be relatives to consider. A natural death . . ."

"It's a bit difficult, I realize, with all the new antibiotics," C said. "Assuming for the moment that it *is* Davis, he's a man of only just over forty. In the prime of life."

"I agree. A heart attack might just possibly be arranged. Unless . . . Does anyone know whether he drinks a lot?"

"You said something about port, didn't you, Daintry?"

"I'm not saying he's guilty," Daintry said.

"None of us are," C said. "We are only taking Davis as a possible example . . . to help us examine the problem."

"I'd like to look at his medical history," Percival said, "and I'd like to get to know him on some excuse. In a way he would be my patient, wouldn't he? That is to say if . . ."

"You and Daintry could arrange that somehow together. There's no great hurry. We have to be quite sure he's our man. And now—it's been a long day—too many hares and too few pheasants—sleep well. Breakfast on a tray. Eggs and bacon? Sausages? Tea or coffee?"

Percival said, "The works, coffee, bacon, eggs and sausages, if that's all right."

"Nine o'clock?"

"Nine o'clock."

"And you, Daintry?"

"Just coffee and toast. Eight o'clock if you don't mind. I can never sleep late and I have a lot of work waiting."

"You ought to relax more," C said.

3

Colonel Daintry was a compulsive shaver. He had shaved already before dinner, but now he went over his chin a second time with his Remington. Then he shook a little dust into the basin and touching it with his fingers felt justified. Afterward he turned on his electric water-pick. The low buzz was enough to drown the tap on his door, so he was surprised when in the mirror he saw the door swing open and Doctor Percival pass diffidently in.

"Sorry to disturb you, Daintry."

"Come in, do. Forgot to pack something? Anything I can lend you?"

"No, no. I just wanted a word before bed. Amusing little gadget, that of yours. Fashionable, too. I suppose it really is better than an ordinary toothbrush?"

"The water gets between the teeth," Daintry said. "My dentist recommended it."

"I always carry a toothpick for that," Percival said. He took a little red Cartier case out of his pocket. "Pretty, isn't it? Eighteen carat. My father used it before me."

"I think this is more hygienic," Daintry said.

"Oh, I wouldn't be so sure of that. This washes easily. I was a general consultant, you know, Harley Street and all, before I got involved in this show. I don't know why they wanted me—perhaps to sign death certificates." He trotted around the room, showing an interest in everything. "I hope you keep clear of all this fluoride nonsense." He paused at a photograph which stood in a folding case on the dressing table. "Is this your wife?"

"No. My daughter."

"Pretty girl."

"My wife and I are separated."

"Never married myself," Percival said. "To tell you the truth I never had much interest in women. Don't mistake me—not in boys either. Now a good trout stream . . . Know the Aube?"

"No."

"A very small stream with very big fish."

"I can't say I've ever had much interest in fishing," Daintry said, and he began to tidy up his gadget.

"How I run on, don't I?" Percival said. "Never can go straight to a subject. It's like fishing again. You sometimes have to make a hundred false casts before you place the fly."

"I'm not a fish," Daintry said, "and it's after midnight."

"My dear fellow, I really am sorry. I promise I won't keep you up a minute longer. Only I didn't want you to go to bed troubled."

"Was I troubled?"

"It seemed to me you were a bit shocked at C's attitude—I mean to things in general."

"Yes, perhaps I was."

"You haven't been a long time with us, have you, or you'd know how we all live in boxes—you know—boxes."

"I still don't understand."

"Yes, you said that before, didn't you? Understanding isn't all that necessary in our business. I see they've given you the Ben Nicholson room."

"I don't . . ."

"I'm in the Miró room. Good lithographs, aren't they? As a matter of fact it was my idea—these decorations. Lady Hargreaves wanted sporting prints. To go with the pheasants."

"I don't understand modern pictures," Daintry said.

"Take a look at that Nicholson. Such a clever balance. Squares of different color. And yet living so happily together. No clash. The man has a wonderful eye. Change just one of the colors—even the size of the square, and it would be no good at all." Percival pointed at a yellow square. "There's your Section 6. That's your square from now on. You don't need to worry about the blue and the red. All you have to do is pinpoint our man and then tell me. You've no responsibility for what happens in the blue or red squares. In fact not even in the yellow. You just report. No bad conscience. No guilt."

"An action has nothing to do with its consequences. Is that what you're telling me?"

"The consequences are decided elsewhere, Daintry. You mustn't take the conversation tonight too seriously. C likes to toss ideas up into the air and see how they fall. He likes to shock. You know the cannibal story. As far as I know, the criminal—if there is a criminal—will be handed over to the police in quite the conservative way. Nothing to keep you awake. Do just try to understand that picture. Particularly the yellow square. If you could only see it with my eyes, you would sleep well tonight."

Part Two

Chapter I

1

An old-young man with hair which dangled over his shoulders and the heaven-preoccupied gaze of some eighteenth-century *abbé* was sweeping out a discotheque at the corner of Little Compton Street as Castle went by.

Castle had taken an earlier train than usual, and he was not due at the office for another three-quarters of an hour. Soho at this hour had still some of the glamor and innocence he remembered from his youth. It was at this corner he had listened for the first time to a foreign tongue, at the small cheap restaurant next door he had drunk his first glass of wine; crossing Old Compton Street in those days had been the nearest he had ever come to crossing the Channel. At nine in the morning the strip-tease clubs were all closed and only the delicatessens of his memory were open. The names against the flat-bells— Lulu, Mimi and the like—were all that indicated the afternoon and evening activities of Old Compton Street. The drains ran with fresh water, and the early housewives passed him under the pale hazy sky, carrying bulging sacks of salami and liverwurst with an air of happy triumph. There was not a policeman in sight, though after dark they would be seen walking in pairs. Castle crossed the peaceful street and entered a bookshop he had frequented for several years now.

It was an unusually respectable bookshop for this area of Soho, quite unlike the bookshop which faced it across the street and bore the simple sign "Books" in scarlet letters. The window below the scarlet sign displayed girlie magazines which nobody was ever seen to buy— they were like a signal in an easy code long broken; they indicated the nature of private wares and interests inside. But the shop of Halliday & Son confronted the scarlet "Books" with a window full of Penguins and Everyman and second-hand copies of World's Classics. The son was never seen there, only old Mr. Halliday himself, bent and white-haired, wearing an air of courtesy like an old suit in which he would probably like to be buried. He wrote all his business letters in longhand: he was busy on one of them now.

"A fine autumn morning, Mr. Castle," Mr. Halliday remarked, as he traced with great care the phrase "Your obedient servant."

"There was a touch of frost this morning in the country."

"A bit early yet," Mr. Halliday said.

"I wonder if you've got a copy of *War and Peace*? I've never read it. It seems about time for me to begin."

"Finished *Clarissa* already, sir?"

"No, but I'm afraid I'm stuck. The thought of all those volumes to come . . . I need a change."

"The Macmillan edition is out of print, but I think I have a clean second-hand copy in the World's Classics in one volume. The Aylmer Maude translation. You can't beat Aylmer Maude for Tolstoy. He wasn't a mere translator, he knew the author as a friend." He put down his pen and looked regretfully at "Your obedient servant." The penmanship was obviously not up to the mark.

"That's the translation I want. Two copies of course."

"How are things with you, if I may ask, sir?"

"My boy's sick. Measles. Oh, nothing to worry about. No complications."

"I'm very glad to hear that, Mr. Castle. Measles in these days can cause a lot of anxiety. All well at the office, I hope? No crises in international affairs?"

"None I've been told about. Everything very quiet. I'm seriously thinking of retiring."

"I'm sorry to hear that, sir. We need traveled gentlemen like you to deal with foreign affairs. They will give you a good pension, I trust?"

"I doubt it. How's your business?"

"Quiet, sir, very quiet. Fashions change. I remember the 1940s, how people would queue for a new World's Classic. There's little demand today for the great writers. The old grow old, and the young—well, they seem to stay young a long time, and their tastes differ from ours . . . My son's doing better than I am—in that shop over the road."

"He must get some queer types."

"I prefer not to dwell on it, Mr. Castle. The two businesses remain distinct—I've always insisted on that. No policeman will ever come in here for what I would call, between you and me, a bribe. Not that any real harm can be done by the things the boy sells. It's like preaching to the converted I say. You can't corrupt the corrupt, sir."

"One day I must meet your son."

"He comes across in the evening to help me go over my books. He has a better head for figures than I ever had. We often speak of you, sir. It interests him to hear what you've been buying. I think he sometimes envies me the kind of clients I have, few though they are. He gets the furtive types, sir. They are not the ones to discuss a book like you and I do."

"You might tell him I have an edition of *Monsieur Nicolas* which I want to sell. Not quite your cup of tea, I think."

"I'm not so sure, sir, that it's quite his either. It's a sort of classic you must admit—the title is not suggestive enough for *his* customers, and it's expensive. It would be described in a catalogue as *erotica* rather than *curiosa*. Of course he might find a borrower. Most of his books are on loan, you understand. They buy a book one day and change it the next. His books are not for keeps—like a good set of Sir Walter Scott used to be."

"You won't forget to tell him? *Monsieur Nicolas*."

"Oh no, sir. Restif de la Bretonne. Limited edition. Published by Rodker. I have a memory like an encyclopedia, so far as the older books are concerned. Will you take *War and Peace* with you? If you'll allow me a five-minute search in the cellar."

"You can post it to Berkhamsted. I shan't have time for reading today. Only do remember to tell your son . . ."

"I've never forgotten a message yet, sir, have I?"

After Castle left the shop he crossed the street and peered for a moment into the other establishment. All he saw was one young spotty man making his way sadly down a rack of *Men Only* and *Penthouse* . . . A green rep curtain hung at the end of the shop. It probably held more erudite and expensive items as well as shyer customers, and perhaps young Halliday too whom Castle had never yet had the good fortune to meet—if good fortune were the right term, he thought, to employ.

2

Davis for once had arrived at the office ahead of him. He told Castle apologetically, "I came in early today. I said to myself—the new broom may still be sweeping around. And so I thought . . . an appearance of zeal . . . It does no harm."

"Daintry won't be here on a Monday morning. He went off somewhere for a shooting weekend. Anything in from Zaire yet?"

"Nothing at all. The Yanks are asking for more information about the Chinese mission in Zanzibar."

"We've nothing new to give them. It's up to MI5."

"You'd think from the fuss they make that Zanzibar was as close to them as Cuba."

"It almost is—in the jet age."

Cynthia, the major-general's daughter, came in with two cups of coffee and a telegram. She wore brown trousers and a turtleneck sweater. She had something in common with Davis, for she played a comedy too. If faithful Davis looked as untrustworthy as a bookie, Cynthia, the domestic-minded, looked as dashing as a young commando. It was a pity that her spelling was so bad, but perhaps there was something Elizabethan about her spelling as well as about her name. She was probably looking for a Philip Sidney, and so far she had only found a Davis.

"From Lourenço Marques," Cynthia told Castle.

"Your pigeon, Davis."

"Of absorbing interest," Davis said. " 'Your 253 of September 10 mutilated. Please repeat.' That's *your* pigeon, Cynthia. Run along and code it again like a good girl and get the spelling right this time. It helps. You know, Castle, when I joined this outfit, I was a romantic. I thought of atom secrets. They only took me on because I was a good mathematician, and my physics were not too bad either."

"Atom secrets belong to Section 8."

"I thought I'd at least learn some interesting gadgets, like using secret ink. I'm sure you know all about secret ink."

"I did once—even to the use of bird shit. I had a course in it before they sent me on a mission at the end of the war. They gave me a handsome little wooden box, full of bottles like one of those chemistry cabinets for children. And an electric kettle—with a supply of plastic knitting needles."

"What on earth for?"

"For opening letters."

"And did you ever? Open one, I mean?"

"No, though I did once try. I was taught not to open an envelope at the flap, but at the side, and then when I closed it again I was supposed to use the same gum. The trouble was I hadn't got the right gum, so I had to burn the letter after reading it. It wasn't important anyway. Just a love letter."

"What about a Luger? I suppose you had a Luger. Or an explosive fountain pen?"

"No. We've never been very James Bond minded here. I wasn't allowed to carry a gun, and my only car was a secondhand Morris Minor."

"We might at least have been given one Luger between us. It's the age of terrorism."

"But we've got a scrambler," Castle said in the hope of soothing Davis. He recognized the kind of embittered dialogue which was always apt to crop up when Davis was out of sorts. A glass of port too many, a disappointment with Cynthia . . .

"Have you ever handled a microdot, Castle?"

"Never."

60

"Not even an old wartime hand like you? What was the most secret information you ever possessed, Castle?"

"I once knew the approximate date of an invasion."

"Normandy?"

"No, no. Only the Azores."

"*Were* they invaded? I'd forgotten—or perhaps I never knew. Oh well, old man, I suppose we've got to set our teeth and go through the bloody Zaire bag. Can you tell me why the Yanks are interested in our forecast for the copper crop?"

"I suppose it affects the budget. And that could affect aid programs. Perhaps the Zaire Government might be tempted to supplement its aid from elsewhere. You see, here we are—Report 397—someone with a rather Slavic name had lunch on the 24th with the President."

"Do we have to pass even that on to the CIA?"

"Of course."

"And do you suppose they will give us one little guided missile secret in return?"

It was certainly one of Davis's worst days. His eyes had a yellow tint. God only knew what mixture he had drunk the night before in his bachelor pad in Davies Street. He said glumly, "James Bond would have had Cynthia a long while ago. On a sandy beach under a hot sun. Pass me Philip Dibba's card, would you?"

"What's his number?"

"59800/3"

"What's he been up to?"

"There's a rumor that his retirement as director of the Post Office in Kinshasa was compulsory. He had too many stamps misprinted for his private collection. There goes our most high-powered agent in Zaire." Davis put his head in his hands and gave a doglike howl of genuine distress.

Castle said, "I know how you feel, Davis. Sometimes I would like to retire myself . . . or change my job."

"It's too late for that."

"I wonder. Sarah always tells me I could write a book."

"Official Secrets."

"Not about us. About apartheid."

"It's not what you'd call a best-selling subject."

Davis stopped writing Dibba's card. He said, "Joking apart, old man, please don't think of it. I couldn't stand this job without you. I'd crack up if there wasn't someone here with whom I could laugh at things. I'm afraid to smile with any of the others. Even Cynthia. I love her, but she's so damned loyal, she might report me as a security risk. To Colonel Daintry. Like James Bond killing the girl he slept with. Only she hasn't even slept with me."

"I wasn't really serious," Castle said. "How *could* I leave? Where would I go from here? Except retire. I'm sixty-two, Davis. Past the official age. I sometimes think they've forgotten me, or perhaps they've lost my file."

"Here they are asking for traces of a fellow called Agbo, an employee in Radio Zaire. 59800 proposes him as a sub-agent."

"What for?"

"He has a contact in Radio Ghana."

"That doesn't sound very valuable. Anyway Ghana's not our territory. Pass it on to 6B and see if they can use him."

"Don't be rash, Castle, we don't want to give away a treasure. Who knows what might spring from agent Agbo? From Ghana we might even penetrate Radio Guinea. That would put Penkovsky in the shade. What a triumph. The CIA have never penetrated as far as that into darkest Africa."

It was one of Davis's worst days.

"Perhaps we only see the dullest side of things in 6A," Castle said.

Cynthia returned with an envelope for Davis. "You have to sign here and acknowledge receipt."

"What's in it?"

"How would I know? It's administration." She collected a single piece of paper from the out-tray. "Is this all?"

"We are not exactly overworked at the moment, Cynthia. Are you free for lunch?"

"No, I have things to get for dinner tonight." She closed the door firmly.

"Oh well, another time. Always another time." Davis opened the envelope. He said, "What will they think up next?"

"What's wrong?" Castle asked.

"Haven't you received one of these?"

"Oh, a medical checkup? Of course. I don't know how many times I've been checked in my time. It's something to do with insurance—or pension. Before they sent me to South Africa, Doctor Percival—perhaps you haven't met Doctor Percival—tried to make out I had diabetes. They sent me to a specialist who found I had too little sugar instead of too much . . . Poor old Percival. I think he was a bit out of practice in general medicine, being mixed up with us. Security is more important than a correct diagnosis in this outfit."

"This chit *is* signed Percival, Emmanuel Percival. What a name. Wasn't Emmanuel the bringer of good tidings? Do you think they might be sending me abroad too?"

"Would you like to go?"

"I've always dreamt of being sent one day to Lourenço Marques. Our man there is due for a change. The port should be good, shouldn't it? I suppose even revolutionaries drink port. If only I could have Cynthia with me . . ."

"I thought you favored a bachelor life."

63

"I wasn't talking about marriage. Bond never had to marry. I like Portuguese cooking."

"It's probably African cooking by now. Do you know anything about the place apart from 69300's cables?"

"I collected a whole file on the nightspots and the restaurants before their damned revolution. Perhaps they are all closed now. All the same I don't suppose 69300 knows the half of what I do about what goes on there. He hasn't got the files, and anyway he's so damned serious—I think he takes his work to bed. Think what the two of us could put down on expenses."

"The two of you?"

"Cynthia and me."

"What a dreamer you are, Davis. She'll never take you on. Remember her father, the major-general."

"Everybody has his dream. What's yours, Castle?"

"Oh, I suppose sometimes I dream of security. I don't mean Daintry's sort of security. To be retired. With a good pension. Enough for me and my wife . . ."

"And your little bastard?"

"Yes, and my little bastard too, of course."

"They aren't very generous with pensions in this department."

"No, I don't suppose either of us will realize his dream."

"All the same—this medical checkup *must* mean something, Castle. That time I went over to Lisbon— our man there took me to a sort of cave beyond Estoril, where you could hear the water washing up under your table . . . I've never eaten any lobsters as good as those were. I've read about a restaurant in Lourenço Marques . . . I even like their green wine, Castle. I really ought to be there—not 69300. He doesn't appreciate good living. You know the place, don't you?"

"I spent two nights there with Sarah—seven years ago. At the Hotel Polana."

"Only two nights?"

"I'd left Pretoria in a hurry—you know that—just ahead of BOSS. I didn't feel safe so near the frontier. I wanted to put an ocean between BOSS and Sarah."

"Oh yes, you had Sarah. Lucky you. At the Hotel Polana. With the Indian Ocean outside."

Castle remembered the bachelor flat—the used glasses, *Penthouse* and *Nature*. "If you are really serious, Davis, I'll talk to Watson. I'll put you up for an exchange."

"I'm serious enough. I want to escape from here, Castle. Desperately."

"Is it as bad as all that?"

"We sit here writing meaningless telegrams. We feel important because we know a little bit more than someone else about the groundnuts or what Mobutu said at a private dinner . . . Do you know I came into this outfit for excitement? Excitement, Castle. What a fool I was. I don't know how you've stood it all these years . . ."

"Perhaps being married helps."

"If I ever married I wouldn't want to live my life here. I'm tired to death of this damned old country, Castle, electricity cuts, strikes, inflation. I'm not worried about the price of food—it's the price of good port which gets me down. I joined this outfit hoping to get abroad, I've even learned Portuguese, but here I stay answering telegrams from Zaire, reporting groundnuts."

"I always thought you were having fun, Davis."

"Oh, I have fun when I get a little drunk. I love that girl, Castle. I can't get her out of my head. And so I clown to please her, and the more I clown the less she likes me. Perhaps if I went to Lourenço Marques . . . She said once she wanted to go abroad too."

The telephone rang. "Is that you, Cynthia?" but it wasn't. It was Watson, the head of Section 6. "Is that you, Castle?"

"It's Davis."

"Give me Castle."

"Yes," Castle said, "I'm here. What is it?"

"C wants to see us. Will you pick me up on the way down?"

3

It was a long way down, for C's office was one floor underground, established in what during the 1890s had been a millionaire's wine cellar. The room where Castle and Watson waited for a green light to go on above C's door had been the adjoining cellar for the coal and wood, and C's office had housed the best wines in London. It was rumored that, when the department had taken over the house in 1946 and the architect started to reconstruct the building, a false wall was discovered in the wine cellar and behind it lay like mummies the millionaire's secret treasure of fabulous vintages. They were sold—so the legend went—by some ignorant clerk in the Office of Works to the Army and Navy Stores for the price of common table wines. The story was probably untrue, but whenever a historic wine came up at a Christie auction, Davis would say with gloom, "That was one of ours."

The red light stayed interminably on. It was like waiting in a car for a traffic accident to be cleared away.

"Do you know what the trouble is?" Castle asked.

"No. He just asked me to introduce all the Section 6 men whom he's never met. He's been through 6B and now it's your turn. I'm to introduce you and then leave you. That's the drill. It sounds like a relic of colonialism to me."

66

"I met the old C once. Before I went abroad the first time. He had a black eyeglass. It was rather daunting being stared at by that black O, but all he did was shake hands and wish me good luck. They aren't thinking of sending me abroad again by any chance?"

"No. Why?"

"Remind me to speak to you about Davis."

The light turned green.

"I wish I'd shaved better this morning," Castle said.

Sir John Hargreaves, unlike the old C, was not daunting at all. He had a brace of pheasants on his desk and he was busy on the telephone. "I brought them up this morning. Mary thought you might like them." He waved his hand toward two chairs.

So that's where Colonel Daintry spent the weekend, Castle thought. To shoot pheasants or report on security? He took the smaller and harder chair with a due sense of protocol.

"She's fine. A bit of rheumatism in her bad leg, that's all," Hargreaves said and rang off.

"This is Maurice Castle, sir," Watson said. "He's in charge of 6A."

"In charge sounds a little too important," Castle said. "There are only two of us."

"You deal with Top Secret sources, don't you? You— and Davis under your direction?"

"And Watson's."

"Yes, of course. But Watson has the whole of 6 in his care. You delegate, I suppose, a good deal, Watson?"

"I find 6C the only section which needs my full attention. Wilkins hasn't been with us long. He has to work himself in."

"Well, I won't keep you any longer, Watson. Thanks for bringing Castle down."

Hargreaves stroked the feathers of one of the dead

birds. He said, "Like Wilkins I'm working myself in. As I see it things are a bit like they were when I was a young man in West Africa. Watson is a sort of Provincial Commissioner and you are a District Commissioner left pretty well to yourself in your own territory. Of course, you know Africa too, don't you?"

"Only South Africa," Castle said.

"Yes, I was forgetting. South Africa never seems quite like the real Africa to me. Nor the north either. That's dealt with by 6C, isn't it? Daintry has been explaining things to me. Over the weekend."

"Did you have a good shoot, sir?" Castle asked.

"Medium. I don't think Daintry was quite satisfied. You must come and have a go yourself next autumn."

"I wouldn't be any good, sir. I've never shot anything in my life, not even a human being."

"Ah, yes, they are the best target. To tell you the truth, birds bore me too."

C looked at a paper on his desk. "You did very good work in Pretoria. You are described as a first-class administrator. You reduced the expenses of the station considerably."

"I took over from a man who was brilliant at recruiting agents, but he hadn't much idea of finance. It came easily to me. I was in a bank for a while before the war."

"Daintry writes here that you had some private trouble in Pretoria."

"I wouldn't call it trouble. I fell in love."

"Yes. So I see. With an African girl. What those fellows call Bantu without distinction. You broke their race laws."

"We're safely married now. But we did have a difficult time out there."

"Yes. So you reported to us. I wish all our people

68

when they are in a bit of trouble would behave as correctly. You were afraid the South African police were getting on to you and would try to tear you in pieces."

"It didn't seem right to leave you with a vulnerable representative."

"You can see I've been looking pretty closely through your file. We told you to get out at once, though we never thought that you'd bring the girl with you."

"HQ had had her vetted. They found nothing wrong with her. Wasn't I right from your point of view to get her out too? I had used her as a contact with my African agents. My cover story was that I was planning a serious critical study of apartheid in my spare time, but the police might have broken her. So I got her away through Swaziland to Lourenço Marques."

"Oh, you did quite right, Castle. And now you're married with a child. All well, I hope?"

"Well, at the moment my son has measles."

"Ah, then you must pay attention to his eyes. The eyes are the weak spot. The thing I really wished to see you about, Castle, was a visit we are going to have in a few weeks' time from a certain Mr. Cornelius Muller, one of the head boys in BOSS. I think you knew him when you were in Pretoria."

"I did indeed."

"We are going to let him see some of the material you deal with. Of course, only enough to establish the fact that we *are* cooperating—in a sort of way."

"He'll know more than we do about Zaire."

"It's Mozambique he's most interested in."

"In that case Davis is your man, sir. He's more abreast of things there than I am."

"Oh yes, of course, Davis. I haven't yet met Davis."

"Another thing, sir. When I was in Pretoria, I didn't get on at all well with this man Muller. If you look further

69

back in my file—it was he who tried to blackmail me under the race laws. That was why your predecessor told me to get out as fast as I could. I don't think that would help our personal relations. It would be better to have Davis deal with him."

"All the same you are Davis's superior, and you are the natural officer to see him. It won't be easy, I know that. Knives out on both sides, but he'll be the one who's taken by surprise. You know exactly what not to show him. It's very important to guard our agents—even if it means keeping some important material dark. Davis hasn't your personal experience of BOSS—and their Mr. Muller."

"Why do we have to show him anything, sir?"

"Have you ever wondered, Castle, what would happen to the West if the South African gold mines were closed by a racial war? And a losing war perhaps, as in Vietnam. Before the politicians have agreed on a substitute for gold. Russia as the chief source. It would be a bit more complicated than the petrol crisis. And the diamond mines . . . De Beers are more important than General Motors. Diamonds don't age like cars. There are even more serious aspects than gold and diamonds, there's uranium. I don't think you've been told yet of a secret White House paper on an operation they call Uncle Remus."

"No. There have been rumors . . ."

"Like it or not, we and South Africa and the States are all partners in Uncle Remus. And that means we have to be pleasant to Mr. Muller—even if he did blackmail you."

"And I have to show him . . .?"

"Information on guerrillas, blockade-running to Rhodesia, the new chaps in power in Mozambique, Russian and Cuban penetration . . . economic information . . ."

"There's not much left, is there?"

"Go a bit carefully on the Chinese. The South Afri-

70

cans are too much inclined to lump them with the Russians. The day may come when we need the Chinese. I don't like the idea of Uncle Remus any more than you do. It's what the politicians call a realistic policy, and realism never got anyone very far in the kind of Africa I used to know. My Africa was a sentimental Africa. I really loved Africa, Castle. The Chinese don't, nor do the Russians nor the Americans—but we have to go with the White House and Uncle Remus and Mr. Muller. How easy it was in the old days when we dealt with chiefs and witch doctors and bush schools and devils and rain queens. My Africa was still a little like the Africa of Rider Haggard. It wasn't a bad place. The Emperor Chaka was a lot better than Field Marshal Amin Dada. Oh well, do your best with Muller. He's the personal representative of the big BOSS himself. I suggest you see him first at home—it would be a salutary shock for him."

"I don't know if my wife would agree."

"Tell her I asked you to. I leave it to her—if it's too painful . . ."

Castle turned at the door, remembering his promise. "Could I have a word with you about Davis, sir?"

"Of course. What is it?"

"He's had too long at a London desk. I think that at the first opportunity we ought to send him to Lourenço Marques. Exchange him for 69300, who must need a change of climate by now."

"Has Davis suggested that?"

"Not exactly, but I think he'd be glad to get away—anywhere. He's in a pretty nervous state, sir."

"What about?"

"A spot of girl trouble, I expect. And desk fatigue."

"Oh, I can understand desk fatigue. We'll see what we can do for him."

"I *am* a little anxious about him."

"I promise you I'll bear him in mind, Castle. By the

way, this visit of Muller's is strictly secret. You know how we like to make our little boxes watertight. This has got to be your personal box. I haven't even told Watson. And you shouldn't tell Davis."

Chapter II

In the second week of October Sam was still officially in quarantine. There had been no complication, so one less danger menaced his future—that future which always appeared to Castle as an unpredictable ambush. Walking down the High Street on a Sunday morning he felt a sudden desire to give a kind of thanks, if it was only to a myth, that Sam was safe, so he took himself in, for a few minutes, to the back of the parish church. The service was nearly at an end and the congregation of the well-dressed, the middle-aged and the old were standing at attention, as they sang with a kind of defiance as though they inwardly doubted the facts, "There is a green hill far away, without a city wall." The simple precise words, with the single *tache* of color, reminded Castle of the local background so often to be found in primitive paintings. The city wall was like the ruins of the keep beyond the station, and up the green hillside of the Common, on top of the abandoned rifle butts, had once stood a tall post on which a man could have been hanged. For a moment he came near to sharing their incredible belief—it would do no harm to mutter a prayer of thanks to the God of his childhood, the God of the Common and the castle, that no ill had yet come to Sarah's child. Then a sonic boom scattered the words of the hymn and shook the old glass of the west window and rattled the crusader's helmet which hung on a pillar, and he was reminded again of the grown-up world. He went quickly out and bought the Sunday papers. The *Sunday Express* had a headline on the front page—"Child's Body Found in Wood."

In the afternoon he took Sam and Buller for a walk across the Common, leaving Sarah to sleep. He would have liked to leave Buller behind, but his angry protest would have wakened Sarah, so he comforted himself with the thought that Buller was unlikely to find a cat astray on the Common. The fear was always there since one summer three years before, when providence played an ill trick by providing suddenly a picnic party among the beech woods who had brought with them an expensive cat with a blue collar round its neck on a scarlet silk leash. The cat—a Siamese—had not even time to give one cry of anger or pain before Buller snapped its back and tossed the corpse over his shoulder like a man loading a sack onto a lorry. Then he had trotted attentively away between the trees, turning his head this way and that— where there was one cat there ought surely to be another—and Castle was left to face alone the angry and grief-stricken picnickers.

In October, however, picnickers were unlikely. All the same Castle waited till the sun had nearly set and he kept Buller on his chain all the way down King's Road past the police station at the corner of the High Street. Once beyond the canal and the railway bridge and the new houses (they had been there for a quarter of a century, but anything which had not existed when he was a boy seemed new to Castle), he let Buller loose, and immediately, like a well-trained dog, Buller splayed out and dropped his *crotte* on the edge of the path, taking his time. The eyes stared ahead, inward-looking. Only on these sanitary occasions did Buller seem a dog of intelligence. Castle did not like Buller—he had bought him for a purpose, to reassure Sarah, but Buller had proved inadequate as a watchdog, so now he was only one responsibility more, though with canine lack of judgment he loved Castle more than any other human being.

The bracken was turning to the dusky gold of a fine autumn, and there were only a few flowers left on the gorse. Castle and Sam searched in vain for the rifle butts which had once stood—a red clay cliff—above the waste of Common. They were drowned now in tired greenery. "Did they shoot spies there?" Sam asked.

"No, no. What gave you that idea? This was simply for rifle practice. In the first war."

"But there are spies, aren't there—real spies?"

"I suppose so, yes. Why do you ask?"

"I just wanted to be sure, that's all."

Castle remembered how at the same age he had asked his father whether there were really fairies, and the answer had been less truthful than his own. His father had been a sentimental man; he wished to reassure his small son at any cost that living was worthwhile. It would have been unfair to accuse him of dishonesty: a fairy, he might well have argued, was a symbol which represented something which was at least approximately true. There were still fathers around even today who told their children that God existed.

"Spies like 007?"

"Well, not exactly." Castle tried to change the subject. He said, "When I was a child I thought there was a dragon living here in an old dugout down there among those trenches."

"Where are the trenches?"

"You can't see them now for the bracken."

"What's a dragon?"

"You know—one of those armored creatures spitting out fire."

"Like a tank?"

"Well, yes, I suppose like a tank." There was a lack of contact between their two imaginations which discouraged him. "More like a giant lizard," he said. Then he realized that the boy had seen many tanks, but they had left the land of lizards before he was born.

"Did you ever see a dragon?"

"Once I saw smoke coming out of a trench and I thought it was the dragon."

"Were you afraid?"

"No, I was afraid of quite different things in those days. I hated my school, and I had few friends."

"Why did you hate school? Will I hate school? I mean *real* school."

"We don't all have the same enemies. Perhaps you won't need a dragon to help you, but I did. All the world hated my dragon and wanted to kill him. They were afraid of the smoke and the flames which came out of his mouth when he was angry. I used to steal out at night from my dormitory and take him tins of sardines from my tuck-box. He cooked them in the tin with his breath. He liked them hot."

"But did that *really* happen?"

"No, of course not, but it almost seems now as though it had. Once I lay in bed in the dormitory crying under the sheet because it was the first week of term and there were twelve endless weeks before the holidays, and I was afraid of—everything around. It was winter, and suddenly I saw the window of my cubicle was misted over with heat. I wiped away the steam with my fingers and looked down. The dragon was there, lying flat in the wet black street, he looked like a crocodile in a stream. He had never left the Common before because every man's hand was against him—just as I thought they were all against me. The police even kept rifles in a cupboard to shoot him if he ever came to town. Yet there he was, lying very still and breathing up at me big warm clouds of breath. You see, he had heard that school had started again and he knew I was unhappy and alone. He was more intelligent than any dog, much more intelligent than Buller."

"You are pulling my leg," Sam said.

"No, I'm just remembering."

"What happened then?"

"I made a secret signal to him. It meant 'Danger. Go away,' because I wasn't sure that he knew about the police with their rifles."

"Did he go?"

"Yes. Very slowly. Looking back over his tail as though he didn't want to leave me. But I never felt afraid or lonely again. At least not often. I knew I had only to give a signal and he would leave his dugout on the Common and come down and help me. We had a lot of private signals, codes, ciphers . . ."

"Like a spy," Sam said.

"Yes," Castle said with disappointment, "I suppose so. Like a spy."

Castle remembered how he had once made a map of the Common with all the trenches marked and the secret paths hidden by ferns. That was like a spy too. He said, "Time to be going home. Your mother will be anxious . . ."

"No, she won't. I'm with you. I want to see the dragon's cave."

"There wasn't really a dragon."

"But you aren't quite sure, are you?"

With difficulty Castle found the old trench. The dugout where the dragon had lived was blocked by blackberry bushes. As he forced his way through them his feet struck against a rusty tin and sent it tumbling.

"You see," Sam said, "you did bring food." He wormed his way forward, but there was no dragon and no skeleton. "Perhaps the police got him in the end," Sam said. Then he picked up the tin.

"It's tobacco," he said, "not sardines."

That night Castle said to Sarah as they lay in bed, "Do you really think it's not too late?"

"For what?"

"To leave my job."

"Of course it isn't. You aren't an old man yet."

"We might have to move from here."

"Why? This place is as good as any."

"Wouldn't you like to go away? This house—it isn't much of a house, is it? Perhaps if I got a job abroad . . ."

"I'd like Sam to stay put in one place so that when he goes away he'll be able to come back. To something he knew in childhood. Like you came back. To something old. Something secure."

"A collection of old ruins by the railway?"

"Yes."

He remembered the bourgeois voices, as sedate as the owners in their Sunday clothes, singing in the flinty church, expressing their weekly moment of belief. "A green hill far away, without a city wall."

"The ruins are pretty," she said.

"But *you* can never go back," Castle said, "to your childhood."

"That's different, I wasn't secure. Until I knew you. And there were no ruins—only shacks."

"Muller is coming over, Sarah."

78

"Cornelius Muller?"

"Yes. He's a big man now. I have to be friendly to him—by order."

"Don't worry. He can't hurt us anymore."

"No. But I don't want you troubled."

"Why should I be?"

"C wants me to bring him here."

"Bring him then. And let him see how you and I . . . and Sam . . ."

"You agree?"

"Of course I agree. A black hostess for Mr. Cornelius Muller. And a black child." They laughed, with a touch of fear.

Chapter III

1

"How's the little bastard?" Davis asked as he had done every day now for three weeks.

"Oh, everything's over. He's quite well again. He wanted to know the other day when you were going to come and see us. He likes you—I can't imagine why. He often talks of that picnic we had last summer and the hide-and-seek. He seems to think no one else can hide like you can. He thinks you are a spy. He talks about spies like children talked about fairies in my day. Or didn't they?"

"Could I borrow his father for tonight?"

"Why? What's on?"

"Doctor Percival was in yesterday when you were away, and we got talking. Do you know, I really think they may be sending me abroad? He was asking if I'd mind a few more tests . . . blood, urine, radio of the kidneys, et cetera, et cetera. He said they had to be careful about the tropics. I liked him. He seems to be a sporting type."

"Racing?"

"No, only fishing as a matter of fact. That's a pretty lonely sport. Percival's a bit like me—no wife. Tonight we thought we'd get together and see the town. I haven't seen the town for a long while. Those chaps from the Department of the Environment are a pretty sad lot. Couldn't you face being a grass widower, old man, just for one evening?"

"My last train leaves Euston at 11:30."

"I've got the flat all to myself tonight. The Environment men have both gone off to a polluted area. You can have a bed. Double or single, whichever you prefer."

"Please—a single bed. I'm getting to be an old man, Davis. I don't know what plans you and Percival have . . ."

"I thought dinner in the Café Grill and afterwards a spot of striptease. Raymond's Revuebar. They've got Rita Rolls . . ."

"Do you think Percival likes that sort of thing?"

"I sounded him out, and can you believe it? He's never been to a striptease in his life. He said he'd love to take a peek with colleagues he can trust. You know how it is with work like ours. He feels the same way. Nothing to talk about at a party for reasons of security. John Thomas doesn't even have a chance to lift his head. He's morose—that's the word. But if John Thomas dies, God help you, you might as well die too. Of course it's different for you—you are a married man. You can always talk to Sarah and . . ."

"We're not supposed to talk even to our wives."

81

"I bet you do."

"I don't, Davis. And if you are thinking of picking up a couple of tarts I wouldn't talk to them either. A lot of them are employed by MI5—oh, I always forget they've changed our names. We are all DI now. I wonder why? I suppose there's a Department of Semantics."

"You sound a bit fed up too."

"Yes. Perhaps a party will do me good. I'll telephone to Sarah and tell her—what?"

"Tell her the truth. You are dining with one of the big boys. Important for your future in the firm. And I'm giving you a bed. She trusts me. She knows I won't lead you astray."

"Yes, I suppose she does."

"And, damn it all, that's true too, isn't it?"

"I'll ring her up when I go out to lunch."

"Why not do it here and save money?"

"I like my calls private."

"Do you really think they bother to listen in to us?"

"Wouldn't you in their position?"

"I suppose I would. But what the hell of a lot of dreary stuff they must have to tape."

2

The evening was only half a success, though it had begun well enough. Doctor Percival in his slow unexciting fashion was a good enough companion. He made neither Castle nor Davis feel he was their superior in the department. When Colonel Daintry's name arose he

poked gentle fun at him—he had met him, he said, at a
shooting weekend. "He doesn't like abstract art and he
doesn't approve of me. That's because I don't shoot,"
Doctor Percival explained, "I only fish."

They were at Raymond's Revuebar by that time,
crushed at a small table, just large enough to hold three
whiskies, while a pretty young thing was going through
curious antics in a hammock.

"I'd like to get my hook into *her*," Davis said.

The girl drank from a bottle of High and Dry sus-
pended above the hammock on a string, and after every
swallow she removed a piece of clothing with an air of
ginny abandon. At long last they could see her naked but-
tocks outlined by the net like the rump of a chicken seen
through a Soho housewife's string bag. A party of busi-
nessmen from Birmingham applauded with some violence, and one man went so far as to wave a Diners Club
card above his head, perhaps to show his financial
standing.

"What do you fish?" Castle asked.

"Mainly trout or grayling," Percival said.

"Is there much difference?"

"My dear fellow, ask a big-game hunter if there's a
difference between lion and tiger."

"Which do you prefer?"

"It's not really a question of preference. I just love
fishing—any fly fishing. The grayling is less intelligent
than the trout, but that doesn't mean he's always easier.
He demands a different technique. And he's a fighter—he
fights until there's no fight left in him."

"And the trout?"

"Oh, he's the king, all right. He scares easily—nail
boots or a stick, any sound you make and he's off. Then
you must place your fly exactly, the first time. Otherwise . . ." Percival made a gesture with his arm as though

he were casting in the direction of yet another naked girl who was striped black and white by the lights like a zebra.

"What a bottom!" Davis said with awe. He sat with a glass of whisky halfway to his lips, watching the cheeks revolve with the same precision as the wheels of a Swiss watch: a diamond movement.

"You aren't doing your blood pressure any good," Percival told him.

"Blood pressure?"

"I told you it was high."

"You can't bother me tonight," Davis said. "That's the great Rita Rolls herself. The one and only Rita."

"You ought to have a more complete checkup if you are really thinking of going abroad."

"I feel all right, Percival. I've never felt better."

"That's where the danger lies."

"You almost begin to scare me," Davis said. "Nail boots and a stick. I can see why a trout . . ." He took a sip of whisky as though it were a disagreeable medicine and laid his glass down again.

Doctor Percival squeezed his arm and said, "I was only joking, Davis. You're more the grayling type."

"You mean I'm a poor fish?"

"You mustn't underestimate the grayling. He has a very delicate nervous system. And he's a fighter."

"Then I'm more of a cod," said Davis.

"Don't talk to me about cod. I don't go in for that sort of fishing."

The lights went up. It was the end of the show. Anything, the management had decided, would be an anticlimax after Rita Rolls. Davis lingered for a moment in the bar to try his luck with a fruit machine. He used up all the coins he had and took two off Castle. "It's not my evening," he said, his gloom returning. Obviously Doctor Percival had upset him.

"What about a nightcap at my place?" Doctor Percival asked.

"I thought you were warning me off the drink."

"My dear chap, I was exaggerating. Anyway whisky's the safest drink there is."

"All the same I begin to feel like bed now."

In Great Windmill Street prostitutes stood inside the doorways under red shades and asked, "Coming up, darling?"

"I suppose you'd warn me off that too?" Davis said.

"Well, the regularity of marriage is safer. Less strain on the blood pressure."

The night porter was scrubbing the steps of Albany as Doctor Percival left them. His chambers in Albany were designated by a letter and a figure—D.6—as though it were one more section of the old firm. Castle and Davis watched him pick his way carefully toward the Ropewalk so as not to wet his shoes—an odd precaution for someone accustomed to wading knee-deep in cold streams.

"I'm sorry he came," Davis said. "We could have had a good evening without him."

"I thought you liked him."

"I did, but he got on my nerves tonight with his damned fishing stories. And all his talk about my blood pressure. What's my blood pressure to do with him? Is he really a doctor?"

"I don't think he's practiced much for years," Castle said. "He's C's liaison officer with the bacteriological warfare people—I suppose someone with a medical degree comes in handy there."

"That place Porton gives me the shivers. People talk so much about the atom bomb, but they quite forget our little country establishment. Nobody has ever bothered to march there. Nobody wears an anti-bacterial button, but if the bomb were abolished, there'd still be that little deadly test-tube . . ."

85

They turned the corner by Claridge's. A tall lean woman in a long dress climbed into a Rolls Royce followed by a sullen man in a white tie who looked furtively at his watch—they looked like actors from an Edwardian play: it was two in the morning. There was a yellow lino worn into holes like a gruyère cheese on the steep stairs up to Davis's flat. With W.1. on the notepaper no one bothered about small details like that. The kitchen door was open, and Castle saw a stack of dirty dishes in the sink. Davis opened a cupboard door; the shelves were stacked with almost empty bottles—the protection of the environment did not begin at home. Davis tried to find a whisky bottle containing enough for two glasses. "Oh well," he said, "we'll mix them. They're all blends anyway." He combined what remained of a Johnnie Walker with a White Horse, and obtained a quarter bottle.

"Does no one here ever wash up?" Castle asked.

"A woman comes in twice a week, and we save it all for her."

Davis opened a door. "Here's your room. I'm afraid the bed's not made. She's due tomorrow." He picked a dirty handkerchief off the floor and stuffed it in a drawer for tidiness' sake. Then he led Castle back into the sitting room and cleared some magazines off a chair onto the floor.

"I'm thinking of changing my name by deed poll," Davis said.

"What to?"

"Davis with an e. Davies of Davies Street has a certain classy ring." He put his feet up on the sofa. "You know, this blend of mine tastes quite good. I shall call it a White Walker. There might be a fortune in the idea—you could advertise it with the picture of a beautiful female ghost. What did you really think of Doctor Percival?"

"He seemed friendly enough. But I couldn't help wondering . . ."

"What?"

"Why he bothered to spend the evening with us. What he wanted."

"An evening out with people he could talk to. Why look further? Don't you get tired of keeping your mouth closed in mixed company?"

"He didn't open his very far. Even with us."

"He did before you came."

"What about?"

"That establishment at Porton. Apparently we are far ahead of the Americans in one range of goods and they've asked us to concentrate on a deadly little fellow suitable for employment at a certain altitude which at the same time can survive desert conditions . . . All the details, temperature and the like, point to China. Or perhaps Africa."

"Why did he tell you all that?"

"Well, we are supposed to know a bit about the Chinese through our African contacts. Ever since that report from Zanzibar our reputation stands quite high."

"That was two years ago and the report's still unconfirmed."

"He said we mustn't take any overt action. No questionnaires to agents. Too secret for that. Just keep our eyes open for any hint in any report that the Chinese are interested in Hell's Parlour and then report direct to him."

"Why did he speak to you and not to me?"

"Oh, I suppose he would have spoken to you, but you were late."

"Daintry kept me. Percival could have come to the office if he wanted to talk."

"What's troubling you?"

"I'm just wondering if he was telling you the truth."

"What earthly reason . . .?"

"He might want to plant a false rumor."

"Not with us. We aren't exactly gossips, you and I and Watson."

"Has he spoken to Watson?"

"No—as a matter of fact—he gave the usual patter about watertight boxes. Top Secret, he said—but that can't apply to you, can it?"

"Better not let them know you told me all the same."

"Old man, you've caught the disease of the profession, suspicion."

"Yes. It's a bad infection. That's why I'm thinking of getting out."

"To grow vegetables?"

"To do anything non-secret and unimportant and relatively harmless. I nearly joined an advertising agency once."

"Be careful. They have secrets too—trade secrets."

The telephone rang at the head of the stairs. "At this hour," Davis complained. "It's anti-social. Who can it be?" He struggled off the sofa.

"Rita Rolls," Castle suggested.

"Give yourself another White Walker."

Castle hadn't time to pour it out before Davis called to him. "It's Sarah, Castle."

The hour was nearly half-past two and fear touched him. Were there complications which a child might get so late in quarantine as this?

"Sarah?" he asked. "What is it? Is it Sam?"

"Darling, I'm sorry. You weren't in bed, were you?"

"No. What's the matter?"

"I'm scared."

"Sam?"

"No, it's not Sam. But the telephone's rung twice since midnight, and no one answers."

"The wrong number," he said with relief. "It's always happening."

88

"Somebody knows you're not in the house. I'm frightened, Maurice."

"What could possibly happen in King's Road? Why, there's a police station two hundred yards away. And Buller? Buller's there, isn't he?"

"He's fast asleep, snoring."

"I'd come back if I could, but there are no trains. And no taxi would take me at this hour."

"I'll drive you down," Davis said.

"No, no, of course not."

"Not what?" Sarah said.

"I was talking to Davis. He said he'd drive me down."

"Oh no, I don't want that. I feel better now I've talked to you. I'll wake Buller up."

"Sam's all right?"

"He's fine."

"You've got the police number. They'd be with you in two minutes."

"I'm a fool, aren't I? Just a fool."

"A beloved fool."

"Say sorry to Davis. Have a good drink."

"Goodnight, darling."

"Goodnight, Maurice."

The use of his name was a sign of love—when they were together it was an invitation to love. Endearments—dear and darling—were everyday currency to be employed in company, but a name was strictly private, never to be betrayed to a stranger outside the tribe. At the height of love she would cry aloud his secret tribal name. He heard her ring off, but he stayed a moment with the receiver pressed against his ear.

"Nothing really wrong?" Davis asked.

"Not with Sarah, no."

He came back into the sitting room and poured himself a whisky. He said, "I think your telephone's tapped."

89

"How do you know?"

"I don't. I have an instinct, that's all. I'm trying to remember what gave me the idea."

"We aren't in the Stone Age. Nobody can tell nowadays when a phone's tapped."

"Unless they're careless. Or unless they want you to know."

"Why should they want me to know?"

"To scare you perhaps. Who can tell?"

"Anyway, why tap *me*?"

"A question of security. They don't trust anyone. Especially people in our position. We are the most dangerous. We are supposed to know those damned Top Secrets."

"I don't feel dangerous."

"Put on the gramophone," Castle said.

Davis had a collection of pop music which was kept more carefully than anything else in the apartment. It was catalogued as meticulously as the British Museum library, and the top of the pops for any given year came as readily to Davis's memory as a Derby winner. He said, "You like something really old-fashioned and classical, don't you?" and put on *A Hard Day's Night*.

"Turn it louder."

"It shouldn't be louder."

"Turn it up all the same."

"It's awful this way."

"I feel more private," Castle said.

"You think they bug us too?"

"I wouldn't be surprised."

"You certainly have caught the disease," Davis said.

"Percival's conversation with you—it worries me—I simply can't believe it . . . it smells to heaven. I think they are on to a leak and are trying to check up."

"OK by me. It's their duty, isn't it? But it doesn't seem very clever if one can spot the dodge so easily."

"Yes—but Percival's story might be true just the

same. True and already blown. An agent, whatever he suspected, would feel bound to pass it on in case . . ."

"And *you* think *they* think we are the leaks?"

"Yes. One of us or perhaps both."

"But as we aren't who cares?" Davis said. "It's long past bedtime, Castle. If there's a mike under the pillow, they'll only hear my snores." He turned the music off. "We aren't the stuff of double agents, you and me."

Castle undressed and put out the light. It was stuffy in the small disordered room. He tried to raise the window, but the sash cord was broken. He stared down into the early morning street. No one went by: not even a policeman. Only a single taxi remained on a rank a little way down Davies Street in the direction of Claridge's. A burglar alarm sent up a futile ringing from somewhere in the Bond Street area, and a light rain had begun to fall. It gave a black glitter to the pavement like a policeman's raincoat. He drew the curtains close and got into bed, but he didn't sleep. A question mark kept him awake for a long while: had there always been a taxi rank so close to Davis's flat? Surely once he had to walk to the other side of Claridge's to find one? Before he fell asleep another question troubled him. Could they possibly, he wondered, be using Davis to watch him? Or were they using an innocent Davis to pass him on a marked bank note? He had small belief in Doctor Percival's story of Porton, and yet, as he had told Davis, it might be true.

Chapter IV

1

Castle had begun to be really worried about Davis. True, Davis made a joke of his own melancholy, but all the same the melancholy was deeply there, and it seemed a bad sign to Castle that Davis no longer chaffed Cynthia. His spoken thoughts too were becoming increasingly irrelevant to any work they had in hand. Once when Castle asked him, "69300/4, who's that?" Davis said, "A double room at the Polana looking out to sea." All the same there could be nothing seriously wrong with his health—he had been given his checkup recently by Doctor Percival.

"As usual we are waiting for a cable from Zaire," Davis said. "59800 never thinks of us, as he sits there on a hot evening swilling his sundowners without a care in the world."

"We'd better send him a reminder," Castle said. He wrote out on a slip of paper, "Our 185 no repeat no answer received," and put it in a tray for Cynthia to fetch.

Davis today had a regatta air. A new scarlet silk handkerchief with yellow dice dangled from his pocket like a flag on a still day, and his tie was bottle-green with a scarlet pattern. Even the handkerchief he kept for use which protruded from his sleeve looked new—a peacock blue. He had certainly dressed ship.

"Had a good weekend?" Castle asked.

"Yes, oh yes. In a way. Very quiet. The pollution boys were away smelling factory smoke in Gloucester. A gum factory."

A girl called Patricia (who had always refused to be known as Pat) came in from the secretaries' pool and collected their one cable. Like Cynthia she was army offspring, the niece of Brigadier Tomlinson: to employ close relations of men already in the department was considered good for security, and perhaps it eased the work of tracing, since many contacts would naturally be duplicated.

"Is this *all*?" the girl asked as though she were accustomed to work for more important sections than 6A.

"I'm afraid that's all we can manage, Pat," Castle told her, and she slammed the door behind her.

"You shouldn't have angered her," Davis said. "She may speak to Watson and we'll all be kept in after school writing telegrams."

"Where's Cynthia?"

"It's her day off."

Davis cleared his throat explosively—like a signal for the regatta to begin—and ran up a Red Ensign all over his face.

"I was going to ask you . . . would you mind if I

slipped away at eleven? I'll be back at one, I promise, and there's nothing doing. If anyone wants me just say that I've gone to the dentist."

"You ought to be wearing black," Castle said, "to convince Daintry. Those glad rags of yours don't go with dentists."

"Of course I'm not really going to the dentist. The fact of the matter is Cynthia said she'd meet me at the Zoo to see the giant pandas. Do you think she's beginning to weaken?"

"You really are in love, aren't you, Davis?"

"All I want, Castle, is a serious adventure. An adventure indefinite in length. A month, a year, a decade. I'm tired of one-night stands. Home from the King's Road after a party at four with a bloody hangover. Next morning—I think oh, that was fine, the girl was wonderful, I wish I'd done better though, if only I hadn't mixed the drinks ... and then I think how it would have been with Cynthia in Lourenço Marques. I could really *talk* to Cynthia. It helps John Thomas when you can talk a bit about your work. Those Chelsea birds, directly the fun's over, they want to find out things. What do I do? Where's my office? I used to pretend I was still at Aldermaston, but everyone now knows the bloody place is closed down. What am I to say?"

"Something in the City?"

"No glamor in that and these birds compare notes." He began arranging his things. He shut and locked his file of cards. There were two typed pages on his desk and he put them in his pocket.

"Taking things out of the office?" Castle said. "Be careful of Daintry. He's found you out once."

"He's finished with our section. 7 are catching it now. Anyway this is only the usual bit of nonsense: For your information only. Destroy after reading. Meaning damn

94

all. I'll 'commit it to memory' while I'm waiting for Cynthia. She's certain to be late."

"Remember Dreyfus. Don't leave it in a rubbish bin for the cleaner to find."

"I'll burn it as an offering in front of Cynthia." He went out and then came quickly back. "I wish you'd wish me luck, Castle."

"Of course. With all my heart."

The hackneyed phrase came warm and unintended to Castle's tongue. It surprised him, as though, in penetrating a familiar cave, on some holiday at the sea, he had observed on a familiar rock the primeval painting of a human face which he had always mistaken before for a chance pattern of fungi.

Half an hour later the telephone rang. A girl's voice said, "J.W. wants to speak to A.D."

"Too bad," Castle said. "A.D. can't speak to J.W."

"Who's that?" the voice asked with suspicion.

"Someone called M.C."

"Hold on a moment, please." A kind of high yapping came back to him over the phone. Then Watson's voice emerged unmistakably from the canine background, "I say, is that Castle?"

"Yes."

"I must speak to Davis."

"He's not here."

"Where is he?"

"He'll be back at one."

"That's too late. Where is he now?"

"At his dentist," Castle said with reluctance. He didn't like being involved in other men's lies: they complicated things.

"We'd better scramble," Watson said. There was the usual confusion: one of them pressing the right button too soon and then going back to normal transmission just when the other scrambled. When their voices were at last sorted out, Watson said, "Can you fetch him back? He's wanted at a conference."

"I can't very well drag him out of a dentist's chair. Anyway I don't know who his dentist is. It's not in the files."

"No?" Watson said with disapproval. "Then he ought to have left a note with the address."

Watson had tried once to be a barrister and failed. His obvious integrity perhaps offended judges; a moral tone, most judges seemed to feel, should be reserved for the Bench and not employed by junior counsel. But in "a department of the Foreign Office" he had risen quickly by the very quality which had served him so ill at the Bar. He easily outdistanced men like Castle of an older generation.

"He ought to have let me know he was going out," Watson said.

"Perhaps it was a very sudden toothache."

"C specially wanted him to be present. There's some report he wanted to discuss with him afterwards. He received it all right, I suppose?"

"He did mention a report. He seemed to think it was the usual average nonsense."

"Nonsense? It was Top Secret. What did he do with it?"

"I suppose he left it in the safe."

"Would you mind checking up?"

"I'll ask his secretary—oh, I'm sorry, I can't, she's off today. Is it all that important?"

"C must think so. I suppose you'd better come to the conference if Davis isn't there, but it was Davis's pigeon. Room 121 at twelve sharp."

2

The conference did not seem of pressing importance. A member of MI5 whom Castle had never seen before was present because the main point on the agenda was to distinguish more clearly than in the past between the responsibilities of MI5 and MI6. Before the last war MI6 had never operated on British territory and security there was left to MI5. The system broke down in Africa with the fall of France and the necessity of running agents from British territory into the Vichy colonies. With the return of peace the old system had never been quite re-established. Tanzania and Zanzibar were united officially as one state, a member of the Commonwealth, but it was difficult to regard the island of Zanzibar as British territory with its Chinese training camps. Confusion had arisen because MI5 and MI6 both had representatives in Dar-es-Salaam, and relations between them had not always been close or friendly.

"Rivalry," C said, as he opened the conference, "is a healthy thing up to a point. But sometimes there has been a lack of trust. We have not always exchanged traces of agents. Sometimes we've been playing the same man, for espionage and counter-espionage." He sat back to let the MI5 man have his say.

There were very few there whom Castle knew except Watson. A lean gray man with a prominent Adam's apple was said to be the oldest man in the firm. His name was Chilton. He dated back to before Hitler's war and surprisingly he had made no enemies. Now he dealt principally with Ethiopia. He was also the greatest living authority on tradesmen's tokens in the eighteenth century and was often called in for consultation by Sotheby's. Laker was an ex-guardsman with ginger hair and a ginger moustache who looked after the Arab republics in North Africa.

The MI5 man stopped talking about the crossed lines. C said, "Well, that's that. The treaty of Room 121. I'm sure we all understand our positions better now. It was very kind of you to look in, Puller."

"Pullen."

"Sorry. Pullen. Now, if you won't think us inhospitable, we have a few little domestic things to discuss . . ." When Pullen had closed the door he said, "I'm never quite happy with those MI5 types. Somehow they always seem to carry with them a kind of police atmosphere. It's natural, of course, dealing as they do with counter-espionage. To me espionage is more of a gentleman's job, but of course I'm old-fashioned."

Percival spoke up from a distant corner. Castle hadn't even noticed that he was there. "I've always rather fancied MI9 myself."

"What does MI9 do?" Laker asked, brushing up his moustache. He was aware of being one of the few genuine military men among all the MI numerals.

"I've long forgotten," Percival said, "but they always seem more friendly." Chilton barked briefly—it was the way he always laughed.

Watson said, "Didn't they deal with escape methods in the war, or was that 11? I didn't know they were still around."

"Oh well, it's true I haven't seen them in a long time," Percival said with his kindly encouraging doctor's air. He might have been describing the symptoms of flu. "Perhaps they've packed up."

"By the way," C asked, "is Davis here? There was a report I wanted to discuss with him. I don't seem to have met him in my pilgrimage around Section 6."

"He's at the dentist's," Castle said.

"He never told me, sir," Watson complained.

"Oh well, it's not urgent. Nothing in Africa ever is. Changes come slowly and are generally impermanent. I wish the same were true of Europe." He gathered his papers and slipped quietly away, like a host who feels that a house party will get on much better without him.

"It's odd," Percival said, "when I saw Davis the other day his crackers seemed to be in good shape. Said he never had any trouble with them. No sign even of tartar. By the way, Castle, you might get me the name of his dentist. Just for my medical files. If he's having trouble we like to recommend our own men. It makes for better security."

Part Three

Chapter I

1

Doctor Percival had invited Sir John Hargreaves to lunch with him at his club, the Reform. They made a habit of lunching alternately at the Reform and the Travellers once a month on a Saturday, when most members had already gone into the country. Pall Mall, a steely gray, like a Victorian engraving, was framed by the long windows. The Indian summer was nearly over, the clocks had all been altered, and you could feel the approach of winter concealed in the smallest wind. They began with smoked trout which led Sir John Hargreaves to tell Doctor Percival that he was now seriously thinking of trying to stock the stream which divided his park from the agricultural land. "I'll need your advice, Emmanuel," he said.

They were on Christian-name terms when they were safely alone.

For a long while they talked of fishing for trout, or rather Doctor Percival talked—it was a subject which always appeared a limited one to Hargreaves, but he knew Doctor Percival would be quite capable of enlarging on it until dinner. However, he was shifted from trout to another favorite topic by a chance diversion to the subject of his club. "If I had a conscience," Doctor Percival said, "I would not remain a member here. I'm a member because the food—and the smoked trout too if you will forgive me, John—is the best in London."

"I like the food at the Travellers just as much," Hargreaves said.

"Ah, but you are forgetting our steak-and-kidney pudding. I know you won't like me saying so, but I prefer it to your wife's pie. Pastry holds the gravy at a distance. Pudding absorbs the gravy. Pudding, you might say, cooperates."

"But why would your conscience be troubled, Emmanuel, even if you had one—which is a most unlikely supposition?"

"You must know that to be a member here I had to sign a declaration in favor of the Reform Act of 1866. True, that Act was not so bad as some of its successors, like giving the vote at eighteen, but it opened the gates to the pernicious doctrine of one man one vote. Even the Russians subscribe to that now for propaganda purposes, but they are clever enough to make sure that the things they can vote for in their own country are of no importance at all."

"What a reactionary you are, Emmanuel. I do believe, though, there's something in what you say about pudding and pastry. We might try out a pudding next year—if we are still able to afford a shoot."

"If you can't, it will be because of one man one vote.

Be honest, John, and admit what a hash that stupid idea has made of Africa."

"I suppose it takes time for true democracy to work."

"That kind of democracy will never work."

"Would you really like to go back to the house-holder's vote, Emmanuel?" Hargreaves could never tell to what extent Doctor Percival was really serious.

"Yes, why not? The income required for a man to vote would be properly adjusted, of course, each year to deal with inflation. Four thousand a year might be the proper level for getting a vote today. That would give the miners and dockers a vote, which would save us a lot of trouble."

After coffee they walked, by common consent, down the great Gladstonian stairs out into the chill of Pall Mall. The old brickwork of St. James's Palace glowed like a dying fire through the gray weather, and the sentry flickered scarlet—a last doomed flame. They crossed into the park and Doctor Percival said, "Returning for a moment to trout . . ." They chose a bench where they could watch the ducks move with the effortlessness of magnetic toys across the surface of the pond. They both wore the same heavy tweed overcoats, the overcoats of men who live by choice in the country. A man wearing a bowler hat passed them; he was carrying an umbrella and he frowned at some thought of his own as he went by. "That's Browne with an e," Doctor Percival said.

"What a lot of people you know, Emmanuel."

"One of the PM's economic advisers. I wouldn't give him a vote whatever he earned."

"Well, let's talk a little business, shall we? Now we are alone. I suppose you are afraid of being bugged at the Reform."

"Why not? Surrounded by a lot of one man one vote fanatics. If they were capable of giving the vote to a bunch of cannibals . . ."

"You mustn't run down cannibals," Hargreaves said, "some of my best friends have been cannibals, and now that Browne with an e is out of earshot . . ."

"I've been going over things very carefully, John, with Daintry, and personally I'm convinced that Davis is the man we are looking for."

"Is Daintry convinced too?"

"No. It's all circumstantial, it has to be, and Daintry's got a very legalistic mind. I can't pretend that I like Daintry. No humor but naturally very conscientious. I spent an evening with Davis, a few weeks ago. He's not an advanced alcoholic like Burgess and Maclean, but he drinks a lot—and he's been drinking more since our check started, I think. Like those two and Philby, he's obviously under some sort of strain. A bit of a manic depressive— and a manic depressive usually has that touch of schizoid about him essential for a double agent. He's anxious to get abroad. Probably because he knows he's being watched and perhaps they've forbidden him to try and bolt. Of course he'd be out of our control in Lourenço Marques and in a very useful spot for them."

"But what about the evidence?"

"It's a bit patchy still, but can we afford to wait for perfect evidence, John? After all we don't intend to put him on trial. The alternative is Castle (you agreed with me that we could rule out Watson), and we've gone into Castle just as thoroughly. Happy second marriage, first wife killed in the blitz, a good family background, the father was a doctor—one of those old-fashioned GPs, a member of the Liberal Party, but not, please note, of the Reform, who looked after his patients through a lifetime and forgot to send in bills, the mother's still alive—she was a head warden in the blitz and won the George Medal. A bit of a patriot and attends Conservative rallies. Pretty good stock, you'll admit. No sign of heavy drinking with Castle, careful about money too. Davis spends a good deal on port and whisky and his Jaguar, bets regularly on the tote—pretends to be a judge of form and to win quite a lot—that's a classic excuse for spending more than you earn. Daintry told me he was caught once taking a report from 59800 out of the office. Said he meant to read it over lunch. Then you remember the day we had the conference with MI5 and you wanted him to be present. Left the office to see his dentist—he never went to his dentist (his teeth are in perfect condition—I know that myself) and then two weeks later we got evidence of another leak."

"Do we know where he went?"

"Daintry was already having him shadowed by Special Branch. He went to the Zoo. Through the members' entrance. The chap who was following him had to queue up at the ordinary entrance and lost him. A nice touch."

"Any idea whom he met?"

"He's a clever one. Must have known he was followed. It turned out that he'd confessed to Castle that he hadn't gone to the dentist. Said he was meeting his secretary (it was her day off) at the pandas. But there was that report you wanted to talk to him about. It was never in the safe—Daintry checked that."

"Not a very important report. Oh, it's all a bit shady, I admit, but I wouldn't call any of it hard evidence, Emmanuel. Did he meet the secretary?"

"Oh, he met her all right. He left the Zoo with her, but what happened in between?"

"Have you tried the marked note technique?"

"I told him in strict confidence a bogus story about researches at Porton, but nothing's turned up yet."

"I don't see how we can act on what you've got at present."

"Suppose he panicked and tried to make a bolt for it?"

"Then we'd have to act quickly. Have you decided on how we should act?"

"I'm working on rather a cute little notion, John. Peanuts."

"Peanuts!"

"Those little salted things you eat with cocktails."

"Of course I know what peanuts are, Emmanuel. Don't forget I was a Commissioner in West Africa."

"Well, they're the answer. Peanuts when they go bad produce a mold. Caused by *aspergillus flavus*—but you can forget the name. It's not important, and I know you were never any good at Latin."

"Go on, for heaven's sake."

"To make it easy for you I'll concentrate on the mold. The mold produces a group of highly toxic substances known collectively as aflatoxin. And aflatoxin is the answer to our little problem."

"How does it work?"

"We don't know for certain about human beings, but no animal seems immune, so it's highly unlikely that we are. Aflatoxin kills the liver cells. They only need to be exposed to the stuff for about three hours. The symptoms in animals are that they lose their appetites and become lethargic. The wings of birds become weak. A postmortem shows hemorrhage and necrosis in the liver and engorgement of the kidneys, if you'll forgive me my medical jargon. Death usually occurs within a week."

"Damnation, Emmanuel, I've always liked peanuts. Now I'll never be able to eat them again."

"Oh, you needn't worry, John. Your salted peanuts are hand picked—though I suppose an accident might just possibly happen, but at the rate you finish a tin they are not likely to go bad."

"You seem to have really enjoyed your researches. Sometimes, Emmanuel, you give me the creeps."

"You must admit it's a very neat little solution to our problem. A postmortem would show only the damage done to the liver, and I expect the coroner would warn the public against the danger of overindulgence in port."

"I suppose you've even worked out how to get this aero—"

"Aflatoxin, John. There's no serious difficulty. I have a fellow at Porton preparing some now. You only need a very small quantity. Point 0063 milligrams per kilogram bodyweight. Of course I've weighed Davis. 0.5 milligrams should do the trick, but to be quite sure let's say .75. Though we might test first with an even smaller dose. One side advantage of all this, of course, is that we should gain valuable information on how aflatoxin works on a human being."

"Do you never find that you shock yourself, Emmanuel?"

"There's nothing shocking about this, John. Think of all the other deaths Davis might die. Real cirrhosis would be much slower. With a dose of aflatoxin he'll hardly suffer at all. Increasing lethargy, perhaps a bit of leg trouble as he doesn't have wings, and of course a certain amount of nausea is to be expected. To spend only a week dying is quite a happy fate, when you think what many people suffer."

"You talk as though he were already condemned."

"Well, John, I'm quite convinced he's our man. I'm only waiting for the green light from you."

"If Daintry were satisfied . . ."

"Oh, Daintry, John, we can't wait for the kind of evidence Daintry demands."

"Give me one piece of *hard* evidence."

"I can't yet, but better not wait for it too long. You remember what you said that night after the shoot—a complaisant husband is always at the mercy of the lover. We can't afford another scandal in the firm, John."

Another bowler-hatted figure went by, coat collar

turned up, into the October dusk. The lights were coming on one by one in the Foreign Office.

"Let's talk a little more about the trout stream, Emmanuel."

"Ah, trout. Let other people boast about salmon—gross oily stupid fellows with that blind urge of theirs to swim upstream which makes for easy fishing. All you need are big boots and a strong arm and a clever gillie. But the trout—oh, the trout—he's the real king of fish."

2

Colonel Daintry had a two-roomed flat in St. James's Street which he had found through the agency of another member of the firm. During the war it had been used by MI6 as a rendezvous for interviewing possible recruits. There were only three apartments in the building, which was looked after by an old housekeeper, who lived in a room somewhere out of sight under the roof. Daintry was on the first floor above a restaurant (the noise of hilarity kept him awake until the small hours when the last taxi ground away). Over his head were a retired businessman who had once been connected with the rival wartime service SOE, and a retired general who had fought in the Western Desert. The general was too old now to be seen often on the stairs, but the businessman, who suffered from gout, used to get as far as the Carlton Club across the road. Daintry was no cook and he usually economized for one meal by buying cold chipolatas at Fortnum's. He had never liked clubs; if he felt hungry, a rare event, there was Overton's just below. His bedroom and his bathroom looked out on a tiny ancient court containing a sun dial and a silversmith. Few people who walked down St. James's Street knew of the court's existence. It was a very discreet flat and not unsuitable for a lonely man.

For the third time with his Remington Daintry went over his face. Scruples of cleanliness grew with loneliness like the hairs on a corpse. He was about to have one of his rare dinners with his daughter. He had suggested giving her dinner at Overton's where he was known, but she told him she wanted roast beef. All the same she refused to go to Simpson's where Daintry was also known because she said the atmosphere was too masculine. She insisted on meeting him at Stone's in Panton Street, where she would expect him at eight. She never came to his flat—that would have shown disloyalty to her mother, even though she knew there was no woman sharing it. Perhaps even Overton's was tainted by the proximity of his flat.

It always irritated Daintry to enter Stone's and to be asked by a man in a ridiculous topper if he had booked a table. The former old-fashioned chophouse which he remembered as a young man had been destroyed in the blitz and been rebuilt with an expense-account décor. Daintry thought with regret of the ancient waiters in dusty black tails and the sawdust on the floor and the strong beer specially brewed at Burton-on-Trent. Now all the way up the stairs there were meaningless panels of giant playing cards more suited to a gambling house, and white naked statues stood under the falling water of a fountain which played beyond the plate glass at the end of the restaurant. They seemed to make the autumn strike colder than the air outside. His daughter was already waiting there.

"I'm sorry if I'm late, Elizabeth," Daintry said. He knew he was three minutes early.

"It's all right. I've given myself a drink."

111

"I'll have a sherry too."

"I've got news to give you. Only Mother knows as yet."

"How is your mother?" Daintry asked with formal politeness. It was always his first question and he was glad when he had disposed of it.

"She's quite well considering. She's spending a week or two at Brighton for a change of air."

It was as if they were speaking of an acquaintance whom he hardly knew—it was odd to think there had ever been a time when he and his wife were close enough to share a sexual spasm which had produced the beautiful girl who sat so elegantly opposite him drinking her Tio Pepe. The sadness which was never far away from Daintry when he met his daughter descended as always—like a sense of guilt. Why guilt? he would argue with himself. He had always been what was called faithful. "I hope the weather will be good," he said. He knew that he had bored his wife, but why should that be a cause of guilt? After all she had consented to marry him knowing all; she had voluntarily entered that chilling world of long silences. He envied men who were free to come home and talk the gossip of an ordinary office.

"Don't you want to know my news, Father?"

Over her shoulder he suddenly noticed Davis. Davis sat alone at a table laid for two. He was waiting, drumming with his fingers, his eyes on his napkin. Daintry hoped he wouldn't look up.

"News?"

"I told you. Only Mother knows. And the other, of course," she added with an embarrassed laugh. Daintry looked at the tables on either side of Davis. He half expected to see Davis's shadow there, but the two elderly couples, well advanced in their meal, certainly didn't look like members of the Special Branch.

112

"You don't seem in the least interested, Father. Your thoughts are miles away."

"I'm sorry. I just saw someone I know. What is the secret news?"

"I'm getting married."

"Married!" Daintry exclaimed. "Does your mother know?"

"I've just said that I told her."

"I'm sorry."

"Why should you be sorry that I'm getting married?"

"I didn't mean that. I meant . . . Of course I'm not sorry if he's worthy of you. You are a very pretty girl, Elizabeth."

"I'm not up for sale, Father. I suppose in your day good legs put up the market price."

"What does he do?"

"He's in an advertising agency. He handles the Jameson's Baby Powder account."

"Is that a good thing?"

"It's very good. They are spending a huge amount trying to push Johnson's Baby Powder into second place. Colin's arranged wonderful television spots. He even wrote a theme song himself."

"You like him a lot? You're *quite* sure . . . ?"

Davis had ordered a second whisky. He was looking at the menu—but he must have read it many times already.

"We are both quite sure, Father. After all, we've been living together for the past year."

"I'm sorry," Daintry said again—it was turning into an evening of apologies. "I never knew. I suppose your mother did?"

"She guessed, naturally."

"She sees more of you than I do."

He felt like a man who was departing into a long

113

exile and who looks back from the deck of a ship at the faint coastline of his country as it sinks below the horizon.

"He wanted to come tonight and be introduced, but I told him this time I wanted to be alone with you." "This time": it had the sound of a long goodbye; now he could see only the bare horizon, the land had gone.

"When are you getting married?"

"On Saturday the twenty-first. At a registry office. We aren't inviting anybody, except of course Mother. And a few of our friends. Colin has no parents."

Colin, he wondered, who's Colin? But of course he was the man at Jameson's.

"You'd be welcome—but I always have the feeling that you're frightened of meeting Mother."

Davis had given up whatever hope he may have had. As he paid for the whiskies, he looked up from the bill and saw Daintry. It was as though two emigrants had come on deck for the same purpose, to look their last on their country, saw each other and wondered whether to speak. Davis turned and made for the door. Daintry looked after him with regret—but after all there was no need to get acquainted yet, they were sailing together on a long voyage.

Daintry put his glass sharply down and spilled some sherry. He felt a sudden irritation against Percival. The man had no evidence against Davis which would stand up in a court of law. He didn't trust Percival. He remembered Percival at the shoot. Percival was never lonely, he laughed as easily as he talked, he knew about pictures, he was at ease with strangers. He had no daughter who was living with a stranger in a flat he had never seen—he didn't even know where it was.

"We thought afterwards we'd have some drinks and sandwiches at a hotel or perhaps at Mother's flat. Mother has to get back to Brighton afterwards. But if you'd like to come . . ."

"I don't think I can. I'm going away that weekend," he lied.

"You do make engagements a long time ahead."

"I have to." He lied again miserably, "There are so many of them. I'm a busy man, Elizabeth. If I'd known . . ."

"I thought I'd give you a surprise."

"We ought to order, oughtn't we? You'll take the roast beef, not the saddle of mutton?"

"Roast beef for me."

"Are you having a honeymoon?"

"Oh, we'll just stay at home for the weekend. Perhaps when the spring comes . . . At the moment Colin's so busy with Jameson's Baby Powder."

"We ought to celebrate," Daintry said. "A bottle of champagne?" He didn't like champagne, but a man must do his duty.

"I'd really rather just have a glass of red wine."

"There's a wedding present to think about."

"A check would be best—and easier for you. You don't want to go shopping. Mother's giving us a lovely carpet."

"I haven't got my checkbook on me. I'll send the check round on Monday."

After dinner they said goodbye in Panton Street—he offered to take her home in a taxi, but she said she preferred to walk. He had no idea where the flat was that she shared. Her private life was as closely guarded as his own, but in his case there had never been anything much to guard. It was not often that he enjoyed their meals together because there was so little for them to talk about, but now, when he realized that they would never again be alone, he felt a sense of abandonment. He said, "Perhaps I could put off that weekend."

"Colin would be glad to meet you, Father."

"Could I perhaps bring a friend with me?"

115

"Of course. Anyone. Who will you bring?"

"I'm not sure. Perhaps someone from the office."

"That would be fine. But you know—you really needn't be scared. Mother likes you." He watched as she made her way east in the direction of Leicester Square— and after?—he had no idea—before he turned west for St. James's Street.

Chapter II

1

The Indian summer had returned for a day, and Castle agreed to a picnic—Sam was growing restive after the long quarantine and Sarah had a fanciful notion that any lingering last germ would be whisked away among the beech woods with the leaves of autumn. She had prepared a thermos of hot onion soup, half a cold chicken to be dismembered in the fingers, some rock buns, a mutton bone for Buller, and a second thermos of coffee. Castle added his flask of whisky. There were two blankets to sit on, and even Sam had consented to take an overcoat in case the wind rose.

"It's crazy to have a picnic in October," Castle said

with pleasure at the rashness of it. The picnic offered escape from office caution, a prudent tongue, foresight. But
then, of course, the telephone rang, clanging away like a
police alarm while they packed the bags on their bicycles.

Sarah said, "It's those men with masks again. They'll
spoil our picnic. I'll be wondering all the time what's happening at home."

Castle replied gloomily (he had his hand over the receiver), "No, no, don't worry, it's only Davis."

"What does he want?"

"He's at Boxmoor with his car. It was such a fine day
he thought he'd look me up."

"Oh, damn Davis. Just when everything's prepared.
There's no other food in the house. Except our supper.
And there's not enough of that for four."

"You go off alone if you like with Sam. I'll lunch at
the Swan with Davis."

"A picnic wouldn't be any fun," Sarah said, "without
you."

Sam said, "Is it Mr. Davis? I want Mr. Davis. We can
play hide-and-seek. We aren't enough without Mr. Davis."

Castle said, "We could take Davis with us, I suppose."

"Half a chicken among four . . . ?"

"There are enough rock buns already for a regiment."

"He won't enjoy a picnic in October unless he's crazy
too."

But Davis proved as crazy as the rest of them. He said
that he loved picnics even on a hot summer's day when
there were wasps and flies, but he much preferred the
autumn. As there was no room in his Jaguar he met them
at a chosen rendezvous on the Common, and at lunch he
won the wishbone of the half chicken with an agile turn
of the wrist. Then he introduced a new game. The others
had to guess his wish by asking questions, and only if
they failed to guess could he expect his wish to be

granted. Sarah guessed it with a flash of intuition. He had wished that one day he would become "top of the pops."

"Oh well, I had little hope of my wish coming true anyway. I can't write a note."

By the time the last rock buns had been eaten the afternoon sun was low above the gorse bushes and the wind was rising. Copper leaves floated down to lie on last year's mast. "Hide-and-seek," Davis suggested, and Castle saw how Sam gazed at Davis with the eyes of a hero-worshipper.

They drew lots to decide which of them should hide first, and Davis won. He went loping away among the trees huddled deep in his camel-hair overcoat, looking like a strayed bear from a zoo. After counting sixty the rest set off in pursuit, Sam toward the edge of the Common, Sarah toward Ashridge, Castle into the woods where he had last seen Davis go. Buller followed him, probably in hope of a cat. A low whistle guided Castle to where Davis hid in a hollow surrounded by bracken.

"It's bloody cold hiding," Davis said, "in the shade."

"You suggested the game yourself. We were all ready to go home. Down, Buller. Down, damn you."

"I know, but I could see how much the little bastard wanted it."

"You seem to know children better than I do. I'd better shout to them. We'll catch our death . . ."

"No, don't do that yet. I was hoping you'd come by. I want a word with you alone. Something important."

"Can't it wait till tomorrow at the office?"

"No, you've made me suspicious of the office. Castle, I really think I'm being followed."

"I told you I thought your phone was tapped."

"I didn't believe you. But since that night . . . On Thursday I took Cynthia out to Scott's. There was a man in the lift as we went down. And later he was in Scott's

119

too drinking Black Velvet. And then today, driving down to Berkhamsted—I noticed a car behind me at Marble Arch—only by chance because for a moment I thought I knew the man—I didn't, but I saw him again behind me at Boxmoor. In a black Mercedes."

"The same man as at Scott's?"

"Of course not. They wouldn't be as stupid as that. My Jaguar's got a turn of speed and there was Sunday traffic on the road. I lost him before Berkhamsted."

"We're not trusted, Davis, nobody is, but who cares if we're innocent?"

"Oh yes, I know all that. Like an old theme song, isn't it? Who cares? 'I'm innocent. Who cares? If they take me unawares, I'll say I only went, To buy some golden apples and some pears . . .' I might be top of the pops yet."

"Did you really lose him before Berkhamsted?"

"Yes. As far as I can tell. But what's it all about, Castle? Is it just a routine check, like Daintry's seemed to be? You've been in this bloody show longer than any of us. You ought to know."

"I told you that night with Percival. I think there must have been a leak of some kind, and they suspect a double agent. So they're putting on a security check, and they don't much mind if you notice it. They think you may lose your nerve, if you are guilty."

"Me a double agent? You don't believe it, Castle?"

"No, of course not. You don't have to worry. Just be patient. Let them finish their check and they won't believe it either. I expect they're checking me too—and Watson."

In the distance Sarah was calling out, "We give up. We give up." A thin voice came from further away, "Oh no, we don't. Keep hiding, Mr. Davis. Please, Mr. Davis . . ."

Buller barked and Davis sneezed. "Children are merciless," he said.

120

There was a rustle in the bracken around their hiding-place and Sam appeared. "Caught," he said, and then he saw Castle. "Oh, but you cheated."

"No," Castle said, "I couldn't call out. He held me up at the point of a gun."

"Where's the gun?"

"Look in his breast pocket."

"There's only a fountain pen," Sam said.

"It's a gas gun," Davis said, "disguised as a fountain pen. You see this knob. It squirts what looks like ink— only it's not really ink, it's nerve gas. James Bond was never allowed one like this—it's too secret. Put up your hands."

Sam put them up. "Are you a real spy?" he asked.

"I'm a double agent for Russia," Davis said, "and if you value your life, you must give me fifty yards start." He burst through the bracken and ran clumsily in his heavy overcoat through the beech woods. Sam pursued him up one slope, down another. Davis reached a bank above the Ashridge road where he had left his scarlet Jaguar. He pointed his fountain pen at Sam and shouted a message as mutilated as one of Cynthia's cables, "Picnic ... love ... Sarah," and then he was gone with a loud explosion from his exhaust.

"Ask him to come again, Sam said, "please ask him to come again."

"Of course. Why not? When the spring comes."

"The spring's a long way off," Sam said. "I'll be at school."

"There'll always be weekends," Castle replied but without conviction. He remembered too well how slowly time limps by in childhood. A car passed them, heading toward London, a black car—perhaps it was a Mercedes, but Castle knew very little about cars.

"I like Mr. Davis," Sam said.

"Yes, so do I."

"Nobody plays hide-and-seek as well as he does. Not even you."

2

"I find I'm not making much headway with *War and Peace*, Mr. Halliday."

"Oh dear, oh dear. It's a great book if you only have the patience. Have you reached the retreat from Moscow?"

"No."

"It's a terrible story."

"It seems a lot less terrible to us today, doesn't it? After all, the French were soldiers—and snow isn't as bad as napalm. You fall asleep, so they say—you don't burn alive."

"Yes, when I think of all those poor children in Vietnam . . . I wanted to join some of the marches they used to have here, but my son would never let me. He's nervous of the police in that little shop of his, though what harm he does with a naughty book or two I can't see. As I always say—the men that buy them—well, you can't very well do much harm to them, can you?"

"No, they are not clean young Americans doing their duty like the napalm bombers were," Castle said. Sometimes he found it impossible not to show one splinter of the submerged iceberg life he led.

"And yet there wasn't a thing any of us could have done," Halliday said. "The Government talk about democracy, but what notice did the Government ever take of all our banners and slogans? Except at election time. It helped them choose which promises to break, that's all. Next day we used to read in the paper how another innocent village had been wiped out in error. Oh, they'll be doing the same thing in South Africa before long. First it was the little yellow babies—no more yellow than we are—and then it will be the little black babies . . ."

"Let's change the subject," Castle said. "Recommend me something to read that isn't about war."

"There's always Trollope," Mr. Halliday said. "My son's very fond of Trollope. Though it doesn't really go with the kind of things he sells, does it?"

"I've never read Trollope. Isn't he a bit ecclesiastical? Anyway, ask your son to choose me one and post it home."

"Your friend didn't like *War and Peace* either?"

"No. In fact he got tired of it before I did. Too much war for him too perhaps."

"I could easily slip across the road and have a word with my son. I know he prefers the political novels—or what he calls the sociological. I've heard him speak well of *The Way We Live Now*. A good title, sir. Always contemporary. Do you want to take it home tonight?"

"No, not today."

"It will be two copies as usual, sir, I suppose? I envy you having a friend with whom you can discuss literature. Too few people nowadays are interested in literature."

After Castle had left Mr. Halliday's shop he walked to Piccadilly Circus station and went to find a telephone. He chose an end box and looked through the glass at his only neighbor: she was a fat spotty girl who giggled and sucked a gum while she listened to something gratifying. A voice said, "Hello," and Castle said, "I'm sorry, wrong number again," and left the box. The girl was parking her gum on the back of the telephone directory while she got

123

down to a long satisfactory conversation. He waited by a ticket machine and watched her for a little while to make sure she had no interest in him.

3

"What are you doing?" Sarah asked. "Didn't you hear me call?"

She looked at the book on his desk and said, "*War and Peace.* I thought you were getting tired of *War and Peace.*"

He gathered up a sheet of paper, folded it and put it in his pocket.

"I'm trying my hand at an essay."

"Show me."

"No. Only if it comes off."

"Where will you send it?"

"The *New Statesman* . . . *Encounter* . . . who knows?"

"It's a very long time since you wrote anything. I'm glad you are starting again."

"Yes. I seem doomed always to try again."

Chapter III

1

Castle helped himself to another whisky. Sarah had been upstairs a long time with Sam, and he was alone, waiting for the bell to ring, waiting ... His mind wandered to that other occasion when he had waited for at least three-quarters of an hour, in the office of Cornelius Muller. He had been given a copy of the *Rand Daily Mail* to read—an odd choice since the paper was the enemy of most things that BOSS, the organization which employed Muller, supported. He had already read that day's issue with his breakfast, but now he reread every page with no other purpose than just to pass the time. Whenever he looked up at the clock he met the eyes of one of the two junior officials who sat stiffly behind their desks and perhaps took it in turn to watch him. Did they expect him to pull out a razor blade and slit open a vein? But torture, he told himself, was always left to the Security Police—or so he believed. And in his case, after all, there could be no fear of torture from any service—he was protected by diplomatic privilege; he was one of the untorturables. No diplomatic privilege, however, could be extended to include Sarah; he had learned during the last year in South Africa the age-old lesson that fear and love are indivisible.

Castle finished his whisky and poured himself another small one. He had to be careful.

Sarah called down to him, "What are you doing, darling?"

"Just waiting for Mr. Muller," he replied, "and drinking another whisky."

"Not too many, darling." They had decided that he should welcome Muller first alone. Muller would no doubt arrive from London in an embassy car. A black Mercedes like the big officials all used in South Africa? "Get over the first embarrassments," C had said, "and leave serious business, of course, for the office. At home you are more likely to pick up a useful indication . . . I mean of what we have and they haven't. But for God's sake, Castle, keep your cool." And now he struggled to keep his cool with the help of a third whisky while he listened and listened for the sound of a car, any car, but there was little traffic at this hour in King's Road—all the commuters had long since arrived safely home.

If fear and love are indivisible, so too are fear and hate. Hate is an automatic response to fear, for fear humiliates. When he had been allowed at last to drop the *Rand Daily Mail* and they interrupted his fourth reading of the same leading article, with its useless routine protest against the evil of petty apartheid, he was deeply aware of

126

his cowardice. Three years of life in South Africa and six months of love for Sarah had turned him, he knew well, into a coward.

Two men waited for him in the inner office: Mr. Muller sat behind a large desk of the finest South African wood which bore nothing but a blank blotting pad and a highly polished pen-stand and one file suggestively open. He was a man a little younger than Castle, approaching fifty perhaps, and he had the kind of face which in ordinary circumstances Castle would have found it easy to forget: an indoors face, as smooth and pale as a bank clerk's or a junior civil servant's, a face unmarked by the torments of any belief, human or religious, a face which was ready to receive orders and obey them promptly without question, a conformist face. Certainly not the face of a bully—though that described the features of the second man in uniform who sat with his legs slung with insolence over the arm of an easy chair as though he wanted to show he was any man's equal; *his* face had not avoided the sun: it had a kind of infernal flush as though it had been exposed too long to a heat which would have been much too fierce for ordinary men. Muller's glasses had gold rims; it was a gold-rimmed country.

"Take a seat," Muller told Castle with just sufficient politeness to pass as courtesy, but the only seat left him to take was a hard narrow chair as little made for comfort as a chair in a church—if he should be required to kneel, there was no hassock available on the hard floor to support his knees. He sat in silence and the two men, the pale one and the heated one, looked back at him and said nothing. Castle wondered how long the silence would continue. Cornelius Muller had a sheet detached from the file in front of him, and after a while he began to tap it with the end of his gold ball-point pen, always in the same place, as though he were hammering in a pin. The

127

small tap tap tap recorded the length of silence like the tick of a watch. The other man scratched his skin above his sock, and so it went on, tap tap and scratch scratch.

At last Muller consented to speak. "I'm glad you found it possible to call, Mr. Castle."

"Yes, it wasn't very convenient, but, well, here I am."

"We wanted to avoid making an unnecessary scandal by writing to your ambassador."

It was Castle's turn now to remain silent, while he tried to make out what they meant by the word scandal.

"Captain Van Donck—this is Captain Van Donck—has brought the matter to us here. He felt it would be more suitably dealt with by us than by the Security Police—because of your position at the British Embassy. You've been under observation, Mr. Castle, for a long time, but an arrest in your case, I feel, would serve no practical purpose—your embassy would claim diplomatic privilege. Of course we could always dispute it before a magistrate and then they would certainly have to send you home. That would probably be the end of your career, wouldn't it?"

Castle said nothing.

"You've been very imprudent, even stupid," Cornelius Muller said, "but then I don't myself consider that stupidity ought to be punished as a crime. Captain Van Donck and the Security Police, though, take a different view, a legalistic view—and they may be right. He would prefer to go through the form of arrest and charge you in court. He feels that diplomatic privileges are often unduly stretched as far as the junior employees of an embassy are concerned. He would like to fight the case as a matter of principle."

The hard chair was becoming painful, and Castle wanted to shift his thigh, but he thought the movement might be taken as a sign of weakness. He was trying very hard to make out what it was they really knew. How many of his agents, he wondered, were incriminated? His own relative safety made him feel shame. In a genuine war an officer can always die with his men and so keep his self-respect.

"Start talking, Castle," Captain Van Donck demanded. He swung his legs off the arm of his chair and prepared to rise—or so it seemed—it was probably bluff. He opened and closed one fist and stared at his signet ring. Then he began to polish the gold ring with a finger as though it were a gun which had to be kept well oiled. In this country you couldn't escape gold. It was in the dust of the cities, artists used it as paint, it would be quite natural for the police to use it for beating in a man's face.

"Talk about what?" Castle asked.

"You are like most Englishmen who come to the Republic," Muller said, "you feel a certain automatic sympathy for black Africans. We can understand your feeling. All the more because we are Africans ourselves. We have lived here for three hundred years. The Bantu are newcomers like yourselves. But I don't need to give you a history lesson. As I said, we understand your point of view, even though it's a very ignorant one, but when it leads a man to grow emotional, then it becomes dangerous, and when you reach the point of breaking the law . . ."

"Which law?"

"I think you know very well which law."

"It's true I'm planning a study on apartheid, the Embassy have no objection, but it's a serious sociological one—quite objective—and it's still in my head. You hardly have the right to censor it yet. Anyway it won't be published, I imagine, in this country."

"If you want to fuck a black whore," Captain Van

129

Donck interrupted with impatience, "why don't you go to a whorehouse in Lesotho or Swaziland? They are still part of your so-called Commonwealth."

Then it was that for the first time Castle realized Sarah, not he, was the one who was in danger.

"I'm too old to be interested in whores," he said.

"Where were you on the nights of February 4th and 7th? The afternoon of February 21st?"

"You obviously know—or think that you know," Castle said. "I keep my engagement book in my office."

He hadn't seen Sarah for forty-eight hours. Was she already in the hands of men like Captain Van Donck? His fear and his hate grew simultaneously. He forgot that in theory he was a diplomat, however junior. "What the hell are you talking about? And you?" he added to Cornelius Muller, "You too, what do you want me for?"

Captain Van Donck was a brutal and simple man who believed in something, however repugnant—he was one of those one could forgive. What Castle could never bring himself to forgive was this smooth educated officer of BOSS. It was men of this kind—men with the education to know what they were about—that made a hell in heaven's despite. He thought of what his Communist friend Carson had so often said to him—"Our worst enemies here are not the ignorant and the simple, however cruel, our worst enemies are the intelligent and the corrupt."

Muller said, "You must know very well that you've broken the Race Relations Act with that Bantu girl friend of yours." He spoke in a tone of reasonable reproach, like a bank clerk who points out to an unimportant customer an unacceptable overdraft. "You must be aware that if it wasn't for diplomatic privilege you'd be in prison now."

"Where have you hidden her?" Captain Van Donck demanded and Castle at the question felt immense relief.

"Hidden her?"

130

Captain Van Donck was on his feet, rubbing at his gold ring. He even spat on it.

"That's all right, Captain," Muller said. "I will look after Mr. Castle. I won't take up any more of your time. Thank you for all the help you've given our department. I want to talk to Mr. Castle alone."

When the door closed Castle found himself facing, as Carson would have said, the real enemy. Muller went on, "You mustn't mind Captain Van Donck. Men like that can see no further than their noses. There are other ways of settling this affair more reasonably than a prosecution which will ruin you and not help us."

"I can hear a car." A woman's voice called to him out of the present.

It was Sarah speaking to him from the top of the stairs. He went to the window. A black Mercedes was edging its way up the indistinguishable commuters' houses in King's Road. The driver was obviously looking for a number, but as usual several of the street lamps had fused.

"It's Mr. Muller all right," Castle called back. When he put down his whisky he found his hand shaking from holding the glass too rigidly.

At the sound of the bell Buller began to bark, but, after Castle opened the door, Buller fawned on the stranger with a total lack of discrimination and left a trail of affectionate spittle on Cornelius Muller's trousers. "Nice dog, nice dog," Muller said with caution.

The years had made a noticeable change in Muller—his hair was almost white now and his face was far less smooth. He no longer looked like a civil servant who knew only the proper answers. Since they last met something had happened to him: he looked more human—perhaps it was that he had taken on with promotion greater responsibilities and with them uncertainties and unanswered questions.

"Good evening, Mr. Castle. I'm sorry I'm so late. The traffic was bad in Watford—I think the place was called Watford."

You might almost have taken him now for a shy man, or perhaps it was only that he was at a loss without his familiar office and his desk of beautiful wood and the presence of two junior colleagues in an outer room. The black Mercedes slid away—the chauffeur had gone to find his dinner. Muller was on his own in a strange town, in a foreign land, where the post boxes bore the initials of a sovereign E II, and there was no statue of Kruger in any market place.

Castle poured out two glasses of whisky. "It's a long time since we met last," Muller said.

"Seven years?"

"It's good of you to ask me to have dinner at your own home."

"C thought it was the best idea. To break the ice. It seems we have to work closely together. On Uncle Remus."

Muller's eyes shifted to the telephone, to the lamp on the table, to a vase of flowers.

"It's all right. Don't worry. If we are bugged here it's only by my own people," Castle said, "and anyway I'm pretty sure we are not." He raised his glass. "To our last meeting. Do you remember you suggested then I might agree to work for you? Well, here I am. We are working together. Historical irony or predestination? Your Dutch church believes in that."

"Of course in those days I hadn't an idea of your real position," Muller said. "If I'd known I wouldn't have threatened you about that wretched Bantu girl. I realize now she was only one of your agents. We might even have worked her together. But, you see, I took you for one of those high-minded anti-apartheid sentimentalists. I was taken completely by surprise when your chief told me

132

you were the man I was to see about Uncle Remus. I hope you don't bear me any grudge. After all you and I were professionals, and we are on the same side now."

"Yes, I suppose we are."

"I do wish though that you'd tell me—it can't matter any longer, can it?—how you got that Bantu girl away. I suppose it was to Swaziland?"

"Yes."

"I thought we had that frontier closed pretty effectively—except for the real guerrilla experts. I never considered you were an expert, though I realized you did have some Communist contacts, but I assumed you needed them for that book of yours on apartheid which was never published. You took me in all right there. Not to speak of Van Donck. You remember Captain Van Donck?"

"Oh, yes. Vividly."

"I had to ask the Security Police for his demotion over your affair. He acted very clumsily. I felt sure that, if we had the girl safe in prison, you'd consent to work for us, and he let her slip. You see—don't laugh—I was convinced it was a real love affair. I've known so many Englishmen who have started with the idea of attacking apartheid and ended trapped by us in a Bantu girl's bed. It's the romantic idea of breaking what they think is an unjust law that attracts them just as much as a black bottom. I never dreamt the girl—Sarah MaNkosi, I think that was the name?—all the time was an agent of MI6."

"She didn't know it herself. She believed in my book too. Have another whisky."

"Thank you. I will."

Castle poured out two glasses, gambling on his better head.

"From all accounts she was a clever girl. We looked pretty closely into her background. Been to the African University in the Transvaal where Uncle Tom professors

133

always produce dangerous students. Personally, though, I've always found that the cleverer the African the more easily he can be turned—one way or another. If we'd had that girl in prison for a month I'm pretty sure we could have turned her. Well, she might have been useful to both of us now in this Uncle Remus operation. Or would she? One forgets that old devil Time. By now she'd be getting a bit long in the tooth, I suppose. Bantu women age so quickly. They are generally finished—anyway to a white taste—long before the age of thirty. You know, Castle, I'm really glad we are working together and you are not what we in BOSS thought—one of those idealistic types who want to change the nature of human beings. We knew the people you were in touch with—or most of them, and we knew the sort of nonsense they'd be telling you. But you outwitted *us*, so you certainly outwitted those Bantu and Communists. I suppose they too thought you were writing a book which would serve their turn. Mind you, I'm not anti-African like Captain Van Donck. I consider myself a hundred percent African myself."

It was certainly not the Cornelius Muller of the Pretoria office who spoke now, the pale clerk doing his conformist job would never have spoken with such ease and confidence. Even the shyness and the uncertainty of a few minutes back had gone. The whisky had cured that. He was now a high officer of BOSS, entrusted with a foreign mission, who took his orders from no one under the rank of a general. He could relax. He could be—an unpleasant thought—himself, and it seemed to Castle that he began to resemble more and more closely, in the vulgarity and brutality of his speech, the Captain Van Donck whom he despised.

"I've taken pleasant enough weekends in Lesotho," Muller said, "rubbing shoulders with my black brothers in the casino at Holiday Inn. I'll admit once I even had a little—well, encounter—it somehow seemed quite differ-

134

ent there—of course it wasn't against the law. I wasn't in the Republic."

Castle called out, "Sarah, bring Sam down to say goodnight to Mr. Muller."

"You are married?" Muller asked.

"Yes."

"I'm all the more flattered to be invited to your home. I brought with me a few little presents from South Africa, and perhaps there's something your wife would like. But you haven't answered my question. Now that we are working together—as I wanted to before, you remember— couldn't you tell me how you got that girl out? It can't harm any of your old agents now, and it does have a certain bearing on Uncle Remus, and the problems we have to face together. Your country and mine—and the States, of course—have a common frontier now."

"Perhaps she'll tell you herself. Let me introduce her and my son, Sam." They came down the stairs together as Cornelius Muller turned.

"Mr. Muller was asking how I got you into Swaziland, Sarah."

He had underestimated Muller. The surprise which he had planned failed completely. "I'm so glad to meet you, Mrs. Castle," Muller said and took her hand.

"We just failed to meet seven years ago," Sarah said.

"Yes. Seven wasted years. You have a very beautiful wife, Castle."

"Thank you," Sarah said. "Sam, shake hands with Mr. Muller."

"This is my son, Mr. Muller," Castle said. He knew Muller would be a good judge of color shades, and Sam was very black.

"How do you do, Sam? Do you go to school yet?"

"He goes to school in a week or two. Run along up to bed now, Sam."

"Can you play hide-and-seek?" Sam asked.

"I used to know the game, but I'm always ready to learn new rules."

"Are you a spy like Mr. Davis?"

"I said go to bed, Sam."

"Have you a poison pen?"

"Sam! Upstairs!"

"And now for Mr. Muller's question, Sarah," Castle said. "Where and how did you cross into Swaziland?"

"I don't think I ought to tell him, do you?"

Cornelius Muller said, "Oh, let's forget Swaziland. It's all past history and it happened in another country."

Castle watched him adapting, as naturally as a chameleon, to the color of the soil. He must have adapted in just that way during his weekend in Lesotho. Perhaps he would have found Muller more likable if he had been less adaptable. All through dinner Muller made his courteous conversation. Yes, thought Castle, I really would have preferred Captain Van Donck. Van Donck would have walked out of the house at the first sight of Sarah. A prejudice had something in common with an ideal. Cornelius Muller was without prejudice and he was without an ideal.

"How do you find the climate here, Mrs. Castle, after South Africa?"

"Do you mean the weather?"

"Yes, the weather."

"It's less extreme," Sarah said.

"Don't you sometimes miss Africa? I came by way of Madrid and Athens, so I've been away some weeks already, and do you know what I miss most? The mine dumps around Johannesburg. Their color when the sun's half set. What do you miss?"

Castle had not suspected Muller of any aesthetic feeling. Was it one of the larger interests which came with promotion or was it adapted for the occasion and the country like his courtesy?

136

"My memories are different," Sarah said. "My Africa was different to yours."

"Oh come, we are both of us Africans. By the way, I've brought a few presents for my friends here. Not knowing that you were one of us, I brought you a shawl. You know how in Lesotho they have those very fine weavers—the Royal Weavers. Would you accept a shawl—from your old enemy?"

"Of course. It's kind of you."

"Do you think Lady Hargreaves would accept an ostrich bag?"

"I don't know her. You must ask my husband."

It would hardly be up to her crocodile standard, Castle thought, but he said, "I'm sure . . . coming from you . . ."

"I take a sort of family interest in ostriches, you see," Muller explained. "My grandfather was what they call now one of the ostrich millionaires—put out of business by the 1914 war. He had a big house in the Cape Province. It was very splendid once, but it's only a ruin now. Ostrich feathers never really came back in Europe, and my father went bankrupt. My brothers still keep a few ostriches though."

Castle remembered visiting one of those big houses, which had been preserved as a sort of museum, camped in by the manager of all that was left of the ostrich farm. The manager was a little apologetic about the richness and the bad taste. The bathroom was the high spot of the tour—visitors were always taken to the bathroom last of all—a bath like a great white double bed with gold-plated taps, and on the wall a bad copy of an Italian primitive: on the haloes real goldleaf was beginning to peel off.

At the end of dinner Sarah left them, and Muller accepted a glass of port. The bottle had remained untouched since last Christmas—a present from Davis. "Seriously though," Muller said, "I wish you would give me a few details about your wife's route to Swaziland. No need to mention names. I know you had some Communist friends—I realize now it was all part of your job. They thought you were a sentimental fellow traveler—just as we did. For example, Carson must have thought you one—poor Carson."

"Why poor Carson?"

"He went too far. He had contacts with the guerrillas. He was a good fellow in his way and a very good advocate. He gave the Security Police a lot of trouble with the pass-laws."

"Doesn't he still?"

"Oh no. He died a year ago in prison."

"I hadn't heard."

Castle went to the sideboard and poured himself yet another double whisky. With plenty of soda the J & B looked no stronger than a single.

"Don't you like this port?" Muller asked. "We used to get admirable port from Lourenço Marques. Alas, those days are over."

"What did he die of?"

"Pneumonia," Muller said. He added, "Well, it saved him from a long trial."

"I liked Carson," Castle said.

"Yes. It's a great pity he always identified Africans with color. It's the kind of mistake second-generation men make. They refuse to admit a white man can be as good an African as a black. My family for instance arrived in 1700. We were early comers." He looked at his watch. "My God, with you I'm a late stayer. My driver must have been waiting an hour. You'll have to excuse me. I ought to be saying goodnight."

Castle said, "Perhaps we should talk a little before you go about Uncle Remus."

"That can wait for the office," Muller said.

At the door he turned. He said, "I'm really sorry

about Carson. If I'd known that you hadn't heard I wouldn't have spoken so abruptly."

Buller licked the bottom of his trousers with undiscriminating affection. "Good dog," Muller said. "Good dog. There's nothing like a dog's fidelity."

2

At one o'clock in the morning Sarah broke a long silence. "You are still awake. Don't pretend. Was it as bad as all that seeing Muller? He was quite polite."

"Oh yes. In England he puts on English manners. He adapts very quickly."

"Shall I get you a Mogadon?"

"No. I'll sleep soon. Only—there's something I have to tell you. Carson's dead. In prison."

"Did they kill him?"

"Muller said he died from pneumonia."

She put her head under the crook of his arm and turned her face into the pillow. He guessed she was crying. He said, "I couldn't help remembering tonight the last note I ever had from him. It was waiting at the Embassy when I came back from seeing Muller and Van Donck. 'Don't worry about Sarah. Take the first possible plane to L.M. and wait for her at the Polana. She's in safe hands.'"

"Yes. I remember that note too. I was with him when he wrote it."

"I was never able to thank him—except by seven years of silence and . . ."

"And?"

"Oh, I don't know what I was going to say." He repeated what he had told Muller, "I liked Carson."

"Yes. I trusted him. Much more than I trusted his friends. During that week while you waited for me in Lourenço Marques we had time for a lot of argument. I used to tell him he wasn't a real Communist."

"Why? He was a member of the Party. One of the oldest members left in the Transvaal."

"Of course. I know that. But there are members and members, aren't there? I told him about Sam even before I told you."

"He had a way of drawing people to him."

"Most of the Communists I knew—they pushed, they didn't draw."

"All the same, Sarah, he was a genuine Communist. He survived Stalin like Roman Catholics survived the Borgias. He made me think better of the Party."

"But he never drew you that far, did he?"

"Oh, there were always some things which stuck in my throat. He used to say I strained at a gnat and swallowed a camel. You know I was never a religious man—I left God behind in the school chapel, but there were priests I sometimes met in Africa who made me believe again—for a moment—over a drink. If all priests had been like they were and I had seen them often enough, perhaps I would have swallowed the Resurrection, the Virgin birth, Lazarus, the whole works. I remember one I met twice—I wanted to use him as an agent as I used you, but he wasn't usable. His name was Connolly—or was it O'Connell? He worked in the slums of Soweto. He said to me exactly what Carson said—you strain at a gnat and you swallow . . . For a while I half believed in his God, like I half believed in Carson's. Perhaps I was born to be a half believer. When people talk about Prague and Budapest and how you can't find a human face in Communism I

140

stay silent. Because I've seen—once—the human face. I say to myself that if it hadn't been for Carson Sam would have been born in a prison and you would probably have died in one. One kind of Communism—or Communist—saved you and Sam. I don't have any trust in Marx or Lenin any more than I have in Saint Paul, but haven't I the right to be grateful?"

"Why do you worry so much about it? No one would say you were wrong to be grateful, I'm grateful too. Gratitude's all right if . . ."

"If . . .?"

"I think I was going to say if it doesn't take you too far."

It was hours before he slept. He lay awake and thought of Carson and Cornelius Muller, of Uncle Remus and Prague. He didn't want to sleep until he was sure from her breathing that Sarah was asleep first. Then he allowed himself to strike, like his childhood hero Allan Quatermain, off on that long slow underground stream which bore him on toward the interior of the dark continent where he hoped that he might find a permanent home, in a city where he could be accepted as a citizen, as a citizen without any pledge of faith, not the City of God or Marx, but the city called Peace of Mind.

Chapter IV

1

Once a month on his day off Castle was in the habit of taking Sarah and Sam for an excursion into the sandy conifered countryside of East Sussex in order to see his mother. No one ever questioned the necessity of the visit, but Castle doubted whether even his mother enjoyed it, though he had to admit she did all she could to please them—according to her own idea of what their pleasures were. Invariably the same supply of vanilla ice cream was waiting for Sam in the deep freeze—he preferred chocolate—and though she only lived half a mile from the station, she ordered a taxi to meet them. Castle, who had never wanted a car since he returned to England, had the impression that she regarded him as an unsuccessful and impecunious son, and Sarah once told him how *she* felt—like a black guest at an anti-apartheid garden party too fussed over to be at ease.

A further cause of nervous strain was Buller. Castle had given up arguing that they should leave Buller at home. Sarah was certain that without their protection he would be murdered by masked men, though Castle pointed out that he had been bought to defend them and not to be defended himself. In the long run it proved easier to give way, though his mother profoundly disliked dogs and had a Burmese cat which it was Buller's fixed ambition to destroy. Before they arrived the cat had to be locked in Mrs. Castle's bedroom, and her sad fate, deprived of human company, would be hinted at from time to time by his mother during the course of the long day. On one occasion Buller was found spread-eagled outside the bedroom door waiting his chance, breathing heavily like a Shakespearian murderer. Afterward Mrs. Castle wrote a long letter of reproach to Sarah on the subject. Apparently the cat's nerves had suffered for more than a week. She had refused her diet of Friskies and existed only on milk—a kind of hunger strike.

Gloom was apt to descend on all of them as soon as the taxi entered the deep shade of the laurel drive which led to the high-gabled Edwardian house that his father had bought for his retirement because it was near a golf course. (Soon after he had a stroke and was unable to walk even as far as the clubhouse.)

Mrs. Castle was invariably standing there on the porch waiting for them, a tall straight figure in an outdated skirt which showed to advantage her fine ankles, wearing a high collar like Queen Alexandra's which disguised the wrinkles of old age. To hide his despondency Castle would become unnaturally elated and he greeted his mother with an exaggerated hug which she barely returned. She believed that any emotions openly expressed must be false emotions. She had deserved to marry an ambassador or a colonial governor rather than a country doctor.

"You are looking wonderful, Mother," Castle said.

"I'm feeling well for my age." She was eighty-five. She offered a clean white cheek which smelled of lavender water for Sarah to kiss. "I hope Sam is feeling quite well again."

"Oh yes, he's never been better."

"Out of quarantine?"

"Of course."

Reassured, Mrs. Castle granted him the privilege of a brief kiss.

"You'll be starting prep school soon, I suppose, won't you?"

Sam nodded.

"You'll enjoy having other boys to play with. Where's Buller?"

"He's gone upstairs looking for Tinker Bell," Sam said with satisfaction.

After lunch Sarah took Sam into the garden along with Buller so as to leave Castle alone with his mother for a little while. That was the monthly routine. Sarah meant well, but Castle had the impression that his mother was glad when the private interview was over. Invariably there was a long silence between them while Mrs. Castle poured out two more unwanted coffees; then she would propose a subject for discussion which Castle knew had been prepared a long time before just to cover this awkward interval.

"That was a terrible air crash last week," Mrs. Castle said, and she dropped the lump sugar in, one for her, two for him.

"Yes. It certainly was. Terrible." He tried to remember which company, where . . . TWA? Calcutta?

144

"I couldn't help thinking what would have happened to Sam if you and Sarah had been on board."

He remembered just in time. "But it happened in Bangladesh, Mother. Why on earth should we . . .?"

"You are in the Foreign Office. They could send you anywhere."

"Oh no, they couldn't. I'm chained to my desk in London, Mother. Anyway you know very well we've appointed you as guardian if anything ever happened."

"An old woman approaching ninety."

"Eighty-five, Mother, surely."

"Every week I read of old women killed in bus crashes."

"You never go in a bus."

"I see no reason why I should make a *principle* of not going in a bus."

"If anything should ever happen to you be sure we'll appoint somebody reliable."

"It might be too late. One must prepare against simultaneous accidents. And in the case of Sam—well, there are special problems."

"I suppose you mean his color."

"You can't make him a Ward in Chancery. Many of those judges—your father always said that—are racialist. And then—has it occurred to you, dear, if we are all dead, there might be people—out there—who might claim him?"

"Sarah has no parents."

"What you leave behind, however small, might be thought quite a fortune—I mean by someone out there. If the deaths are simultaneous, the eldest is judged to have died first, or so I'm told. My money would then be added to yours. Sarah must have *some* relations and they might claim . . ."

"Mother, aren't you being a bit racialist yourself?"

"No, dear. I'm not at all racialist, though perhaps I'm

145

old-fashioned and patriotic. Sam is English by birth whatever anyone may say."

"I'll think about it, Mother." That statement was the end of most of their discussions, but it was always well to try a diversion too. "I've been wondering, Mother, whether to retire."

"They don't give you a very good pension, do they?"

"I've saved a little. We live very economically."

"The more you've saved the more reason for a spare guardian—just in case. I hope I'm as liberal as your father was, but I would hate to see Sam dragged back to South Africa . . ."

"But you wouldn't see it, Mother, if you were dead."

"I'm not so certain of things, dear, as all that. I'm not an *atheist*."

It was one of their most trying visits and he was only saved by Buller, who returned with heavy determination from the garden and lumbered upstairs looking for the imprisoned Tinker Bell.

"At least," Mrs. Castle said, "I hope I will never have to be a guardian for Buller."

"I can promise you that, Mother. In the event of a fatal accident in Bangladesh which coincides with a Grandmothers' Union bus crash in Sussex I have left strict directions for Buller to be put away—as painlessly as possible."

"It's not the sort of dog that I would personally have chosen for my grandson. Watchdogs like Buller are always very color-conscious. And Sam's a nervous child. He reminds me of you at his age—except for the color of course."

"Was I a nervous child?"

"You always had an exaggerated sense of gratitude for the least kindness. It was a sort of insecurity, though why you should have felt insecure with me and your father . . .

146

You once gave away a good fountain pen to someone at school who had offered you a bun with a piece of chocolate inside."

"Oh well, Mother. I always insist on getting my money's worth now."

"I wonder."

"And I've quite given up gratitude." But as he spoke he remembered Carson dead in prison, and he remembered what Sarah had said. He added, "Anyway, I don't let it go too far. I demand more than a penny bun nowadays."

"There's something I've always found strange about you. Since you met Sarah you never mention Mary. I was very fond of Mary. I wish you had had a child with her."

"I try to forget the dead," he said, but that wasn't true. He had learned early in his marriage that he was sterile, so there was no child, but they were happy. It was as much an only child as a wife who was blown to pieces by a buzz bomb in Oxford Street when he was safe in Lisbon, making a contact. He had failed to protect her, and he hadn't died with her. That was why he never spoke of her even to Sarah.

2

"What always surprises me about your mother," Sarah said, when they began to go over in bed the record of their day in the country, "is that she accepts so easily the fact that Sam's your child. Does it never occur to her that he's very black to have a white father?"

"She doesn't seem to notice shades."

"Mr. Muller did. I'm sure of that."

Downstairs the telephone rang. It was nearly midnight.

"Oh hell," Castle said, "who would ring us at this hour? Your masked men again?"

"Aren't you going to answer?"

The ringing stopped.

"If it's your masked men," Castle said, "we'll have a chance to catch them."

The telephone rang a second time. Castle looked at his watch.

"For God's sake answer them."

"It's certain to be a wrong number."

"I'll answer if you won't."

"Put on your dressing gown. You'll catch cold." But as soon as she got out of bed the telephone stopped ringing.

"It's sure to ring again," Sarah said. "Don't you remember last month—three times at one o'clock in the morning?" But this time the telephone remained silent.

There was a cry from across the passage. Sarah said, "Damn them, they've woken up Sam. Whoever they are."

"I'll go to him. You're shivering. Get back into bed."

Sam asked, "Was it burglars? Why didn't Buller bark?"

"Buller knew better. There are no burglars, Sam. It was just a friend of mine ringing up late."

"Was it that Mr. Muller?"

"No. He's not a friend. Go to sleep. The telephone won't ring again."

"How do you know?"

"I know."

"It rang more than once."

"Yes."

"But you never answered. So how do you know it was a friend?"

"You ask too many questions, Sam."

"Was it a secret signal?"

"Do you have secrets, Sam?"

"Yes. Lots of them."

"Tell me one."

"I won't. It wouldn't be a secret if I told you."

"Well, I have my secrets too."

Sarah was still awake. "He's all right now," Castle said. "He thought they were burglars ringing up."

"Perhaps they were. What did you tell him?"

"Oh, I said they were secret signals."

"You always know how to calm him. You love him, don't you?"

"Yes."

"It's strange. I never understand. I wish he were really your child."

"I don't wish it. You know that."

"I've never really understood why."

"I've told you many times. I see enough of myself every day when I shave."

"All you see is a kind man, darling."

"I wouldn't describe myself that way."

"For me a child of yours would have been something to live for when you are not there anymore. You won't live forever."

"No, thank God for that." He brought the words out without thinking and regretted having spoken them. It was her sympathy which always made him commit himself too far; however much he tried to harden himself he was tempted to tell her everything. Sometimes he compared her cynically with a clever interrogator who uses sympathy and a timely cigarette.

149

Sarah said, "I know you are worried. I wish you could tell me why—but I know you can't. Perhaps one day . . . when you are free . . ." She added sadly, "If you are ever free, Maurice."

Chapter V

1

Castle left his bicycle with the ticket collector at Berkhamsted station and went upstairs to the London platform. He knew nearly all the commuters by sight—he was even on nodding terms with a few of them. A cold October mist was lying in the grassy pool of the castle and dripping from the willows into the canal on the other side of the line. He walked the length of the platform and back; he thought he recognized all the faces except for one woman in a shabby rabbity fur—women were rare on this train. He watched her climb into a compartment and he chose the same one so as to watch her more closely. The men opened newspapers and the woman opened a

151

paperbound novel by Denise Robins. Castle began reading in Book II of *War and Peace*. It was a breach of security, even a small act of defiance, to read this book publicly for pleasure. "One step beyond that boundary line, which resembles the line dividing the living from the dead, lies uncertainty, suffering and death. And what is there? Who is there—there beyond that field, that tree . . ." He looked out of the window and seemed to see with the eyes of Tolstoy's soldier the motionless spirit-level of the canal pointing toward Boxmoor. "That roof lit up by the sun? No one knows, but one wants to know. You fear and yet long to cross that line . . ."

When the train stopped at Watford, Castle was the only one to leave the compartment. He stood beside the list of train departures and watched the last passenger go through the barrier—the woman was not among them. Outside the station he hesitated at the tail of the bus queue while he again noted the faces. Then he looked at his watch and with a studied gesture of impatience for any observer who cared to notice him walked on. Nobody followed him, he was sure of that, but all the same he was a little worried by the thought of the woman in the train and his petty defiance of the rules. One had to be meticulously careful. At the first post office to which he came he rang the office and asked for Cynthia—she always arrived half an hour at least before Watson or Davis or himself.

He said, "Will you tell Watson I shall be in a little late? I've had to stop at Watford on the way to see a vet. Buller's got an odd sort of rash. Tell Davis too." He considered for a moment whether it would be necessary for his alibi actually to visit the vet, but he decided that taking too much care could sometimes be as dangerous as taking too little—simplicity was always best, just as it paid to speak the truth whenever possible, for the truth is so much easier to memorize than a lie. He went into the third coffee bar on the list which he carried in his head and there he waited. He didn't recognize the tall lean man who followed him, in an overcoat which had seen better days. The man stopped at his table and said, "Excuse me, but aren't you William Hatchard?"

"No, my name's Castle."

"I'm sorry. An extraordinary likeness."

Castle drank two cups of coffee and read *The Times*. He valued the air of respectability that paper always seemed to lend the reader. He saw the man tying up his shoelace fifty yards down the road, and he experienced a similar sense of security to that which he had once felt while he was being carried from his ward in a hospital toward a major operation—he found himself again an object on a conveyor belt which moved him to a destined end with no responsibility, to anyone or anything, even to his own body. Everything would be looked after for better or worse by somebody else. Somebody with the highest professional qualifications. That was the way death ought to come in the end, he thought, as he moved slowly and happily in the wake of the stranger. He always hoped that he would move toward death with the same sense that before long he would be released from anxiety forever.

The road they were now in, he noticed, was called Elm View, although there were no elms anywhere in sight or any other trees, and the house to which he was guided was as anonymous and uninteresting as his own. There were even rather similar stained glass panels in the front door. Perhaps a dentist had once worked there too. The lean man ahead of him stopped for a moment by an iron gate to a front garden which was about the size of a billiard table, and then walked on. There were three bells by the door, but only one had an indicating card—very worn with illegible writing ending in the words "ition Limited." Castle rang the bell and saw that his guide had crossed Elm View and was walking back on the other side. When he was opposite the house he took a handkerchief from his sleeve and wiped his nose. It was probably an all-clear signal, for Castle almost immediately heard a creak-creak descending the stairs inside. He wondered whether "they" had taken their precautions in order to protect him from a possible follower or to protect themselves against his possible treachery—or both of course. He didn't care—he was on the conveyor belt.

The door opened on a familiar face he had not expected to see—eyes of a very startling blue over a wide welcoming grin, a small scar on the left cheek which he knew dated from a wound inflicted on a child in Warsaw when the city fell to Hitler.

"Boris," Castle exclaimed, "I thought I was never going to see *you* again."

"It's good to see you, Maurice."

Strange, he thought, that Sarah and Boris were the only people in the world who ever called him Maurice. To his mother he was simply "dear" in moments of affection, and at the office he lived among surnames or initials. Immediately he felt at home in this strange house which he had never visited before: a shabby house with worn carpeting on the stairs. For some reason he thought of his father. Perhaps when a child he had gone with him to see a patient in just such a house.

From the first landing he followed Boris into a small square room with a desk, two chairs and a large picture on rollers which showed a numerous family eating in a garden at a table laden with an unusual variety of food. All the courses seemed to be simultaneously displayed—an apple pie stood beside a joint of roast beef, and a salmon and a plate of apples beside a soup tureen. There was a jug of water and a bottle of wine and a coffeepot. Several dictionaries lay on a shelf and a pointer leaned against a blackboard on which was written a half-obliterated word in a language he couldn't identify.

"They decided to send me back after your last

report," Boris said. "The one about Muller. I'm glad to be here. I like England so much better than France. How did you get on with Ivan?"

"All right. But it wasn't the same." He felt for a packet of cigarettes which was not there. "You know how Russians are. I had the impression that he didn't trust me. And he was always wanting more than I ever promised to do for any of you. He even wanted me to try to change my section."

"I think it's Marlboros you smoke?" Boris said, holding out a packet. Castle took one.

"Boris, did you know all the time you were here that Carson was dead?"

"No. I didn't know. Not until a few weeks ago. I don't even know the details yet."

"He died in prison. From pneumonia. Or so they say. Ivan must surely have known—but they let me learn it first from Cornelius Muller."

"Was it such a great shock? In the circumstances. Once arrested—there's never much hope."

"I know that, and yet I'd always believed that one day I would see him again—somewhere in safety far away from South Africa—perhaps in my home—and then I would be able to thank him for saving Sarah. Now he's dead and gone without a word of thanks from me."

"All you've done for us has been a kind of thanks. He will have understood that. You don't have to feel any regret."

"No? One can't reason away regret—it's a bit like falling in love, falling into regret."

He thought, with a sense of revulsion: The situation's impossible, there's no one in the world with whom I can talk of everything, except this man Boris whose real name even is unknown to me. He couldn't talk to Davis—half his life was hidden from Davis, nor to Sarah, who didn't even know that Boris existed. One day he had even told

Boris about the night in the Hotel Polana when he learned the truth about Sam. A control was a bit like a priest must be to a Catholic—a man who received one's confession whatever it might be without emotion. He said, "When they changed my control and Ivan took over from you, I felt unbearably lonely. I could never speak about anything but business to Ivan."

"I'm sorry I had to go. I argued with them about it. I did my best to stay. But you know how it is in your own outfit. It's the same in ours. We live in boxes and it's they who choose the box." How often he had heard that comparison in his own office. Each side shares the same clichés.

Castle said, "It's time to change the book."

"Yes. Is that all? You gave an urgent signal on the phone. Is there more news of Porton?"

"No. I'm not sure I trust their story."

They were sitting on uncomfortable chairs on either side of the desk like a master and a pupil. Only the pupil in this case was so much older than the master. Well, it happened, Castle supposed, in the confessional too that an old man spoke his sins to a priest young enough to be his son. With Ivan at their rare meetings the dialogue had always been short, information was passed, questionnaires were received, everything was strictly to the point. With Boris he had been able to relax. "Was France promotion for you?" He took another cigarette.

"I don't know. One never does know, does one? Perhaps coming back here may be promotion. It may mean they took your last report very seriously, and thought I could deal with it better than Ivan. Or was Ivan compromised? You don't believe the Porton story, but have you really hard evidence that your people suspect a leak?"

"No. But in a game like ours one begins to trust one's instincts and they've certainly made a routine check on the whole section."

156

"You say yourself *routine.*"

"Yes, it could be routine, some of it's quite open, but I believe it's a bit more than that. I think Davis's telephone is tapped and mine may be too, though I don't believe so. Anyway we'd better drop those call-signals to my house. You've read the report I made on Muller's visit and the Uncle Remus operation. I hope to God that's been channeled differently on your side if there *is* a leak. I have a feeling they might be passing me a marked note."

"You needn't be afraid. We've been most careful over that report. Though I don't think Muller's mission can be what you call a marked note. Porton perhaps, but not Muller. We've had confirmation of that from Washington. We take Uncle Remus very seriously, and we want you to concentrate on that. It could affect us in the Mediterranean, the Gulf, the Indian Ocean. Even the Pacific. In the long term . . ."

"There's no long term for me, Boris. I'm over retirement age as it is."

"I know."

"I want to retire now."

"We wouldn't like that. The next two years may be very important."

"For me too. I'd like to live them in my own way."

"Doing what?"

"Looking after Sarah and Sam. Going to the movies. Growing old in peace. It would be safer for you to drop me, Boris."

"Why?"

"Muller came and sat at my own table and ate our food and was polite to Sarah. Condescending. Pretending there was no color bar. How I dislike that man! And how I hate the whole bloody BOSS outfit. I hate the men who killed Carson and now call it pneumonia. I hate them for trying to shut Sarah up and let Sam be born in prison. You'd do much better to employ a man who doesn't hate,

157

Boris. Hate's liable to make mistakes. It's as dangerous as love. I'm doubly dangerous, Boris, because I love too. Love's a fault in both our services."

He felt the enormous relief of speaking without prudence to someone who, he believed, understood him. The blue eyes seemed to offer complete friendship, the smile encouraged him to lay down for a short time the burden of secrecy. He said, "Uncle Remus is the last straw—that behind the scenes we should be joining with the States to help those apartheid bastards. Your worst crimes, Boris, are always in the past, and the future hasn't arrived yet. I can't go on parroting, 'Remember Prague! Remember Budapest!'—they were years ago. One has to be concerned about the present, and the present is Uncle Remus. I became a naturalized black when I fell in love with Sarah."

"Then why do you think you're dangerous?"

"Because for seven years I've kept my cool, and I'm losing it now. Cornelius Muller is making me lose it. Perhaps C sent him to me for that very reason. Perhaps C wants me to break out."

"We are only asking you to hold on a little longer. Of course the early years of this game are always the easiest, aren't they? The contradictions are not so obvious and the secrecy hasn't had time to build up like hysteria or a woman's menopause. Try not to worry so much, Maurice. Take your Valium and a Mogadon at night. Come and see me whenever you feel depressed and have to talk to someone. It's the lesser danger."

"I've done enough, haven't I, by now to pay my debt to Carson?"

"Yes, of course, but we can't lose you yet—because of Uncle Remus. As you put it, you're a naturalized black now."

Castle felt as though he were emerging from an anesthetic, an operation had been completed successfully. He

158

said, "I'm sorry. I made a fool of myself." He couldn't remember exactly what he had said. "Give me a shot of whisky, Boris."

Boris opened the desk and took out a bottle and a glass. He said, "I know you like J & B." He poured out a generous measure and he watched the speed with which Castle drank. "You are taking a bit too much these days, aren't you, Maurice?"

"Yes. But no one knows that. Only at home. Sarah notices."

"How are things there?"

"Sarah's worried by the telephone rings. She always thinks of masked burglars. And Sam has bad dreams because soon he will be going to prep school—a white school. I'm worried about what will happen to both of them if something happens to me. Something always does happen in the end, doesn't it?"

"Leave all that to us. I promise you—we've got your escape route very carefully planned. If an emergency . . ."

"*My* escape route? What about Sarah's and Sam's?"

"They'll follow you. You can trust us, Maurice. We'll look after them. We know how to show our gratitude too. Remember Blake—we look after our own." Boris went to the window. "All's clear. You ought to be getting on to the office. My first pupil comes in a quarter of an hour."

"What language do you teach him?"

"English. You mustn't laugh at me."

"Your English is nearly perfect."

"My first pupil today is a Pole like myself. A refugee from *us,* not from the Germans. I like him—he's a ferocious enemy of Marx. You smile. That's better. You must never let things build up so far again."

"This security check. It's even getting Davis down—and he's innocent."

"Don't worry. I think I see a way of drawing their fire."

159

"I'll try not to worry."

"From now on we'll shift to the third drop, and if things get difficult signal me at once—I'm only here to help you. You do trust me?"

"Of course I trust you, Boris. I only wish your people really trusted *me*. This book code—it's a terribly slow and old-fashioned way of communicating, and you know how dangerous it is."

"It's not that we don't trust you. It's for your own safety. Your house might be searched any time as a routine check. At the beginning they wanted to give you a microdot outfit—I wouldn't let them. Does that satisfy your wish?"

"I have another."

"Tell me."

"I wish the impossible. I wish all the lies were unnecessary. And I wish we were on the same side."

"We?"

"You and I."

"Surely we are?"

"Yes, in this case . . . for the time being. You know Ivan tried to blackmail me once?"

"A stupid man. I suppose that's why I've been sent back."

"It has always been quite clear between you and me. I give you all the information you want in my section. I've never pretended that I share your faith—I'll never be a Communist."

"Of course. We've always understood your point of view. We need you for Africa only."

"But what I pass to you—I have to be the judge. I'll fight beside you in Africa, Boris—not in Europe."

"All we need from you is all the details you can get of Uncle Remus."

"Ivan wanted a lot. He threatened me."

160

"Ivan has gone. Forget him."

"You would do better without me."

"No. It would be Muller and his friends who would do better," Boris said.

Like a manic depressive Castle had had his outbreak, the recurrent boil had broken, and he felt a relief he never felt elsewhere.

2

It was the turn of the Travellers, and here, where he was on the Committee, Sir John Hargreaves felt quite at home, unlike at the Reform. The day was much colder than at their last lunch together and he saw no reason to go and talk in the park.

"Oh, I know what you are thinking, Emmanuel, but they all know you here only too well," he said to Doctor Percival. "They'll leave us quite alone with our coffee. They've learned by this time that you talk about nothing except fish. By the way, how was the smoked trout?"

"Rather dry," Doctor Percival said, "by Reform standards."

"And the roast beef?"

"Perhaps a little overdone?"

"You're an impossible man to please, Emmanuel. Have a cigar."

"If it's a real Havana."

"Of course."

"I wonder if you'll get them in Washington?"

"I doubt whether *détente* has got as far as cigars. Anyway, the question of laser beams will take priority. What a game it all is, Emmanuel. Sometimes I wish I was back in Africa."

"The old Africa."

"Yes. You are right. The old Africa."

"It's gone forever."

"I'm not so sure. Perhaps if we destroy the rest of the world, the roads will become overgrown and all the new luxury hotels will crumble, the forests will come back, the chiefs, the witch doctors—there's still a rain queen in the northeast Transvaal."

"Are you going to tell them that in Washington too?"

"No. But I shall talk without enthusiasm about Uncle Remus."

"You are against it?"

"The States, ourselves and South Africa—we are incompatible allies. But the plan will go ahead because the Pentagon want to play war games now that they haven't got a real war. Well, I'm leaving Castle behind to play it with their Mr. Muller. By the way, he's left for Bonn. I hope West Germany isn't in the game too."

"How long will you be away?"

"Not more than ten days, I hope. I don't like the Washington climate—in all senses of the word." With a smile of pleasure he tipped off a satisfactory length of ash. "Doctor Castro's cigars," he said, "are every bit as good as Sergeant Batista's."

"I wish you weren't going just at this moment, John, when we seem to have a fish on the line."

"I can trust you to land it without my help—anyway it may be only an old boot."

"I don't think it is. One gets to know the tug of an old boot."

"I leave it with confidence in your hands, Emmanuel. And in Daintry's too, of course."

162

"Suppose we don't agree?"

"Then it must be your decision. You are my deputy in this affair. But for God's sake, Emmanuel, don't do anything rash."

"I'm only rash when I'm in my Jaguar, John. When I'm fishing I have a great deal of patience."

Chapter VI

1

Castle's train was forty minutes late at Berkhamsted. There were repairs to the line somewhere beyond Tring, and when he arrived at the office his room seemed empty in an unaccustomed way. Davis wasn't there, but that hardly explained the sense of emptiness; Castle had often enough been alone in the room—with Davis at lunch, Davis in the lavatory, Davis off to the Zoo to see Cynthia. It was half an hour before he came on the note in his tray from Cynthia: "Arthur's not well. Colonel Daintry wants to see you." For a moment Castle wondered who the hell Arthur was; he was unused to thinking of Davis as anyone but Davis. Was Cynthia, he wondered, beginning to yield

164

at last to the long siege? Was that why she now used his Christian name? He rang for her and asked, "What's wrong with Davis?"

"I don't know. One of the Environment men rang up for him. He said something about stomach cramps."

"A hangover?"

"He'd have rung up himself if it had been only that. I didn't know what I ought to do with you not in. So I rang Doctor Percival."

"What did he say?"

"The same as you—a hangover. Apparently they were together last night—drinking too much port and whisky. He's going to see him at lunchtime. He's busy till then."

"You don't think it's serious, do you?"

"I don't think it's serious but I don't think it's a hangover. If it was serious Doctor Percival would have gone at once, wouldn't he?"

"With C away in Washington I doubt if he's got much time for medicine," Castle said. "I'll go and see Daintry. Which room?"

He opened the door marked 72. Daintry was there and Doctor Percival—he had the sense of interrupting a dispute.

"Oh yes, Castle," Daintry said. "I did want to see you."

"I'll be pushing off," Doctor Percival said.

"We'll talk later, Percival. I don't agree with you. I'm sorry, but there it is. I can't agree."

"You remember what I said about boxes—and Ben Nicholson."

"I'm not a painter," Daintry said, "and I don't understand abstract art. Anyway, I'll be seeing you later."

Daintry was silent for quite a while after the shutting of the door. Then he said, "I don't like people jumping to conclusions. I've been brought up to believe in evidence—real evidence."

165

"Is something bothering you?"

"If it was a question of sickness, he'd take blood tests, X-rays . . . He wouldn't just *guess* a diagnosis."

"Doctor Percival?"

Daintry said, "I don't know how to begin. I'm not supposed to talk to you about this."

"About what?"

There was a photograph of a beautiful girl on Daintry's desk. Daintry's eyes kept returning to it. He said, "Don't you get damned lonely sometimes in this outfit?"

Castle hesitated. He said, "Oh well, I get on well with Davis. That makes a lot of difference."

"Davis? Yes. I wanted to talk to you about Davis."

Daintry rose and walked to the window. He gave the impression of a prisoner cooped up in a cell. He stared out morosely at the forbidding sky and was not reassured. He said, "It's a gray day. The autumn's really here at last."

" 'Change and decay in all around I see,' " Castle quoted.

"What's that?"

"A hymn I used to sing at school."

Daintry returned to his desk and faced the photograph again. "My daughter," he said, as though he felt the need of introducing the girl.

"Congratulations. She's a beautiful girl."

"She's getting married at the weekend, but I don't think I shall go."

"You don't like the man?"

"Oh, I dare say he's all right. I've never met him. But what would I talk to him about? Jameson's Baby Powder?"

"Baby powder?"

"Jameson's are trying to knock out Johnson's—or so she tells me." He sat down and lapsed into an unhappy silence.

Castle said, "Apparently Davis is ill. I was in late this

166

morning. He's chosen a bad day. I've got the Zaire bag to deal with."

"I'm sorry. I'd better not keep you then. I didn't know that Davis was ill. It's nothing serious?"

"I don't think so. Doctor Percival is going to see him at lunchtime."

"Percival?" Daintry said. "Hasn't he a doctor of his own?"

"Well, if Doctor Percival sees him the cost is on the old firm, isn't it?"

"Yes. It's only that—working with us—he must get a bit out of date—medically, I mean."

"Oh well, it's probably a very simple diagnosis." He heard the echo of another conversation.

"Castle, all I wanted to see you about was—you *are* quite satisfied with Davis?"

"How do you mean 'satisfied'? We work well together."

"Sometimes I have to ask rather silly questions— oversimple ones—but then security's my job. They don't necessarily mean a great deal. Davis gambles, doesn't he?"

"A little. He likes to talk about horses. I doubt if he wins much, or loses much."

"And drinks?"

"I don't think he drinks more than I do."

"Then you *have* got complete confidence in him?"

"Complete. Of course we are all liable to make mistakes. Has there been a complaint of some kind? I wouldn't want to see Davis shifted unless it's to L.M."

"Forget I asked you," Daintry said. "I ask the same sort of thing about everyone. Even about you. Do you know a painter called Nicholson?"

"No. Is he one of us?"

"No, no. Sometimes," Daintry said, "I feel out of touch. I wonder if—but I suppose at night you always go home to your family?"

167

"Well, yes . . . I do."

"If, for some reason, you had to stay up in town one night . . . we might have dinner together."

"It doesn't often happen," Castle said.

"No, I suppose not."

"You see, my wife's nervous when she's left alone."

"Of course. I understand. It was only a passing idea." He was looking at the photograph again. "We used to have dinner together now and then. I hope to God she'll be happy. There's nothing one can ever do, is there?"

Silence fell like an old-fashioned smog, separating them from each other. Neither of them could see the pavement: they had to feel their way with a hand stretched out.

Castle said, "My son's not of marriageable age. I'm glad I don't have to worry about that."

"You come in on Saturday, don't you? I suppose you couldn't just stay up an hour or two longer . . . I won't know a soul at the wedding except my daughter—and her mother, of course. She said—my daughter, I mean—that I could bring someone from the office if I wanted to. For company."

Castle said, "Of course I'd be glad . . . if you really think . . ." He could seldom resist a call of distress however it was encoded.

2

For once Castle went without his lunch. He didn't suffer from hunger—he suffered only from a breach in his routine. He was uneasy. He wanted to see that Davis was all right.

As he was leaving the great anonymous building at one o'clock, after he had locked all his papers in the safe, even a humorless note from Watson, he saw Cynthia in the doorway. He told her, "I'm going to see how Davis is. Will you come?"

"No, why should I? I have a lot of shopping to do. Why are *you* going? It's nothing serious, is it?"

"No, but I thought I'd just look in. He's all alone in that flat except for those Environment types. And they never come home till evening."

"Doctor Percival promised to see him."

"Yes, I know, but he's probably gone by now. I thought perhaps you might like to come along with me . . . just to see . . ."

"Oh well, if we don't have to stay too long. We don't need to take flowers, do we? Like to a hospital." She was a harsh girl.

Davis opened the door to them wearing a dressing gown. Castle noticed how for a moment his face lit up at the sight of Cynthia, but then he realized that she had a companion.

He commented without enthusiasm, "Oh, *you* are here."

"What's wrong, Davis?"

"I don't know. Nothing much. The old liver's playing it up."

"I thought your friend said stomach cramps on the telephone," Cynthia said.

"Well, the liver's somewhere near the stomach, isn't it? Or is it the kidneys? I'm awfully vague about my own geography."

"I'll make your bed, Arthur," Cynthia said, "while you two talk."

169

"No, no, please no. It's only a bit rumpled. Sit down and make yourself comfortable. Have a drink."

"You and Castle can drink, but I'm going to make your bed."

"She has a very strong will," Davis said. "What'll you take, Castle? A whisky?"

"A small one, thank you."

Davis laid out two glasses.

"You'd better not have one if your liver's bad. What did Doctor Percival say exactly?"

"Oh, he tried to scare me. Doctors always do, don't they?"

"I don't mind drinking alone."

"He said if I didn't pull up a bit I was in danger of cirrhosis. I have to go and have an X-ray tomorrow. I told him that I don't drink more than anyone else, but he said some livers are weaker than others. Doctors always have the last word."

"I wouldn't drink that whisky if I were you."

"He said 'Cut down,' and I've cut this whisky down by half. And I've told him that I'd drop the port. So I will for a week or two. Anything to please. I'm glad you looked in, Castle. D'you know, Doctor Percival really did scare me a bit? I had the impression he wasn't telling me everything he knew. It would be awful, wouldn't it, if they had decided to send me to L.M. and then *he* wouldn't let me go. And there's another fear—have they spoken to you about me?"

"No. At least Daintry asked me this morning if I was satisfied with you, and I said I was—completely."

"You're a good friend, Castle."

"It's only that stupid security check. You remember the day you met Cynthia at the Zoo . . . I told them you were at the dentist, but all the same . . ."

"Yes. I'm the sort of man who's always found out. And yet I nearly always obey the rules. It's my form of loyalty, I suppose. You aren't the same. If I take out a report once to read at lunch, I'm spotted. But I've seen you take them out time after time. You take risks—like they say priests have to do. If I really leaked something—without meaning to, of course—I'd come to you for confession."

"Expecting absolution?"

"No. But expecting a bit of justice."

"Then you'd be wrong, Davis. I haven't the faintest idea what the word 'justice' means."

"So you'd condemn me to be shot at dawn?"

"Oh no. I would always absolve the people I liked."

"Why, then it's you who are the real security risk," Davis said. "How long do you suppose this damned check is going on?"

"I suppose till they find their leak or decide there was no leak after all. Perhaps some man in MI5 has misread the evidence."

"Or some woman, Castle. Why not a woman? It could be one of our secretaries, if it's not me or you or Watson. The thought gives me the creeps. Cynthia promised to dine with me the other night. I was waiting for her at Stone's, and there at the table next door was a pretty girl waiting for someone too. We half smiled at each other because we had both been stood up. Companions in distress. I'd have spoken to her—after all, Cynthia had let me down—and then the thought came—perhaps she's been planted to catch me, perhaps they heard me reserve the table on the office phone. Perhaps Cynthia kept away under orders. And then who should come in and join the girl—guess who—Daintry."

"It was probably his daughter."

"They use daughters in our outfit, don't they? What a damn silly profession ours is. You can't trust anyone. Now I even distrust Cynthia. She's making my bed, and God knows what she hopes to find in it. But all she'll get are yesterday's breadcrumbs. Perhaps they'll analyze those. A crumb could contain a microdot."

"I can't stay much longer. The Zaire bag is in."

Davis laid down his glass. "I'm damned if whisky tastes the same, since Percival put ideas in my head. Do *you* think I've got cirrhosis?"

"No. Just go easy for a while."

"Easier said than done. When I'm bored, I drink. You're lucky to have Sarah. How's Sam?"

"He asks after you a lot. He says nobody plays hide-and-seek like you do."

"A friendly little bastard. I wish I could have a little bastard too—but only with Cynthia. What a hope!"

"The climate of Lourenço Marques isn't very good . . ."

"Oh, people say that it's OK for children up to six."

"Well, perhaps Cynthia's weakening. After all, she *is* making your bed."

"Yes, she'd mother me, I daresay, but she's one of those girls who are looking all the time for someone to admire. She'd like someone serious—like you. The trouble is that when I'm serious I can't *act* serious. Acting serious embarrasses me. Can you picture anyone ever admiring me?"

"Well, Sam does."

"I doubt if Cynthia enjoys hide-and-seek."

Cynthia came back. She said, "Your bed was in an unholy mess. When was it made last?"

"Our daily comes in on Mondays and Fridays and today is Thursday."

"Why don't you make it yourself?"

"Well, I do sort of pull it up around me when I get in."

"Those Environment types? What do they do?"

"Oh, they're trained not to notice pollution until it's brought officially to their notice."

Davis saw the two of them to the door. Cynthia said,

172

"See you tomorrow," and went down the stairs. She called over her shoulder that she had a lot of shopping to do.

> " 'She should never have looked at me
> If she meant I should not love her,' "

Davis quoted. Castle was surprised. He would not have imagined Davis reading Browning—except at school, of course.

"Well," he said, "back to the bag."

"I'm sorry, Castle. I know how that bag irritates you. I'm not malingering, really I'm not. And it's not a hangover. It's my legs, my arms—they feel like jelly."

"Go back to bed."

"I think I will. Sam wouldn't find me any good now at hide-and-seek," Davis added, leaning over the banisters, watching Castle go. As Castle reached the top of the stairs he called out, "Castle!"

"Yes?" Castle looked up.

"You don't think, do you, this might stop me?"

"Stop you?"

"I'd be a different man if I could get to Lourenço Marques."

"I've done my best. I spoke to C."

"You're a good chap, Castle. Thank you, whatever happens."

"Go back to bed and rest."

"I think I will." But he continued to stand there looking down while Castle turned away.

Chapter VII

1

Castle and Daintry arrived last at the registry office and took seats in the back row of the grim brown room. They were divided by four rows of empty chairs from the other guests of whom there were about a dozen, separated into rival clans as in a church marriage, each clan regarding the other with critical interest and some disdain. Only champagne might possibly lead to a truce later between them.

"I suppose that's Colin," Colonel Daintry said, indicating a young man who had just joined his daughter in front of the registrar's table. He added, "I don't even know his surname."

"Who's the woman with the handkerchief? She seems upset about something."

"That's my wife," Colonel Daintry said. "I hope we can slip away before she notices."

"You can't do that. Your daughter won't even know you've come."

The registrar began to speak. Someone said "Shhh," as though they were in a theater and the curtain had risen.

"Your son-in-law's name is Clutters," Castle whispered.

"Are you sure?"

"No, but it sounded like that."

The registrar gave the kind of brief Godless good wishes which are sometimes described as a lay sermon and a few people left, looking at watches as an excuse. "Don't you think we could go too?" Daintry asked.

"No."

All the same no one seemed to notice them as they stood in Victoria Street. The taxis came winging in like birds of prey and Daintry made one more effort to escape.

"It's not fair to your daughter," Castle argued.

"I don't even know where they're all going," Daintry said. "To a hotel, I suppose."

"We can follow."

And follow they did—all the way to Harrods and beyond through a thin autumnal mist.

"I can't think what hotel . . ." Daintry said. "I believe we've lost them." He leaned forward to examine the car ahead. "No such luck. I can see the back of my wife's head."

"It's not much to go by."

"All the same I'm pretty sure of it. We were married for fifteen years." He added gloomily, "And we haven't spoken for seven."

"Champagne will help," Castle said.

175

"But I don't like champagne. It's awfully good of you, Castle, to come with me. I couldn't have faced this alone."

"We'll just have one glass and go away."

"I can't imagine where we are heading. I haven't been down this way for years. There seem to be so many new hotels."

They proceeded in fits and starts down the Brompton Road.

"One generally goes to the bride's home," Castle said, "if it's not to a hotel."

"She hasn't got a home. Officially she shares a flat with some girlfriend, but apparently she's been living quite a while with this chap Clutters. Clutters! What a name!"

"The name may not have been Clutters. The registrar was very indistinct."

The taxis began to deliver the other guests like gift-wrapped parcels at a small too-pretty house in a crescent. It was lucky there were not many of them—the houses here had not been built for large parties. Even with two dozen people one felt the walls might bend or the floors give way.

"I think I know where we are—my wife's flat," Daintry said. "I heard she'd bought something in Kensington."

They edged their way up the overloaded stairs into a drawing room. From every table, from the bookshelves, the piano, from the mantel, china owls gazed at the guests, alert, predatory, with cruel curved beaks. "Yes, it *is* her flat," Daintry said. "She always had a passion for owls—but the passion's grown since my day."

They couldn't see his daughter in the crowd which clustered before the buffet. Champagne bottles popped intermittently. There was a wedding cake, and a plaster owl was even balanced on the top of the pink sugar scaffolding. A tall man with a moustache trimmed exactly like

Daintry's came up to them and said, "I don't know who you are, but do help yourselves to the champers." Judging by the slang he must have dated back nearly to the First World War. He had the absent-minded air of a rather ancient host. "We've saved on waiters," he explained.

"I'm Daintry."

"Daintry?"

"This is my daughter's marriage," Daintry said in a voice as dry as a biscuit.

"Oh, then you must be Sylvia's husband?"

"Yes. I didn't catch *your* name."

The man went away calling, "Sylvia! Sylvia!"

"Let's get out," Daintry said in desperation.

"You must say hello to your daughter."

A woman burst her way through the guests at the buffet. Castle recognized the woman who had wept at the registrar's, but she didn't look at all like weeping now. She said, "Darling, Edward told me you were here. How nice of you to come. I know how desperately busy you always are."

"Yes, we really have to be going. This is Mr. Castle. From the office."

"That damned office. How do you do, Mr. Castle? I must find Elizabeth—and Colin."

"Don't disturb them. We really have to be going."

"I'm only up for the day myself. From Brighton. Edward drove me up."

"Who's Edward?"

"He's been awfully helpful. Ordering the champagne and things. A woman needs a man on these occasions. You haven't changed a bit, darling. How long is it?"

"Six—seven years?"

"How time flies."

"You've collected a lot more owls."

"Owls?" She went away calling, "Colin, Elizabeth,

177

come over here." They came hand in hand. Daintry didn't associate his daughter with childlike tenderness, but she probably thought hand-holding a duty at a wedding.

Elizabeth said, "How sweet of you to make it, Father. I know how you hate this sort of thing."

"I've never experienced it before." He looked at her companion, who wore a carnation and a very new pin-stripe suit. His hair was jet black and well combed around the ears.

"How do you do, sir. Elizabeth has spoken such a lot about you."

"I can't say the same," Daintry said. "So you are Colin Clutters?"

"Not Clutters, Father. Whatever made you think that? His name's Clough. I mean *our* name's Clough."

A surge of latecomers who had not been at the registry office had separated Castle from Colonel Daintry. A man in a double-breasted waistcoat told him, "I don't know a soul here—except Colin, of course."

There was a smash of breaking china. Mrs. Daintry's voice rose above the clamor. "For Christ's sake, Edward, is it one of the owls?"

"No, no, don't worry, dear. Only an ashtray."

"Not a soul," repeated the man with the waistcoat. "My name's Joiner, by the way."

"Mine's Castle."

"You know Colin?"

"No, I came with Colonel Daintry."

"Who's he?"

"The bride's father."

Somewhere a telephone began to ring. No one paid any attention.

"You ought to have a word with young Colin. He's a bright lad."

"He's got a strange surname, hasn't he?"

"Strange?"

178

"Well . . . Clutters . . ."

"His name's Clough."

"Oh, then I heard it wrong."

Again something broke. Edward's voice rose reassuringly above the din. "Don't worry, Sylvia. Nothing serious. All the owls are safe."

"He's quite revolutionized our publicity."

"You work together?"

"You might say I *am* Jameson's Baby Powder."

The man called Edward grasped Castle's arm. He said, "Is your name Castle?"

"Yes."

"Somebody wants you on the telephone."

"But no one knows I'm here."

"It's a girl. She's a bit upset. Said it was urgent."

Castle's thoughts went to Sarah. She knew that he was attending this wedding, but not even Daintry knew where they were going to end up. Was Sam ill again? He asked, "Where's the telephone?"

"Follow me," but when they reached it—a white telephone beside a white double bed, guarded by a white owl—the receiver had been put back. "Sorry," Edward said, "I expect she'll ring again."

"Did she give a name?"

"Couldn't hear it with all this noise going on. Had an impression that she'd been crying. Come and have some more champers."

"If you don't mind, I'll stay here near the phone."

"Well, excuse me if I don't stay here with you. I have to look after all these owls, you see. Sylvia would be heartbroken if one of them got damaged. I suggested we tidied them away, but she's got more than a hundred of them. The place would have looked a bit bare without them. Are you a friend of Colonel Daintry?"

"We work in the same office."

"One of those hush-hush jobs, isn't it? A bit embar-

179

rassing for me meeting him like this. Sylvia didn't think he'd come. Perhaps I ought to have stayed away myself. Tactful. But then who would have looked after the owls?"

Castle sat down on the edge of the great white bed, and the white owl glared at him beside the white telephone as if it recognized him as an illegal immigrant who had just perched on the edge of this strange continent of snow—even the walls were white and there was a white rug under his feet. He was afraid—afraid for Sam, afraid for Sarah, afraid for himself—fear poured like an invisible gas from the mouth of the silent telephone. He and all he loved were menaced by the mysterious call. The clamor of voices from the living room seemed now no more than a rumor of distant tribes beyond the desert of snow. Then the telephone rang. He pushed the white owl to one side and lifted the receiver.

To his relief he heard Cynthia's voice. "Is that M.C.?"

"Yes, how did you know where to find me?"

"I tried the registry office, but you'd left. So I found a Mrs. Daintry in the telephone book."

"What's the matter, Cynthia? You sound odd."

"M.C., an awful thing has happened. Arthur's dead."

Again, as once before, he wondered for a moment who Arthur was.

"Davis? Dead? But he was coming back to the office next week."

"I know. The daily found him when she went to—to make his bed." Her voice broke.

"I'll come back to the office, Cynthia. Have you seen Doctor Percival?"

"He rang me up to tell me."

"I must go and tell Colonel Daintry."

"Oh, M.C., I wish I'd been nicer to him. All I ever did for him was—was to make his bed." He could hear her catch her breath, trying not to sob.

"I'll be back as soon as I can." He rang off.

180

The living room was as crowded as ever and just as noisy. The cake had been cut and people were looking for unobtrusive places to hide their portions. Daintry stood alone with a slice in his fingers behind a table littered with owls. He said, "For God's sake, let's be off, Castle. I don't understand this sort of thing."

"Daintry, I've had a call from the office. Davis is dead."

"Davis?"

"He's dead. Doctor Percival . . ."

"Percival!" Daintry exclaimed. "My God, that man . . ." He pushed his slice of cake among the owls and a big gray owl toppled off and smashed on the floor.

"Edward," a woman's voice shrieked, "John's broken the gray owl."

Edward thrust his way toward them. "I can't be everywhere at once, Sylvia."

Mrs. Daintry appeared behind him. She said, "John, you damned old boring fool. I'll never forgive you for this—never. What the hell are you doing anyway in *my* house?"

Daintry said, "Come away, Castle. I'll buy you another owl, Sylvia."

"It's irreplaceable, that one."

"A man's dead," Daintry said. "He's irreplaceable too."

2

"I had not expected this to happen," Doctor Percival told them.

To Castle it seemed an oddly indifferent phrase for him to use, a phrase as cold as the poor body which lay in crumpled pajamas stretched out upon the bed, the jacket wide open and the bare chest exposed, where no doubt they had long since listened and searched in vain for the least sound of a heartbeat. Doctor Percival had struck him hitherto as a very genial man, but the geniality was chilled in the presence of the dead, and there was an incongruous note of embarrassed apology in the strange phrase he had uttered.

The sudden change had come as a shock to Castle, when he found himself standing in this neglected room, after all the voices of strangers, the flocks of china owls and the explosion of corks at Mrs. Daintry's. Doctor Percival had fallen silent again after that one unfortunate phrase and nobody else spoke. He stood back from the bed rather as though he were exhibiting a picture to a couple of unkind critics, and was waiting in apprehension for their judgment. Daintry was silent too. He seemed content to watch Doctor Percival as if it were up to him to explain away some obvious fault which he was expected to find in the painting.

Castle felt an urge to break the long silence.

"Who are those men in the sitting room? What are they doing?"

Doctor Percival turned with reluctance away from the bed. "What men? Oh, those. I asked the Special Branch to take a look around."

"Why? Do you think he was killed?"

"No, no. Of course not. Nothing of that kind. His liver was in a shocking state. He had an X-ray a few days ago."

"Then why did you say you didn't expect . . .?"

"I didn't expect things to go so rapidly."

"I suppose there'll be a postmortem?"

"Of course. Of course."

The "of courses" multiplied like flies round the body.

Castle went back into the sitting room. There was a bottle of whisky and a used glass and a copy of *Playboy* on the coffee table.

"I told him he had to stop drinking," Doctor Percival called after Castle. "He wouldn't pay attention."

There were two men in the room. One of them picked up *Playboy* and ruffled and shook the pages. The other was going through the drawers of the bureau. He told his companion, "Here's his address book. You'd better go through the names. Check the telephone numbers in case they don't correspond."

"I still don't understand what they are after," Castle said.

"Just a security check," Doctor Percival explained. "I tried to get hold of you, Daintry, because it's really your pigeon, but apparently you were away at some wedding or other."

"Yes."

"There seems to have been some carelessness recently at the office. C's away but he would have wanted us to be sure that the poor chap hadn't left anything lying about."

"Like telephone numbers attached to the wrong names?" Castle asked. "I wouldn't call that exactly carelessness."

"These chaps always follow a certain routine. Isn't that so, Daintry?"

But Daintry didn't reply. He stood in the doorway of the bedroom looking at the body.

One of the men said, "Take a squint at this, Taylor." He handed the other a sheet of paper. The other read aloud, "Bonne chance, Kalamazoo, Widow Twanky."

"Bit odd, isn't it?"

Taylor said, "Bonne chance is French, Piper. Kalamazoo sounds like a town in Africa."

"Africa, eh? Might be important."

183

Castle said, "Better look in the *Evening News.* You'll probably find that they are three horses. He always bet on the tote at the weekend."

"Ah," Piper said. He sounded a little discouraged.

"I think we ought to leave our friends of the Special Branch to do their job in peace," Doctor Percival said.

"What about Davis's family?" Castle asked.

"The office has been seeing to that. The only next of kin seems to be a cousin in Droitwich. A dentist."

Piper said, "Here's something that looks a bit off-color to me, sir." He held out a book to Doctor Percival, and Castle intercepted it. It was a small selection of Robert Browning's poems. Inside was a book plate with a coat of arms and the name of a school, the Droitwich Royal Grammar School. Apparently the prize had been awarded in 1910 to a pupil called William Davis for English Composition and William Davis had written in black ink in a small finicky hand, "Passed on to my son Arthur from his father on his passing First in Physics, June 29, 1953." Browning and physics and a boy of sixteen certainly seemed a bit strange in conjunction, but presumably it was not this that Piper meant by "off-color."

"What is it?" Doctor Percival asked.

"Browning's poems. I don't see anything off-color about them."

All the same he had to admit that the little book didn't go with Aldermaston and the tote and *Playboy*, the dreary office routine and the Zaire bag; does one always discover clues to the complexity even of the most simple life if one rummages enough after death? Of course, Davis might have kept the book from filial piety, but it was obvious that he had read it. Hadn't he quoted Browning the last time Castle saw him alive?

"If you look, sir, there are passages marked," Piper said to Doctor Percival. "You know more about book codes than I do. I thought I ought to draw attention."

"What do you think, Castle?"

"Yes, there *are* marks." He turned the pages. "The book belonged to his father and of course they might be his father's marks—except that the ink looks too fresh: he puts a 'c' against them."

"Significant?"

Castle had never taken Davis seriously, not his drinking, not his gambling, not even his hopeless love for Cynthia, but a dead body could not be so easily ignored. For the first time he felt real curiosity about Davis. Death had made Davis important. Death gave Davis a kind of stature. The dead are perhaps wiser than we are. He turned the pages of the little book like a member of the Browning Society keen on interpreting a text.

Daintry dragged himself away from the bedroom door. He said, "There isn't anything, is there . . . in those marks?"

"Anything what?"

"Significant." He repeated Percival's question.

"Significant? I suppose there might be. Of a whole state of mind."

"What do you mean?" Percival asked. "Do you really think . . .?" He sounded hopeful, as if he positively wished that the man who was dead next door might have represented a security risk and, well, in a way he had, Castle thought. Love and hate are both dangerous, as he had warned Boris. A scene came to his mind: a bedroom in Lourenço Marques, the hum of an air conditioner, and Sarah's voice on the telephone, "Here I am," and then the sudden sense of great joy. His love of Sarah had led him to Carson, and Carson finally to Boris. A man in love walks through the world like an anarchist, carrying a time bomb.

"You really mean there is some evidence . . .?" Doctor Percival went on. "You've been trained in codes. I haven't."

"Listen to this passage. It's marked with a vertical line and the letter 'c.'

'Yet I will but say what mere friends say,
Or only a thought stronger:
I will hold your hand but as long as all may . . .' "

"Have you any idea what 'c' stands for?" Percival asked—and again there was that note of hope which Castle found irritating. "It could mean, couldn't it, 'code,' to remind him that he had already used that particular passage? In a book code I suppose one must be careful not to use the same passage twice."

"True enough. Here's another marked passage.

'Worth how well, those dark gray eyes,
That hair so dark and dear, how worth,
That a man should strive and agonize,
And taste a veriest hell on earth . . .' "

"It sounds to me like poetry, sir," Piper said.

"Again a vertical line and a 'c,' Doctor Percival."

"You really think then . . .?"

"Davis said to me once, 'I can't be serious when I'm serious.' So I suppose he had to go to Browning for words."

"And 'c'?"

"It only stands for a girl's name, Doctor Percival. Cynthia. His secretary. A girl he was in love with. One of us. Not a case for the Special Branch."

Daintry had been a brooding restless presence, silent, locked in thoughts of his own. He said now with a sharp note of accusation, "There should be a postmortem."

"Of course," Doctor Percival said, "if his doctor wants it. I'm not his doctor. I'm only his colleague— though he did consult me, and we have the X-rays."

"His doctor should be here now."

"I'll have him called as soon as these men have finished their work. You of all people, Colonel Daintry, will appreciate the importance of that. Security is the first consideration."

"I wonder what a postmortem will show, Doctor Percival."

"I think I can tell you that—his liver is almost totally destroyed."

"Destroyed?"

"By drink, of course, Colonel. What else? Didn't you hear me tell Castle?"

Castle left them to their subterranean duel. It was time to have a last look at Davis before the pathologist got to work on him. He was glad that the face showed no indication of pain. He drew the pajamas together across the hollow chest. A button was missing. Sewing on buttons was not part of a daily woman's job. The telephone beside the bed gave a small preliminary tinkle which came to nothing. Perhaps somewhere far away a microphone and a recorder were being detached from the line. Davis would no longer be under surveillance. He had escaped.

Chapter VIII

1

Castle sat over what he meant to be his final report. Davis being dead the information from the African section must obviously cease. If the leaks continued there could be no doubt whose was the responsibility, but if the leaks stopped the guilt would be attributed with certainty to the dead man. Davis was beyond suffering; his personal file would be closed and sent to some central store of records, where no one would bother to examine it. What if it contained a story of treachery? Like a Cabinet secret it would be well guarded for thirty years. In a sad way it had been a providential death.

Castle could hear Sarah reading aloud to Sam before packing him off for the night. It was half an hour after his usual bedtime, but tonight he had needed that extra childish comfort for the first week of school had passed unhappily.

What a long slow business it was transcribing a report into book code. He would never now get to an end of *War and Peace*. The next day he would burn his copy for security in a bonfire of autumn leaves without waiting for the Trollope to arrive. He felt relief and regret—relief because he had repaid as far as he could his debt of gratitude to Carson, and regret that he would never be able to close the dossier on Uncle Remus and complete his revenge on Cornelius Muller.

When he had finished his report he went downstairs to wait for Sarah. Tomorrow was Sunday. He would have to leave the report in the drop, that third drop which would never be used again; he had signaled its presence there from a call box in Piccadilly Circus before he caught his train at Euston. It was an inordinately slow business, this way of making his last communication, but a quicker and more dangerous route had been reserved for use only in a final emergency. He poured himself a triple J & B and the murmur of voices upstairs began to give him a temporary sense of peace. A door was closed softly, footsteps passed along the corridor above; the stairs always creaked on the way down—he thought how to some people this would seem a dull and domestic, even an intolerable routine. To him it represented a security he had been afraid every hour he might lose. He knew exactly what Sarah would say when she came into the sitting room, and he knew what he would answer. Familiarity was a protection against the darkness of King's Road outside and the lighted lamp of the police station at the corner. He had always pictured a uniformed policeman, whom he would probably know well by sight, accompanying the man from the Special Branch when the hour struck.

"You've taken your whisky?"

"Can I give *you* one?"

"A small one, darling."

"Sam all right?"

"He was asleep before I tucked him in."

As in an unmutilated cable, there was not one numeral wrongly transcribed.

He handed her the glass: he hadn't been able to speak until now of what had happened.

"How was the wedding, darling?"

"Pretty awful. I was sorry for poor Daintry."

"Why poor?"

"He was losing a daughter and I doubt if he has got any friends."

"There seem to be such a lot of lonely people in your office."

"Yes. All those that don't pair off for company. Drink up, Sarah."

"What's the hurry?"

"I want to get both of us another glass."

"Why?"

"I've got bad news, Sarah. I couldn't tell you in front of Sam. It's about Davis. Davis is dead."

"Dead? *Davis?*"

"Yes."

"How?"

"Doctor Percival talks of his liver."

"But a liver doesn't go like that—from one day to another."

"It's what Doctor Percival says."

"You don't believe him?"

"No. Not altogether. I don't think Daintry does either."

190

She gave herself two fingers of whisky—he had never seen her do that before. "Poor, poor Davis."

"Daintry wants an independent postmortem. Percival was quite ready for that. He's obviously quite sure his diagnosis will be confirmed."

"If he's sure, then it must be true?"

"I don't know. I really don't know. They can arrange so many things in our firm. Perhaps even a postmortem."

"What are we going to tell Sam?"

"The truth. It's no good keeping deaths from a child. They happen all the time."

"But he loved Davis so much. Darling, let me say nothing for a week or two. Until he finds his feet at school."

"You know best."

"I wish to God you could get away from all those people."

"I shall—in a few years."

"I mean now. This minute. We'd take Sam out of bed and go abroad. The first plane to anywhere."

"Wait till I've got my pension."

"I could work, Maurice. We could go to France. It would be easier there. They're used to my color."

"It isn't possible, Sarah. Not yet."

"Why? Give me one good reason . . ."

He tried to speak lightly. "Well, you know a man has to give proper notice."

"Do *they* bother about things like notice?"

He was scared by the quickness of her perception when she said, "Did they give Davis notice?"

He said, "If it was his liver . . ."

"You don't believe that, do you? Don't forget that I worked for you once—for them. I was your agent. Don't think I haven't noticed the last month how anxious you've been—even about the meter man. There's been a leak, is that it? In your section?"

"I think they think so."

"And they pinned it on Davis. Do you believe Davis was guilty?"

"It may not have been a deliberate leak. He was very careless."

"You think they may have killed him because he was careless."

"I suppose that in our outfit there's such a thing as criminal carelessness."

"It might have been you they suspected, not Davis. And then you'd have died. From too much J & B."

"Oh, I've always been very careful," and he added as a sad joke, "except when I fell in love with you."

"Where are you going?"

"I want a breath of air and so does Buller."

2

On the other side of the long ride through the Common known for some reason as Cold Harbour the beech woods began, sloping down toward the Ashridge road. Castle sat on a bank while Buller rummaged among last year's leaves. He knew he had no business to linger there. Curiosity was no excuse. He should have made his drop and gone. A car came slowly up the road from the direction of Berkhamsted and Castle looked at his watch. It was four hours since he had made his signal from the call box in Piccadilly Circus. He could just make out the number plate of the car, but as he might have expected it was just as strange to him as the car, a small red Toyota. Near the lodge at the entrance to Ashridge Park, the car stopped. No other car was in sight and no pedestrian. The driver turned off his lights, and then as though he had second thoughts turned them on again. A noise behind Castle made his heart leap, but it was only Buller bumbling through the bracken.

Castle climbed away through the tall olive-skinned trees which had turned black against the last light. It was over fifty years since he had discovered the hollow in one trunk . . . four, five, six trees back from the road. In those days he had been forced to stretch almost his full height to reach the hole, but his heart had knocked in the same erratic fashion as it did now. At ten years old he was leaving a message for someone he loved: the girl was only seven. He had shown her the hiding place when they were together on a picnic, and he had told her he would leave something important there for her the next time he came.

On the first occasion he left a large peppermint humbug wrapped in greaseproof paper, and when he revisited the hole it had gone. Then he left a note which declared his love—in capital letters because she had only just begun to read—but when he came back the third time he found the note was still there but disfigured by a vulgar drawing. Some stranger, he thought, must have discovered the hiding-place; he wouldn't believe that she was responsible until she put her tongue out at him, as she went by on the other side of the High Street, and he realized she was disappointed because she had not found another humbug. It had been his first experience of sexual suffering, and he never returned to the tree until almost fifty years later he was asked by a man in the lounge of the Regent Palace, whom he never saw again, to suggest another safe drop.

He put Buller on his lead and watched from his hiding place in the bracken. The man from the car had to use

193

a torch to find the hole. Castle saw his lower half outlined for a moment as the torch descended the trunk: a plump belly, an open fly. A clever precaution—he had even stored up a reasonable amount of urine. When the torch turned and lit the way back toward the Ashridge road, Castle started home. He told himself, "This is the last report," and his thoughts went back to the child of seven. She had seemed lonely at the picnic, where they had first met, she was shy and she was ugly, and perhaps he was drawn to her for those reasons.

Why are some of us, he wondered, unable to love success or power or great beauty? Because we feel unworthy of them, because we feel more at home with failure? He didn't believe that was the reason. Perhaps one wanted the right balance, just as Christ had, that legendary figure whom he would have liked to believe in. "Come unto me all ye that travail and are heavy laden." Young as the girl was at that August picnic she was heavily laden with her timidity and shame. Perhaps he had merely wanted her to feel that she was loved by someone and so he began to love her himself. It wasn't pity, any more than it had been pity when he fell in love with Sarah pregnant by another man. He was there to right the balance. That was all.

"You've been out a long time," Sarah said.

"Well, I needed a walk badly. How's Sam?"

"Fast asleep, of course. Shall I give you another whisky?"

"Yes. A small one again."

"A small one? Why?"

"I don't know. Just to show I can slow up a bit perhaps. Perhaps because I'm feeling happier. Don't ask me why, Sarah. Happiness goes when you speak of it."

The excuse seemed good enough to both of them. Sarah, during their last year in South Africa, had learned not to probe too far, but in bed that night he lay awake a long time, repeating to himself over and over again the

194

final words of the last report which he had concocted with the aid of *War and Peace*. He had opened the book at random several times, seeking a *sortes Virgilianae*, before he chose the sentences on which his code was to be based. "You say: I am not free. But I have lifted my hand and let it fall." It was as if, in choosing that passage, he were transmitting a signal of defiance to both the services. The last word of the message, when it was decoded by Boris or another, would read "goodbye."

Part Four

Chapter I

1

The nights after Davis died were full of dreams for
Castle, dreams formed out of broken fragments of a past
which pursued him till the daylight hours. Davis played
no part in them—perhaps because the thought of him, in
their now reduced and saddened sub-section, filled
many waking hours. The ghost of Davis hovered over the
bag from Zaire and the telegrams which Cynthia encoded
were now more mutilated than ever.

So at night Castle dreamt of a South Africa recon-
structed with hatred, though sometimes the bits and
pieces were jumbled up with an Africa which he had forgotten how much he loved. In one dream he came on

Sarah suddenly in a litter-strewn Johannesburg park sitting on a bench for blacks only: he turned away to find a different bench. Carson separated from him at a lavatory door and chose the door reserved for blacks, leaving him on the outside ashamed of his lack of courage, but then quite another sort of dream came to him on the third night.

When he woke he said to Sarah, "It's funny. I dreamt of Rougemont. I haven't thought of him for years."

"Rougemont?"

"I forgot. You never knew Rougemont."

"Who was he?"

"A farmer in the Free State. I liked him in a way as much as I liked Carson."

"Was he a Communist? Surely not if he was a farmer."

"No. He was one of those who will have to die when your people take control."

"My people?"

"I meant of course 'our people,' " he said with sad haste as though he had been in danger of breaking a promise.

Rougemont lived on the edge of a semi-desert not far from an old battlefield of the Boer War. His ancestors, who were Huguenot, had fled from France at the time of the persecution, but he spoke no French, only Afrikaans and English. He had been, before he was born, assimilated to the Dutch way of life—but not to apartheid. He stood aside from it—he wouldn't vote Nationalist, he despised the United Party, and some undetermined sense of loyalty to his ancestors kept him from voting for the small band of progressives. It was not a heroic attitude, but perhaps in his eyes, as in his grandfather's, heroism began where politics stopped. He treated his laborers with kindness and understanding, with no condescension. Castle listened to him one day as he debated with his black foreman on the state of the crops—they argued with each other as equals. The family of Rougemont and the tribe of the foreman had arrived in South Africa at much the same time. Rougemont's grandfather had not been an ostrich millionaire from the Cape, like Cornelius Muller's: when he was sixty years old grandfather Rougemont had ridden with De Wet's commando against the English invaders and he had been wounded there on the local *kopje*, which leaned with the winter clouds over the farm, where the Bushmen hundreds of years earlier had carved the rocks with animal forms.

"Fancy climbing up that under fire with a pack on your back," Rougemont had remarked to Castle. He admired the British troops for their courage and endurance far from home rather as though they were legendary marauders in a history book, like the Vikings who had once descended on the Saxon coast. He had no resentment against those of the Vikings who remained, only perhaps a certain pity for a people without roots in this old tired beautiful land where his family had settled three hundred years ago. He had said to Castle one day over a glass of whisky, "You say you are writing a study of apartheid, but you'll never understand our complexities. I hate apartheid as much as you do, but you are much more a stranger to me than any of my laborers. We belong here—you are as much an outsider as the tourists who come and go." Castle felt sure that, when the time for decision came, he would take the gun on his living-room wall in defense of this difficult area of cultivation on the edge of a desert. He would not die fighting for apartheid or for the white race, but for so many *morgen* which he called his own, subject to drought and floods and earthquakes and cattle disease, and snakes which he regarded as a minor pest like mosquitoes.

"Was Rougemont one of your agents?" Sarah asked.

"No, but oddly enough it was through him that I met Carson." He might have added, "And through Carson I

201

have joined Rougemont's enemies." Rougemont had hired Carson to defend one of his laborers accused by the local police of a crime of violence of which he was innocent.

Sarah said, "I sometimes wish I was still your agent. You tell me so much less than you did then."

"I never told you much—perhaps you thought I did, but I told you as little as I could, for your own safety, and then it was often lies. Like the book I intended to write on apartheid."

"I thought things would be different," Sarah said, "in England. I thought there would be no more secrets." She drew in her breath and was again immediately asleep, but Castle lay awake a long time. He had at such moments an enormous temptation to trust her, to tell her everything, much as a man who has had a passing affair with a woman, an affair which is finished, wants suddenly to trust his wife with the whole sad history—to explain once and for all the unexplained silences, the small deceptions, the worries they haven't been able to share, and in the same way as that other man he came to the conclusion, "Why worry her when it's all over?" for he really believed, if only for a while, that it was over.

2

It seemed very strange to Castle to be sitting in the same room he had occupied for so many years alone with Davis and to see, facing him across the table, the man called Cornelius Muller—a Muller curiously transformed, a Muller who said to him, "I was so sorry to hear the news when I got back from Bonn . . . I hadn't met your colleague, of course . . . but to you it must have been a great shock . . ." a Muller who began to resemble an ordinary human being, not an officer of BOSS but a man whom he might have met by chance in the train on the way to Euston. He was struck by the note of sympathy in the tone of Muller's voice—it sounded oddly sincere. In England, he thought, we have become increasingly cynical about all deaths which do not concern us closely, and even in those cases it is polite to fit on quickly a mask of indifference in the presence of a stranger; death and business don't go together. But in the Dutch Reformed Church to which Muller belonged, a death, Castle remembered, was still the most important event in family life. Castle had attended a funeral once in the Transvaal, and it was not the sorrow which he recalled but the dignity, even the protocol, of the occasion. Death remained socially important to Muller, even though he was an officer of BOSS.

"Well," Castle said, "it was certainly unexpected." He added, "I've asked my secretary to bring me in the Zaire and Mozambique files. For Malawi we have to depend on MI5, and I can't show you their material without permission."

"I'll be seeing them when I've finished with you," Muller said. He added, "I enjoyed so much the evening I spent at your house. Meeting your wife . . ." He hesitated a little before he continued, "and your son."

Castle hoped that these opening remarks were only a polite preparation before Muller took up again his inquiries about the route Sarah had taken into Swaziland. An enemy had to remain a caricature if he was to be kept at a safe distance: an enemy should never come alive. The generals were right—no Christmas cheer ought to be exchanged between the trenches.

He said, "Of course Sarah and I were very happy to

see you." He rang his bell. "I'm sorry. They're taking the hell of a long time over those files. Davis's death has a bit upset our routine."

A girl he didn't know answered the bell. "I telephoned five minutes ago for the files," he said. "Where's Cynthia?"

"She isn't in."

"Why isn't she in?"

The girl looked at him with stone-cold eyes. "She's taken the day off."

"Is she sick?"

"Not exactly."

"Who are you?"

"Penelope."

"Well, will you tell me, Penelope, what exactly you mean by not exactly?"

"She's upset. It's natural, isn't it? Today's the funeral. Arthur's funeral."

"Today? I'm sorry. I forgot." He added, "All the same, Penelope, I would like you to get us the files."

When she had left the room he said to Muller, "I'm sorry for all this confusion. It must give you a strange impression of the way we do things. I really had forgotten—they're burying Davis today—they're having a funeral service at eleven. It's been delayed because of the postmortem. The girl remembered. I forgot."

"I'm sorry," Muller said, "I would have changed our date if I'd known."

"It's not your fault. The fact is—I have an official diary and a private diary. Here I have you marked, you see, for 10 Thursday. The private diary I keep at home, and I must have written the funeral down in that one. I'm always forgetting to compare the two."

"All the same . . . forgetting the funeral . . . isn't that a bit odd?"

"Yes, Freud would say I wanted to forget."

"Just fix another date for me and I'll be off. Tomorrow or the next day?"

"No, no. Which is more important anyway? Uncle Remus or listening to prayers being said over poor Davis? Where was Carson buried by the way?"

"At his home. A small town near Kimberley. I suppose you'll be surprised when I tell you that I was there?"

"No, I imagine you had to watch and observe who the mourners were."

"Someone—you're right—someone had to watch. But I chose to go."

"Not Captain Van Donck?"

"No. He would have been easily recognized."

"I can't think what they are doing with those files."

"This man Davis—perhaps he didn't mean very much to you?" Muller asked.

"Well, not as much as Carson. Whom you people killed. But my son was fond of him."

"Carson died of pneumonia."

"Yes. Of course. So you told me. I had forgotten that too."

When the files at last came Castle went through them, seeking to answer Muller's questions, but with only half of his mind. "We have no reliable information about that yet," he found himself saying for the third time. Of course it was a deliberate lie—he was protecting a source from Muller—for they were approaching dangerous ground, working together up to that point of non-cooperation which was still undetermined by either of them.

He asked Muller, "Is Uncle Remus really practicable? I can't believe the Americans will ever get involved again—I mean with troops in a strange continent. They are just as ignorant of Africa as they were of Asia—except, of course, through novelists like Hemingway. He would go off on a month's safari arranged by a travel agency and write about white hunters and shooting lions—the poor half-starved brutes reserved for tourists."

"The ideal that Uncle Remus has in mind," Muller said, "is to make the use of troops almost unnecessary. At any rate in great numbers. A few technicians, of course, but they're already with us. America maintains a guided missile tracking station and a space tracking station in the Republic, and they have over-flying rights to support those stations—you certainly know all that. No one has protested, no one has marched. There have been no student riots in Berkeley, no questions in Congress. Our internal security so far has proved excellent. You see, our race laws have in a way been justified: they prove an excellent cover. We don't have to charge anyone with espionage—that would only draw attention. Your friend Carson was dangerous—but he'd have been more dangerous still if we had had to try him for espionage. A lot is going on now at the tracking stations—that's why we want a close cooperation with your people. You can pinpoint any danger and we can deal with it quietly. In some ways you're much better placed than we are to penetrate the liberal elements, or even the black nationalists. Take an example. I'm grateful for what you've given me on Mark Ngambo—of course we knew it already. But now we can be satisfied that we've missed nothing important. There's no danger from that particular angle—for the time anyway. The next five years, you see, are of vital importance—I mean for our survival."

"But I wonder, Muller—can you survive? You've got a long open frontier—too long for minefields."

"Of the old-fashioned kind, yes," Muller said. "It's as well for us that the hydrogen bomb made the atom bomb just a tactical weapon. Tactical is a reassuring word. No one will start a nuclear war because a tactical weapon has been used in almost desert country very far away."

206

"How about the radiation?"

"We are lucky in our prevailing winds and our deserts. Besides, the tactical bomb is reasonably clean. Cleaner than the bomb at Hiroshima and we know how limited the effect of that was. In the areas which may for a few years be radioactive there are few white Africans. We plan to canalize any invasions there are."

"I begin to see the picture," Castle said. He remembered Sam, as he remembered him when he looked at the newspaper photograph of the drought—the spread-eagled body and the vulture, but the vulture would be dead too of radiation.

"That's what I came here to show you—the general picture—we needn't go into all the details—so that you can properly evaluate any information you obtain. The tracking stations are at this moment the sensitive point."

"Like the race laws they can cover a multitude of sins?"

"Exactly. You and I needn't go on playing with each other. I know you've been instructed to keep certain things from me, and I quite understand. I've received just the same orders as you have. The only important thing is—we should both look at identically the same picture; we shall be fighting on the same side, so we've got to see the same picture."

"In fact we're in the same box?" Castle said, making his private joke against them all, against BOSS, against his own service, even against Boris.

"Box? Yes, I suppose you could put it that way." He looked at his watch. "Didn't you say the funeral was at eleven? It's ten to eleven now. You'd better be off."

"The funeral can go on without me. If there's an after-life Davis will understand, and if there isn't . . ."

"I'm quite sure there *is* an after-life," Cornelius Muller said.

"You are? Doesn't the idea frighten you a bit?"

207

"Why should it? I've always tried to do my duty."

"But those little tactical atomic weapons of yours. Think of all the blacks who will die before you do and be there waiting for you."

"Terrorists," Muller said. "I don't expect to meet them again."

"I didn't mean the guerrillas. I mean all the families in the infected area. Children, girls, the old grannies."

"I expect they'll have their own kind of heaven," Muller said.

"Apartheid in heaven?"

"Oh, I know you are laughing at me. But I don't suppose they'd enjoy our sort of heaven, do you? Anyway I leave all that to the theologians. You didn't exactly spare the children in Hamburg, did you?"

"Thank God, I didn't participate as I'm doing now."

"I think if you aren't going to the funeral, Castle, we should get on with our business."

"I'm sorry. I agree." Indeed he was sorry; he was even afraid, as he had been in the office of BOSS that morning in Pretoria. For seven years he had trodden with unremitting care through the minefields, and now with Cornelius Muller he had taken his first wrong step. Was it possible that he had fallen into a trap set by someone who understood his temperament?

"Of course," Muller said, "I know that you English like arguing for the sake of arguing. Why, even your C pulled my leg about apartheid, but when it comes to Uncle Remus . . . well, you and I have to be serious."

"Yes, we'd better get back to Uncle Remus."

"I have permission to tell you—in broad lines, of course—how things went with me in Bonn."

"You had difficulties?"

"Not serious ones. The Germans—unlike other ex-colonial powers—have a lot of secret sympathy for us. You could say that it goes back as far as the Kaiser's telegram to President Kruger. They are worried about South-West Africa; they would rather see us control South-West Africa than a vacuum there. After all they ruled the South-West more brutally than we have ever done, and the West needs our uranium."

"You brought back an agreement?"

"One shouldn't talk of an agreement. We are no longer in the days of secret treaties. I only had contact with my opposite number, not with the Foreign Secretary or the Chancellor. Just the same way as your C has been talking with the CIA in Washington. What I hope is that we've all three reached a clearer understanding."

"A secret understanding instead of a secret treaty?"

"Exactly."

"And the French?"

"No trouble there. If we are Calvinist they're Cartesian. Descartes didn't worry about the religious persecution of his time. The French have a great influence on Senegal, the Ivory Coast, they even have a fair understanding with Mobutu in Kinshasa. Cuba won't seriously interfere in Africa again (America has seen to that), and Angola won't be a danger for a good many years. No one is apocalyptic today. Even a Russian wants to die in his bed, not in a bunker. At the worst, with the use of a few atomic bombs—small tactical ones, of course—we shall gain five years of peace if we are attacked."

"And afterwards?"

"That's the real point of our understanding with Germany. We need a technical revolution and the latest mining machines, although we've gone further than anyone realizes on our own. In five years we can more than halve the labor force in the mines: we can more than double wages for skilled men and we can begin to produce what they have in America, a black middle class."

209

"And the unemployed?"

"They can go back to their homelands. That is what the homelands were for. I'm an optimist, Castle."

"And apartheid stays?"

"There'll always be a certain apartheid as there is here—between the rich and the poor."

Cornelius Muller took off his gold-rimmed glasses and polished the gold till it gleamed. He said, "I hope your wife liked her shawl. You know you will always be welcome to come back now that we realize your true position. With your family too, of course. You may be sure they will be treated as honorary whites."

Castle wanted to reply, "But I am an honorary black," but this time he showed a little prudence. "Thank you."

Muller opened his briefcase and took out a sheet of paper. He said, "I have made a few notes for you on my meetings in Bonn." He produced a ball-point pen—gold again. "You might have some useful information on these points when we next meet. Would Monday suit you? The same time?" He added, "Please destroy that when you've read it. BOSS wouldn't like it to go on even your most secret file."

"Of course. As you wish."

When Muller had gone he put the paper in his pocket.

Chapter II

1

There were very few people at St. George's in Hanover Square when Doctor Percival arrived with Sir John Hargreaves, who had only returned from Washington the night before.

A man with a black band around his arm stood alone by the aisle in the front row; presumably, Doctor Percival thought, he was the dentist from Droitwich. He refused to make way for anyone—it was as though he were safeguarding his right to the whole front row as the nearest living relative. Doctor Percival and C took their seats near the back of the church. Davis's secretary, Cynthia, was two rows behind them. Colonel Daintry sat beside Watson on the other side of the aisle, and there were a number of faces only half known to Doctor Percival. He had glimpsed them once perhaps in a corridor or at a conference with MI5, perhaps there were even intruders—a funeral attracts strangers like a wedding. Two tousled men in the last row were almost certainly Davis's fellow lodgers from the Department of the Environment. Someone began to play softly on the organ.

Doctor Percival whispered to Hargreaves, "Did you have a good flight?"

"Three hours late at Heathrow," Hargreaves said. "The food was uneatable." He sighed—perhaps he was remembering with regret his wife's steak-and-kidney pie, or the smoked trout at his club. The organ breathed a last note and fell silent. A few people knelt and a few stood up. There was a lack of certainty about what to do next.

The Vicar, who was probably known to nobody there, not even to the dead man in the coffin, intoned "Take Thy plague away from me; I am even consumed by means of Thy heavy hand."

"What plague was it that killed Davis, Emmanuel?"

"Don't worry, John. The postmortem was all in order."

The service seemed to Doctor Percival, who had not attended a funeral for many years, full of irrelevant information. The Vicar had begun reading the lesson from the First Epistle to the Corinthians: "All flesh is not the same flesh: but there is one kind of flesh of men, another flesh of beasts, another of fishes, and another of birds." The statement was undeniably true, Doctor Percival thought. The coffin did not contain a fish; he would have been more interested in it if it had—an enormous trout perhaps. He took a quick look round. There was a tear caged behind the girl's lashes. Colonel Daintry had an angry or perhaps a sullen expression which might bode ill. Watson too was obviously worried about something—probably he was wondering whom to promote in Davis's place. "I want to have a word with you after the service," Hargreaves said, and that might be tiresome too.

"Behold I show you a mystery," the Vicar read. The mystery of whether I killed the right man? Doctor Percival wondered, but that will never be solved unless the leaks continue—that would certainly suggest he had made an unfortunate mistake. C would be very upset and so would Daintry. It was a pity one couldn't throw a man back into the river of life as one could throw a fish. The Vicar's voice, which had risen to greet a familiar passage of English literature, "O Death, where is thy sting?" as a bad actor playing Hamlet picks out from its context the famous soliloquy, fell to a drone again for the dull and academic conclusion, "The sting of death is sin, and the strength of sin is the law." It sounded like a proposition of Euclid.

"What did you say?" C whispered.

"Q.E.D.," Doctor Percival replied.

2

"What exactly did you mean by Q.E.D.?" Sir John Hargreaves asked when they managed to get outside.

"It seemed a more suitable response to what the Vicar was saying than Amen."

They walked after that in a near silence toward the Travellers Club. By a mute consent the Travellers seemed a spot more suited for lunch that day than the Reform—Davis had become an honorary traveller by this voyage of his into unexplored regions and he certainly had lost his claim to one man one vote.

"I don't remember when I last attended a funeral," Doctor Percival said. "An old great-aunt, I think, more than fifteen years ago. A rather stiff ceremony, isn't it?"

"I used to enjoy funerals in Africa. Lots of music— even if the only instruments were pots and pans and empty sardine tins. They made one think that death after all might be a lot of fun. Who was the girl I saw crying?"

"Davis's secretary. Her name is Cynthia. Apparently he was in love with her."

"A lot of that goes on, I imagine. It's inevitable in an outfit like ours. Daintry checked on her thoroughly, I suppose?"

"Oh yes, yes. In fact—quite unconsciously—she gave us some useful information—you remember that business at the Zoo."

"The Zoo?"

"When Davis . . ."

"Oh yes, I remember now."

As usual at the weekend, the club was almost empty. They would have begun lunch—it was an almost automatic reflex—with smoked trout, but it was not available. Doctor Percival reluctantly accepted as a substitute smoked salmon. He said, "I wish I had known Davis better. I think I might have come to like him quite a lot."

"And yet you still believe he was the leak?"

"He played the role of a rather simple man very cleverly. I admire cleverness—and courage too. He must have needed a lot of courage."

"In a wrong cause."

"John, John! You and I are not really in a position to talk about cause. We aren't Crusaders—we are in the wrong century. Saladin was long ago driven out of Jerusalem. Not that Jerusalem has gained much by that."

214

"All the same, Emmanuel...I can't admire treachery."

"Thirty years ago when I was a student I rather fancied myself as a kind of Communist. Now . . .? Who is the traitor—me or Davis? I really believed in internationalism, and now I'm fighting an underground war for nationalism."

"You've grown up, Emmanuel, that's all. What do you want to drink—claret or burgundy?"

"Claret, if it's all the same to you."

Sir John Hargreaves crouched in his chair and buried himself deep in the wine list. He looked unhappy—perhaps only because he couldn't make up his mind between St. Emilion and Médoc. At last he made his decision and his order. "I sometimes wonder why you are with us, Emmanuel."

"You've just said it, I grew up. I don't think Communism will work—in the long run—any better than Christianity has done, and I'm not the Crusader type. Capitalism or Communism? Perhaps God is a Capitalist. I want to be on the side most likely to win during my lifetime. Don't look shocked, John. You think I'm a cynic, but I just don't want to waste a lot of time. The side that wins will be able to build the better hospitals, and give more to cancer research—when all this atomic nonsense is abandoned. In the meanwhile I enjoy the game we're all playing. Enjoy. Only enjoy. I don't pretend to be an enthusiast for God or Marx. Beware of people who believe. They aren't reliable players. All the same one grows to like a good player on the other side of the board—it increases the fun."

"Even if he's a traitor?"

"Oh, traitor—that's an old-fashioned word, John. The player is as important as the game. I wouldn't enjoy the game with a bad player across the table."

"And yet . . . you did kill Davis? Or didn't you?"

"He died of his liver, John. Read the postmortem."

"A happy coincidence?"

"The marked card—you suggested it—turned up, you see—the oldest trick of all. Only he and I knew of my little fantasy about Porton."

"You should have waited till I came home. Did you discuss it with Daintry?"

"You had left me in charge, John. When you feel the fish on the line you don't stand waiting on the bank for someone else to advise you what to do."

"This Château Talbot—does it seem to you quite up to the mark?"

"It's excellent."

"I think they must have ruined my palate in Washington. All those dry martinis." He tried his wine again. "Or else it's your fault. Does nothing ever worry you, Emmanuel?"

"Well, yes, I am a little worried about the funeral service—you noticed they even had an organ—and then there's the interment. All that must cost a lot, and I don't suppose Davis left many pennies behind. Do you suppose that poor devil of a dentist has paid for it all—or did our friends from the East? That doesn't seem quite proper to me."

"Don't worry about that, Emmanuel. The office will pay. We don't have to account for secret funds." Hargreaves pushed his glass on one side. He said, "This Talbot doesn't taste to me like '71."

"I was taken aback myself, John, by Davis's quick reaction. I'd calculated his weight exactly and I gave him what I thought would be less than lethal. You see, aflatoxin had never been tested before on a human being, and I wanted to be sure in case of a sudden emergency that we gave the right dose. Perhaps his liver was in a bad way already."

"How did you give it to him?"

"I dropped in for a drink and he gave me some hideous whisky which he called a White Walker. The flavor was quite enough to drown the aflatoxin."

"I can only pray you got the right fish," Sir John Hargreaves said.

3

Daintry turned gloomily into St. James's Street, and as he passed White's on the way to his flat a voice hailed him from the steps. He looked up from the gutter in which his thoughts had lain. He recognized the face, but he couldn't for a moment put a name to it, nor even remember in what circumstances he had seen it before. Boffin occurred to him. Buffer?

"Got any Maltesers, old man?"

Then the scene of their encounter came back to him with a sense of embarrassment.

"What about a spot of lunch, Colonel?"

Buffy was the absurd name. Of course, the fellow must certainly possess another, but Daintry had never learned it. He said, "I'm sorry. I've got lunch waiting for me at home." This was not exactly a lie. He had put out a tin of sardines before he went to Hanover Square, and there remained some bread and cheese from yesterday's lunch.

"Come and have a drink then. Meals at home can always wait," Buffy said, and Daintry could think of no excuse not to join him.

As it was still early only two people were in the bar. They seemed to know Buffy a thought too well, for they greeted him without enthusiasm. Buffy didn't seem to mind. He waved his hand in a wide gesture that included the barman. "This is the Colonel." Both of them grunted at Daintry with weary politeness. "Never caught your name," Buffy said, "at that shoot."

"I never caught yours."

"We met," Buffy explained, "at Hargreaves' place. The Colonel is one of the hush-hush boys. James Bond and all that."

One of the two said, "I never could read those books by Ian."

"Too sexy for me," the other one said. "Exaggerated. I like a good screw as much as the next man, but it's not all that important, is it? Not the way you do it, I mean."

"What'll you have?" Buffy asked.

"A dry martini," Colonel Daintry said, and, remembering his meeting with Doctor Percival, he added, "very dry."

"One large very dry, Joe, and one large pink. Really large, old chap. Don't be stingy."

A deep silence fell over the little bar as though each one was thinking of something different—of a novel by Ian Fleming, of a shooting party, or a funeral. Buffy said, "The Colonel and I have a taste in common—Maltesers."

One of the men emerged from his private thoughts and said, "Maltesers? I prefer Smarties."

"What the hell are Smarties, Dicky?"

"Little chocolate things all different colors. They taste much the same, but, I don't know why, I prefer the red and yellow ones. I don't like the mauve."

Buffy said, "I saw you coming down the street, Colonel. You seemed to be having quite a talk with yourself, if you don't mind my saying so. State secrets? Where were you off to?"

"Only home," Daintry said. "I live near here."

"You looked properly browned off. I said to myself, the country must be in serious trouble. The hush-hush boys know more than we do."

"I've come from a funeral."

"No one close, I hope?"

"No. Someone from the office."

"Oh well, a funeral's always better to my mind than a wedding. I can't bear weddings. A funeral's final. A wedding—well, it's only an unfortunate stage to something else. I'd rather celebrate a divorce—but then that's often a stage too, to just another wedding. People get into the habit."

"Come off it, Buffy," said Dicky, the man who liked Smarties, "you thought of it once yourself. We know all about that marriage bureau of yours. You were damned lucky to escape. Joe, give the Colonel another martini."

Daintry, with a feeling of being lost among strangers, drank the first down. He said, like a man picking a sentence from a phrase book in a language he doesn't know, "I was at a wedding too. Not long ago."

"Hush-hush again? I mean, one of your lot?"

"No. It was my daughter. She got married."

"Good God," Buffy said, "I never thought you were one of those—I mean one of those married fellows."

"It doesn't necessarily follow," Dicky said.

The third man, who had hardly spoken up till then, said, "You needn't be so damned superior, Buffy. I was one of those too once. Though it seems the hell of a long time ago. As a matter of fact it was my wife who introduced Dicky to Smarties. You remember that afternoon, Dicky? We'd had a pretty gloomy lunch, because we sort of knew we were breaking up the old home. Then she said, 'Smarties,' just like that, 'Smarties' . . . I don't know why. I suppose she thought we had to talk about something. She was a great one for appearances."

219

"I can't say I do remember, Willie. Smarties seem to me to date back a long time in my life. Thought I'd discovered them for myself. Give the Colonel another dry, Joe."

"No, if you don't mind . . . I've really got to get home."

"It's my turn," the man called Dicky said. "Top up his glass, Joe. He's come from a funeral. He needs cheering up."

"I got used to funerals very early," Daintry said to his own surprise after he had taken a swig of the third dry martini. He realized he was talking more freely than he usually did with strangers and most of the world to him were strangers. He would have liked to pay for a round himself, but of course it was their club. He felt very friendly toward them, but he remained—he was sure of it—in their eyes a stranger still. He wanted to interest them, but so many subjects were barred to him.

"Why? Were there a lot of deaths in your family?" Dicky asked with alcoholic curiosity.

"No, it wasn't exactly that," Daintry said, his shyness drowning in the third martini. For some reason he remembered a country railway station where he had arrived with his platoon more than thirty years ago—the signs naming the place had all been removed after Dunkirk against a possible German invasion. It was as though once again he were delivering himself of a heavy pack, which he let drop resoundingly on the floor of White's. "You see," he said, "my father was a clergyman, so I went to a lot of funerals when I was a child."

"I would never have guessed it," Buffy said. "Thought you'd come from a military family—son of a general, the old regiment, and all that cock. Joe, my glass is crying to be refilled. But, of course, when you come to think of it, your father being a clergyman does explain quite a lot."

"What does it explain?" Dicky asked. For some reason he seemed to be annoyed and in the mood to question everything. "The Maltesers?"

"No, no, the Maltesers are a different story. I can't tell you about them now. It would take too long. What I meant was the Colonel belongs to the hush-hush boys, and so in a way does a clergyman, when you come to think of it . . . You know, the secrets of the confessional and all that, they are in the hush-hush business too."

"My father wasn't a Roman Catholic. He wasn't even High Church. He was a naval chaplain. In the first war."

"The first war," said the morose man called Willie who had once been married, "was the one between Cain and Abel." He made his statement flatly as though he wanted to close an unnecessary conversation.

"Willie's father was a clergyman too," Buffy explained. "A big shot. A bishop against a naval chaplain. Trumps."

"My father was in the Battle of Jutland," Daintry told them. He didn't mean to challenge anyone, to set up Jutland against a bishopric. It was just another memory which had returned.

"As a non-combatant, though. That hardly counts, does it?" Buffy said. "Not against Cain and Abel."

"You don't look all that old," Dicky said. He spoke with an air of suspicion, sucking at his glass.

"My father wasn't married then. He married my mother after the war. In the twenties." Daintry realized the conversation was becoming absurd. The gin was acting like a truth drug. He knew he was talking too much.

"He married your mother?" Dicky asked sharply like an interrogator.

"Of course he married her. In the twenties."

"She's still alive?"

"They've both been dead a long time. I really must be getting home. My meal will be spoiled," Daintry added, thinking of the sardines drying on a plate. The sense of being among friendly strangers left him. The conversation threatened to turn ugly.

"And what has all this to do with a funeral? What funeral?"

"Don't mind Dicky," Buffy said. "He likes interrogating. He was in MI5 during the war. More gins, Joe. He's already told us, Dicky. It was some poor bugger in the office."

"Did you see him properly into the ground?"

"No, no. I just went to the service. In Hanover Square."

"That would be St. George's," said the son of the bishop. He held his glass out to Joe as though it were a communion cup.

It took quite a time for Daintry to detach himself from the bar at White's. Buffy even conducted him as far as the steps. A taxi passed. "You see what I mean," Buffy said. "Buses in St. James's. No one was safe." Daintry had no idea what he meant. As he walked down the street toward the palace he was aware that he had drunk more than he had drunk for years at this hour of the day. They were nice fellows, but one had to be careful. He had spoken far too much. About his father, his mother. He walked past Lock's hat shop; past Overton's Restaurant; he halted on the pavement at the corner of Pall Mall. He had overshot the mark—he realized that in time. He turned on his heel and retraced his steps to the door of the flat where his lunch awaited him.

The cheese was there all right and the bread, and the tin of sardines which after all he had not yet decanted. He was not very clever with his fingers, and the small leaf of the tin broke before the tin was a third open. All the same he managed to fork out half the sardines in bits and pieces. He wasn't hungry—that was enough. He hesitated whether he should drink any more after the dry martinis and then chose a bottle of Tuborg.

222

His lunch lasted for less than four minutes, but it seemed to him quite a long time because of his thoughts. His thoughts wobbled like a drunken man's. He thought first of Doctor Percival and Sir John Hargreaves going off together down the street in front of him when the service was over, their heads bent like conspirators. He thought next of Davis. It wasn't that he had any personal liking for Davis, but his death worried him. He said aloud to the only witness, which happened to be a sardine tail balanced on his fork, "A jury would never convict on that evidence." Convict? He hadn't any proof that Davis had not died, as the postmortem showed, a natural death—cirrhosis was what one called a natural death. He tried to remember what Doctor Percival had said to him on the night of the shoot. He had drunk too much that night, as he had done this morning, because he was ill at ease with people whom he didn't understand, and Percival had come uninvited to his room and talked about an artist called Nicholson.

Daintry didn't touch the cheese; he carried it back with the oily plate to the kitchen—or kitchenette as it would be called nowadays—there was only room for one person at a time. He remembered the vast spaces of the basement kitchen in that obscure rectory in Suffolk where his father had been washed up after the Battle of Jutland, and he remembered Buffy's careless words about the confessional. His father had never approved of confession nor of the confessional box set up by a High Church celibate in the next parish. Confessions came to him, if they came at all, secondhand, for people did confess sometimes to his mother, who was much loved in the village, and he had heard her filter these confessions to his father, with any grossness, malice or cruelty removed. "I think you ought to know what Mrs. Baines told me yesterday."

Daintry spoke aloud—the habit was certainly growing on him—to the kitchen sink, "There was *no* real evidence

223

against Davis." He felt guilty of failure—a man in late middle age near to retirement—retirement from what? He would exchange one loneliness for another. He wanted to be back in the Suffolk rectory. He wanted to walk up the long weedy path lined with laurels that never flowered and enter the front door. Even the hall was larger than his whole flat. A number of hats hung from a stand on the left and on the right a brass shell-case held the umbrellas. He crossed the hall and, very softly opening the door in front of him, he surprised his parents where they sat on the chintz sofa hand in hand because they thought they were alone. "Shall I resign," he asked them, "or wait for retirement?" He knew quite well that the answer would be "No" from both of them—from his father because the captain of his cruiser had shared in his eyes something of the divine right of kings—his son couldn't possibly know better than his commanding officer the right action to take— and from his mother—well, she would always tell a girl in the village who was in trouble with her employer, "Don't be hasty. It's not so easy to find another situation." His father, the ex-naval chaplain, who believed in his captain and his God, would have given him what he considered to be the Christian reply, and his mother would have given him the practical and worldly answer. What greater chance had he to find another job if he resigned now than a daily maid would have in the small village where they had lived?

Colonel Daintry went back into his sitting room, forgetting the oily fork he carried. For the first time in some years he possessed his daughter's telephone number—she had sent it to him after her marriage on a printed card. It was the only link he had with her day-to-day life. Perhaps it would be possible, he thought, to invite himself to dinner. He wouldn't actually suggest it, but if she made an offer. . .

He didn't recognize the voice which answered. He said, "Is that 6731075?"

"Yes. Who do you want?" It was a man speaking—a stranger.

He lost his nerve and his memory for names. He replied, "Mrs. Clutter."

"You've got the wrong number."

"I'm sorry." He rang off. Of course he should have said, "I meant Mrs. Clough," but it was too late now. The stranger, he supposed, was his son-in-law.

4

"You didn't mind," Sarah asked, "that I couldn't go?"

"No. Of course not. I couldn't go myself—I had a date with Muller."

"I was afraid of not being back here before Sam returned from school. He'd have asked me where I'd been."

"All the same, he has to know sometime."

"Yes, but there's still a lot of time. Were there many people there?"

"Not many, so Cynthia said. Watson, of course, as the head of the section. Doctor Percival. C. It was decent of C to go. It wasn't as though Davis was anyone important in the firm. And there was his cousin—Cynthia thought it was his cousin, because he wore a black band."

"What happened after the service?"

"I don't know."

"I meant—to the body."

"Oh, I think they took it out to Golders Green to be burned. That was up to the family."

"The cousin?"

"Yes."

"We used to have better funerals in Africa," said Sarah.

"Oh well . . . other countries, other manners."

"Yours is supposed to be an older civilization."

"Yes, but old civilizations are not always famous for feeling deeply about death. We are no worse than the Romans."

Castle finished his whisky. He said, "I'll go up and read to Sam for five minutes—otherwise he may think something's wrong."

"Swear that you won't say anything to him," Sarah said.

"Don't you trust me?"

"Of course I trust you, but . . ." The "but" pursued him up the stairs. He had lived a long time with "buts"— we trust you, but . . . Daintry looking in his briefcase, the stranger at Watford, whose duty it was to make sure he had come alone to the rendezvous with Boris. Even Boris. He thought: Is it possible that one day life will be as simple as childhood, that I shall have finished with buts, that I will be trusted naturally by everyone, as Sarah trusts me—and Sam?

Sam was waiting for him, his face black against the clean pillowcase. The sheets must have been changed that day, which made the contrast stronger like an advertisement for Black and White whisky. "How are things?" he asked because he could think of nothing else to say, but Sam didn't reply—he had his secrets too.

"How did school go?"

"It was all right."

"What lessons today?"

226

"Arithmetic."

"How did that go?"

"All right."

"What else?"

"English compo—"

"Composition. How was that?"

"All right."

Castle knew that the time had almost come when he would lose the child forever. Each "all right" fell on the ear like the sound of distant explosions that were destroying the bridges between them. If he asked Sam, "Don't you trust me?" perhaps he would answer, "Yes, but . . ."

"Shall I read to you?"

"Yes, please."

"What would you like?"

"That book about a garden."

Castle for a moment was at a loss. He looked along the single shelf of battered volumes which were held in place by two china dogs that bore a likeness to Buller. Some of the books belonged to his own nursery days: the others had nearly all been chosen by himself, for Sarah had come late to books and her books were all adult ones. He took down a volume of verse which was one he had guarded from his childhood. There was no tie of blood between Sam and himself, no guarantee that they would have any taste in common, but he always hoped—even a book could be a bridge. He opened the book at random, or so he believed, but a book is like a sandy path which keeps the indent of footsteps. He had read in this one to Sam several times during the last two years, but the footprints of his own childhood had dug deeper and the book opened on a poem he had never read aloud before. After a line or two he realized that he knew it almost by heart. There are verses in childhood, he thought, which shape one's life more than any of the scriptures.

"Over the borders a sin without pardon,
  Breaking the branches and crawling below,
Out through the breach in the wall of the garden,
  Down by the banks of the river, we go."

"What are borders?"

"It's where one country ends and another begins." It seemed, as soon as he spoke, a difficult definition, but Sam accepted it.

"What's a sin without pardon? Are they spies?"

"No, no, not spies. The boy in the story has been told not to go out of the garden, and . . ."

"Who told him?"

"His father, I suppose, or his mother."

"And that's a sin?"

"This was written a long time ago. People were more strict then, and anyway it's not meant seriously."

"I thought murder was a sin."

"Yes, well, murder's wrong."

"Like going out of the garden?"

Castle began to regret he had chanced on that poem, that he had trodden in that one particular footprint of his own long walk. "Don't you want me to go on reading?" He skimmed through the lines ahead—they seemed innocuous enough.

"Not that one. I don't understand that one."

"Well, which one then?"

"There's one about a man . . ."

"The lamplighter?"

"No, it's not that one."

"What does the man do?"

"I don't know. He's in the dark."

"That's not much to go by." Castle turned back the pages, looking for a man in the dark.

"He's riding a horse."

"Is it this one?"

Castle read,

"Whenever the moon and stars are set,
  Whenever the wind is high,
All night long in the dark and wet ..."

"Yes, yes, that's the one."

"A man goes riding by.
Late in the night when the fires are out,
Why does he gallop and gallop about?"

"Go on. Why do you stop?"

"Whenever the trees are crying aloud,
  And ships are tossed at sea,
By, on the highway, low and loud,
  By at the gallop goes he.
By at the gallop he goes, and then
By he comes back at the gallop again."

"That's the one. That's the one I like best."

"It's a bit frightening," Castle said.

"That's why I like it. Does he wear a stocking mask?"

"It doesn't say he's a robber, Sam."

"Then why does he go up and down outside the house? Has he a white face like you and Mr. Muller?"

"It doesn't say."

"I think he's black, black as my hat, black as my cat."

"Why?"

"I think all the white people are afraid of him and lock their house in case he comes in with a carving knife and cuts their throats. Slowly," he added with relish.

Sam had never looked more black, Castle thought. He put his arm round him with a gesture of protection, but he couldn't protect him from the violence and vengeance which were beginning to work in the child's heart.

He went into his study, unlocked a drawer and took out Muller's notes. There was a heading: "A Final Solution." Muller apparently had felt no hesitation at all in speaking that phrase into a German ear, and the solution,

229

it was obvious, had not been rejected—it was still open for discussion. The same image recurred like an obsession—of the dying child and the vulture.

He sat down and made a careful copy of Muller's notes. He didn't even bother to type them. The anonymity of a typewriter, as the Hiss case indicated, was very partial and anyway he had no desire to take trivial precautions. As for the book code, he had abandoned that with his last message which ended in "goodbye." Now as he wrote "Final Solution" and copied the words which followed with exactitude he identified himself truly for the first time with Carson. Carson at this point would have taken the ultimate risk. He was, as Sarah had once put it, "going too far."

5

At two o'clock in the morning Castle was still awake when he was startled by a cry from Sarah. "No!" she cried, "No!"

"What is it?"

There was no reply, but when he turned on the light, he could see that her eyes were wide with fear.

"You've had another nightmare. It's only a nightmare."

She said, "It was terrible."

"Tell me. A dream never comes back if you tell it quickly before you forget."

He could feel how she trembled against his side. He began to catch her fear. "It's only a dream, Sarah, just tell me. Get rid of it."

She said, "I was in a railway train. It was moving off. You were left on the platform. I was alone. You had the tickets. Sam was with you. He didn't seem to care. I didn't even know where we were supposed to be going. And I could hear the ticket collector in the next compartment. I knew I was in the wrong coach, reserved for whites."

"Now you've told it the dream won't come back."

"I knew he'd say, Get out of there. You've no business there. This is a white coach."

"It's only a dream, Sarah."

"Yes. I know. I'm sorry I woke you. You need your sleep."

"It was a bit like the dreams Sam had. Remember?"

"Sam and I are color conscious, aren't we? It haunts us both in sleep. Sometimes I wonder whether you love me only because of my color. If you were black you wouldn't love a white woman only because she was white, would you?"

"No. I'm not a South African off on a weekend in Swaziland. I knew you for nearly a year before I fell in love. It came slowly. All those months when we worked secretly together. I was a so-called diplomat, safe as houses. You ran all the risks. I didn't have nightmares, but I used to lie awake, wondering whether you'd come to our next rendezvous or whether you'd disappear and I'd never know what happened to you. Just a message perhaps from one of the others saying that the line was closed."

"So you worried about the line."

"No. I worried about what would happen to you. I'd loved you for months. I knew I couldn't go on living if you disappeared. Now we are safe."

"Are you sure?"

"Of course I'm sure. Haven't I proved it over seven years?"

231

"I don't mean that you love me. I mean are you sure we are safe?"

To that question there was no easy answer. The last encoded report with the final word "goodbye" had been premature and the passage he had chosen, "I have lifted my hand and let it fall," was no mark of freedom in the world of Uncle Remus.

Part Five

Chapter I

1

Darkness had fallen early with the mist and the drizzle of November, when he left the telephone box. There had been no reply to any of his signals. In Old Compton Street the blurred red light of the sign "Books," marking where Halliday Junior carried on his dubious trade, shone down the pavement with less than its normal effrontery; Halliday Senior in the shop across the way stooped as usual under a single globe, economizing fuel. When Castle came into the shop the old man touched a switch without raising his head so as to light up on either side the shelves of outmoded classics.

"You don't waste your electricity," Castle said.

"Ah! It's you, sir. Yes, I do my little bit to help the Government, and anyway I don't get many real customers after five. A few shy sellers, but their books are seldom in good enough condition, and I have to send them away disappointed—they think there's value in any book that's a hundred years old. I'm sorry, sir, about the delay over the Trollope if that's what you are seeking. There's been difficulty about the second copy—it was on television once, that's the trouble—even the Penguins are sold out."

"There's no hurry now. One copy will do. I came in to tell you that. My friend has gone to live abroad."

"Ah, you'll miss your literary evenings, sir. I was saying to my son only the other day . . ."

"It's odd, Mr. Halliday, but I've never met your son. Is he in? I thought I might discuss with him some books I can spare. I've rather grown out of my taste for *curiosa*. Age, I suppose. Would I find him in?"

"You won't, sir, not now. To tell you the truth he's got himself into a bit of trouble. From doing too well. He opened another shop last month in Newington Butts and the police there are far less understanding than those here—or more expensive if you care to be cynical. He had to attend the magistrate's court all the afternoon about some of those silly magazines of his and he's not back yet."

"I hope his difficulties don't make trouble for you, Mr. Halliday."

"Oh dear me, no. The police are very sympathetic. I really think they're sorry for me having a son in that way of business. I tell them, if I was young, I might be doing the same thing, and they laugh."

It had always seemed strange to Castle that "they" had chosen so dubious an intermediary as young Halliday, whose shop might be searched at any time by the police. Perhaps, he thought, it was a kind of double bluff. The Vice Squad would hardly be trained in the niceties of intelligence. It was even possible that Halliday Junior was as unaware as his father of the use to which he was being put. That was what he wanted very much to know, for he was going to entrust him with what amounted to his life.

He stared across the road at the scarlet sign and the girlie magazines in the window and wondered at the strange emotion that was driving him to take so open a risk. Boris would not have approved, but now he had sent "them" his last report and resignation he felt an irresistible desire to communicate directly by word of mouth, without the intervention of safe drops and book codes and elaborate signals on public telephones.

"You've no idea when he'll return?" he asked Mr. Halliday.

"No idea, sir. Couldn't I perhaps help you myself?"

"No, no. I won't bother you." He had no code of telephone rings to attract the attention of Halliday Junior. They had been kept so scrupulously apart he sometimes wondered whether their only meeting might be scheduled for the final emergency.

He asked, "Has your son by any chance a scarlet Toyota?"

"No, but he sometimes uses mine in the country—for sales, sir. He helps me there now and then, for I can't get about as much as I used to do. Why did you ask?"

"I thought I saw one outside the shop once."

"That wouldn't be ours. Not in town it wouldn't. With all the traffic jams it wouldn't be economic. We have to do our best to economize when the Government asks."

"Well, I hope the magistrate has not been too severe with him."

"It's a kind thought, sir. I'll tell him you called."

"As it happens I brought a note with me you might let him have. It's confidential, mind. I wouldn't want people to know the kind of books I collected when I was young."

"You can trust me, sir. I've never failed you yet. And the Trollope?"

"Oh, forget the Trollope."

At Euston Castle took a ticket to Watford—he didn't want to show his season to and from Berkhamsted. Ticket collectors have a memory for seasons. In the train he read, to keep his mind occupied, a morning paper which had been left behind on the next seat. It contained an interview with a film star whom he had never seen (the cinema at Berkhamsted had been turned into a Bingo hall). Apparently the actor had married for a second time. Or was it a third? He had told the reporter during an interview several years before that he was finished with marriage. "So you've changed your mind?" the gossip writer impudently asked.

Castle read the interview to the last word. Here was a man who could talk to a reporter about the most private things in his life: "I was very poor when I married my first wife. She didn't understand . . . our sex life went all wrong. It's different with Naomi. Naomi knows that when I come back exhausted from the studio . . . whenever we can we take a week's holiday all alone in some quiet spot like St. Tropez and work it all off." I'm hypocritical to blame him, Castle thought: I am going to talk if I can to Boris: a moment arrives when one has to talk.

At Watford he went carefully through his previous routine, hesitating at the bus stop, finally walking on, waiting round the next corner for any followers. He reached the coffee shop, but he didn't go in but walked straight on. Last time he had been guided by the man with the loose shoelace, but now he had no guide. Did he turn left or right at the corner? All the streets in this part of Watford looked alike—rows of identical gabled houses with small front gardens planted with rose trees that dripped with moisture—one house joined to another by a garage for one car.

He took another cast at random, and another, but he found always the same houses, sometimes in streets, sometimes in crescents, and he felt himself mocked by the similarity of the names—Laurel Drive, Oaklands, The Shrubbery—to the name he was seeking, Elm View. Once a policeman seeing him at a loss asked whether he could be of help. Muller's original notes seemed to weigh like a revolver in his pocket and he said no, that he was only looking for a To Let notice in the area. The policeman told him that there were two of these some three or four turns to the left, and by a coincidence the third brought him into Elm View. He hadn't remembered the number, but a lamp in the street shone on to the stained glass of a door and he recognized that. There was no light in any window, and it was without much hope that, peering closely, he made out the mutilated card "ition Limited" and rang the bell. It was unlikely Boris would be here at this hour: indeed, he might not be in England at all. He had severed his connection with them, so why should they preserve a dangerous channel open? He tried the bell a second time, but there was no reply. He would have welcomed at that moment even Ivan who had tried to blackmail him. There was no one—literally no one—left to whom he could speak.

He had passed a telephone box on his way and now he returned to it. At a house across the road he could see through the uncurtained window a family sitting down to a high tea or an early dinner: a father and two teenage children, a boy and a girl, took their seats, the mother entered carrying a dish, and the father seemed to be saying grace, for the children bowed their heads. He remembered that custom in his childhood but thought it had died out a long time ago—perhaps they were Roman Catholics, customs seemed to survive much longer with them. He began to dial the only number left for him to try, a number to be used only in the final emergency, re-

239

placing the receiver at intervals which he timed on his watch. After he had dialed five times with no response he left the box. It was as though he had cried aloud five times in the empty street for help—and he had no idea whether he had been heard. Perhaps after his final report all lines of communication had been cut forever.

He looked across the road. The father made a joke and the mother smiled her approval and the girl winked at the boy, as much as to say "The old boy's at it again." Castle went on down the road toward the station—nobody followed him, no one looked at him through a window as he went by, nobody passed him. He felt invisible, set down in a strange world where there were no other human beings to recognize him as one of themselves.

He stopped at the end of the street which was called The Shrubbery beside a hideous church so new it might have been constructed overnight with the glittering bricks of a build-it-yourself kit. The lights were on inside and the same emotion of loneliness which had driven him to Halliday's drove him to the building. He recognized from the gaudy bedizened altar and the sentimental statues that it was a Roman Catholic church. There was no sturdy band of bourgeois faithful standing shoulder to shoulder singing of a green hill far away. One old man slumbered over his umbrella knob not far from the altar, and two women who might have been sisters in their similar subfusc clothing waited by what he guessed was a confessional box. A woman in a macintosh came out from behind a curtain and a woman without one went in. It was like a weather house indicating rain. Castle sat down not far away. He felt tired—the hour had struck long past for his triple J & B; Sarah would be growing anxious, and as he listened to the low hum of conversation in the box the desire to talk openly, without reserve, after seven years of silence grew in him. Boris had been totally withdrawn, he thought, I shall never be able to speak again—unless, of

240

course, I end up in the dock. I could make what they call a "confession" there—*in camera,* of course, the trial would be *in camera.*

The second woman emerged, and the third went in. The other two had got rid briskly enough of their secrets—*in camera.* They were kneeling separately down before their respective altars with looks of smug satisfaction at a duty well performed. When the third woman emerged there was no one left waiting but himself. The old man had woken and accompanied one of the women out. Between a crack in the priest's curtain he caught a glimpse of a long white face; he heard a throat being cleared of the November damp. Castle thought: I want to talk; why don't I talk? A priest like that has to keep my secret. Boris had said to him, "Come to me whenever you feel you have to talk: it's a smaller risk," but he was convinced Boris had gone forever. To talk was a therapeutic act—he moved slowly toward the box like a patient who is visiting a psychiatrist for the first time with trepidation.

A patient who didn't know the ropes. He drew the curtain to behind him and stood hesitating in the little cramped space which was left. How to begin? The faint smell of eau-de-cologne must have been left by one of the women. A shutter clattered open and he could see a sharp profile like a stage detective's. The profile coughed, and muttered something.

Castle said, "I want to talk to you."

"What are you standing there for like that?" the profile said. "Have you lost the use of your knees?"

"I only want to talk to you," Castle said.

"You aren't here to talk to me," the profile said. There was a chink–chink–chink. The man had a rosary in his lap and seemed to be using it like a chain of worry beads. "You are here to talk to God."

"No, I'm not. I'm just here to talk."

The priest looked reluctantly round. His eyes were

241

bloodshot. Castle had an impression that he had fallen by a grim coincidence on another victim of loneliness and silence like himself.

"Kneel down, man, what sort of a Catholic do you think you are?"

"I'm not a Catholic."

"Then what business have you here?"

"I want to talk, that's all."

"If you want instruction you can leave your name and address at the presbytery."

"I don't want instruction."

"You are wasting my time," the priest said.

"Don't the secrets of the confessional apply to non-Catholics?"

"You should go to a priest of your own Church."

"I haven't got a Church."

"Then I think what you need is a doctor," the priest said. He slammed the shutter to, and Castle left the box. It was an absurd end, he thought, to an absurd action. How could he have expected the man to understand him even if he had been allowed to talk? He had far too long a history to tell, begun so many years ago in a strange country.

2

Sarah came out to greet him as he was hanging his coat in the hall. She asked, "Has something happened?"

"No."

"You've never been as late as this without telephoning."

"Oh, I've been going here and there, trying to see people. I couldn't find any of them in. I suppose they are all taking long weekends."

"Will you have your whisky? Or do you want dinner straight away?"

"Whisky. Make it a large one."

"Larger than usual?"

"Yes, and no soda."

"Something *has* happened."

"Nothing important. But it's cold and wet almost like winter. Is Sam asleep?"

"Yes."

"Where's Buller?"

"Looking for cats in the garden."

He sat down in the usual chair and the usual silence fell between them. Normally he felt the silence like a comforting shawl thrown round his shoulders. Silence was relaxation, silence meant that words were unnecessary between the two of them—their love was too established to need assurance; they had taken out a life policy in their love. But this night, with the original of Muller's notes in his pocket and his copy of it by this time in the hands of young Halliday, silence was like a vacuum in which he couldn't breathe: silence was a lack of everything, even trust, it was a foretaste of the tomb.

"Another whisky, Sarah."

"You *are* drinking too much. Remember poor Davis."

"He didn't die of drink."

"But I thought . . ."

"You thought like all the others did. And you're wrong. If it's too much trouble to give me another whisky, say so and I'll help myself."

"I only said remember Davis . . ."

"I don't want to be looked after, Sarah. You are Sam's mother, not mine."

"Yes, I *am* his mother and you aren't even his father."

243

They looked at each other with astonishment and dismay. Sarah said, "I didn't mean . . ."

"It's not your fault."

"I'm sorry."

He said, "This is what the future will be like if we can't talk. You asked me what I'd been doing. I've been looking for someone to talk to all this evening, but no one was there."

"Talk about what?"

The question silenced him.

"Why can't you talk to *me*? Because They forbid it, I suppose. The Official Secrets Act—all that stupidity."

"It's not them."

"Then who?"

"When we came to England, Sarah, Carson sent someone to see me. He had saved you and Sam. All he asked in return was a little help. I was grateful and I agreed."

"What's wrong with that?"

"My mother told me that when I was a child I always gave away too much in a swap, but it wasn't too much for the man who had saved you from BOSS. So there it is—I became what they call a double agent, Sarah. I rate a lifetime in jail."

He had always known that one day this scene would have to be played out between them, but he had never been able to imagine the kind of words they would say to each other. She said, "Give me your whisky." He handed her his glass and she drank a finger from it. "Are you in danger?" she asked. "I mean now. Tonight."

"I've been in danger all our life together."

"But is it worse now?"

"Yes. I think they've discovered there's a leak and I think they thought it was Davis. I don't believe Davis died a natural death. Something Doctor Percival said . . ."

"You think they killed him?"

"Yes."

"So it might have been you?"

"Yes."

"Are you still going on with it?"

"I wrote what I thought was my last report. I said goodbye to the whole business. But then—something else happened. With Muller. I had to let them know. I hope I have. I don't know."

"How did the office discover the leak?"

"I suppose they have a defector somewhere—probably in place—who had access to my reports and passed them back to London."

"But if he passes back this one?"

"Oh, I know what you are going to say. Davis is dead. I'm the only man at the office who deals with Muller."

"Why have you gone on, Maurice? It's suicide."

"It may save a lot of lives—lives of your people."

"Don't talk to me of my people. I have no people any longer. You are 'my people.' " He thought, Surely that's something out of the Bible. I've heard that before. Well, she'd been to a Methodist school.

She put her arm round him and held the glass of whisky to his mouth. "I wish you hadn't waited all these years to tell me."

"I was afraid to—Sarah." The Old Testament name came back to him with hers. It had been a woman called Ruth who had said what she had said—or something very like it.

"Afraid of me and not of Them?"

"Afraid for you. You can't know how long it seemed, waiting for you in the Hotel Polana. I thought you'd never come. While it was daylight I used to watch car numbers through a pair of binoculars. Even numbers meant Muller had got you. Odd numbers that you were on the way. This

245

time there'll be no Hotel Polana and no Carson. It doesn't happen twice the same way."

"What do you want me to do?"

"The best thing would be for you to take Sam and go to my mother's. Separate yourself from me. Pretend there's been a bad quarrel and you are getting a divorce. If nothing happens I'll stay here and we can come together again."

"What should I do all that time? Watch car numbers? Tell me the next best thing."

"If they are still looking after me—I don't know whether they are—they promised me a safe escape route, but I'll have to go alone. So that way too you must go to my mother with Sam. The only difference is we won't be able to communicate. You won't know what has happened—perhaps for a long time. I think I'd prefer the police to come—at least that way we'd see each other again in court."

"But Davis never reached a court, did he? No, if they are looking after you, go, Maurice. Then at least I'll know you are safe."

"You haven't said a word of blame, Sarah."

"What sort of word?"

"Well, I'm what's generally called a traitor."

"Who cares?" she said. She put her hand in his: it was an act more intimate than a kiss—one can kiss a stranger. She said, "We have our own country. You and I and Sam. You've never betrayed that country, Maurice."

He said, "It's no good worrying any more tonight. We've still time and we've got to sleep."

But when they were in bed, they made love at once without thinking, without speaking, as though it had been something they had agreed together an hour ago and all their discussion had only been a postponement of it. It had been months since they had come together in this way. Now that his secret was spoken love was released,

246

and he fell asleep almost as soon as he withdrew. His last thought was: There is still time—it will be days, perhaps weeks, before any leak can be reported back. Tomorrow is Saturday. We have a whole weekend before us in which to decide.

Chapter II

Sir John Hargreaves sat in his study in the country reading Trollope. It should have been a period of almost perfect peace—the weekend calm, which only a duty officer was allowed to break with an urgent message, and urgent messages were of extreme rarity in the Secret Service—the hour of tea when his wife respected his absence, as she knew that Earl Grey in the afternoons spoiled for him the Cutty Sark at six. During his service in West Africa he had grown to appreciate the novels of Trollope, though he was not a novel reader. At moments of irritation, he had found *The Warden* and *Barchester Towers* reassuring books, they reinforced the patience which Africa required. Mr. Slope would remind him of an importunate and self-righteous District Commissioner, and Mrs. Proudie of the Governor's wife. Now he found himself disturbed by a piece of fiction which should have soothed him in England as he had been soothed in Africa.

The novel was called *The Way We Live Now*—somebody, he couldn't remember who it was, had told him the novel had been turned into a good television series. He didn't like television, yet he had been sure he would like the Trollope.

So all that afternoon he felt for a while the same smooth pleasure he always received from Trollope—the sense of a calm Victorian world, where good was good and bad was bad and one could distinguish easily between them. He had no children who might have taught him differently—he had never wanted a child nor had his wife; they were at one in that, though perhaps for different reasons. He hadn't wanted to add to his public responsibilities private responsibilities (children would have been a constant anxiety in Africa), and his wife—well—he would think with affection—she wished to guard her figure and her independence. Their mutual indifference to children reinforced their love for each other. While he read Trollope with a whisky at his elbow, she drank tea in her room with equal content. It was a weekend of peace for both of them—no shoot, no guests, darkness falling early in November over the park—he could even imagine himself in Africa, at some resthouse in the bush, on one of the long treks which he always enjoyed, far from headquarters. The cook would now be plucking a chicken behind the resthouse and the pie-dogs would be gathering in the hope of scraps . . . The lights in the distance where the motorway ran might well have been the lights of the village where the girls would be picking the lice out of each other's hair.

He was reading of old Melmotte—the swindler as his fellow members judged him. Melmotte took his place in the restaurant of the House of Commons—"It was impossible to expel him—almost as impossible to sit next him. Even the waiters were unwilling to serve him; but with patience and endurance he did at last get his dinner."

Hargreaves, unwillingly, felt drawn to Melmotte in his isolation, and he remembered with regret what he had said to Doctor Percival when Percival expressed a liking for Davis. He had used the word "traitor" as Melmotte's colleagues used the word "swindler." He read on, "They who watched him declared among themselves that he was happy in his own audacity;—but in truth he was probably at that moment the most utterly wretched man in London." He had never known Davis—he wouldn't have recognized him if he had met him in a corridor of the office. He thought: Perhaps I spoke hastily—I reacted stupidly—but it was Percival who eliminated him—I shouldn't have left Percival in charge of the case . . . He went on reading: "But even he, with all the world now gone from him, with nothing before him but the extremest misery which the indignation of offended laws could inflict, was able to spend the last moments of his freedom in making a reputation at any rate for audacity." Poor devil, he thought, one has to grant him courage. Did Davis guess what potion Doctor Percival might be dropping into his whisky when he left the room for a moment?

It was then the telephone rang. He heard it intercepted by his wife in her room. She was trying to protect his peace better than Trollope had done, but all the same, owing to some urgency at the other end, she was forced to transfer the call. Unwillingly he lifted the receiver. A voice he didn't recognize said, "Muller speaking."

He was still in the world of Melmotte. He said, "Muller?"

"Cornelius Muller."

There was an uneasy pause and then the voice explained, "From Pretoria."

For a moment Sir John Hargreaves thought the stranger must be calling from the remote city, and then he remembered. "Yes. Yes. Of course. Can I be of any help?" He added, "I hope Castle . . ."

250

"I would like to talk to you, Sir John, *about* Castle."

"I'll be in the office on Monday. If you'd ring my secretary . . ." He looked at his watch. "She will still be at the office."

"You won't be there tomorrow?"

"No. I'm taking this weekend at home."

"Could I come and see you, Sir John?"

"Is it so very urgent?"

"I think it is. I have a strong feeling I've made a most serious mistake. I do want badly to talk to you, Sir John."

There goes Trollope, Hargreaves thought, and poor Mary—I try to keep the office away from us when we are here and yet it's always intruding. He remembered the evening of the shoot when Daintry had been so difficult . . . He asked, "Have you a car?"

"Yes. Of course."

He thought, I can still have Saturday free if I'm reasonably hospitable tonight. He said, "It's less than two hours' drive if you'd care to come to dinner."

"Of course. It's very kind of you, Sir John. I wouldn't have disturbed you if I hadn't thought it important. I . . ."

"We may not be able to rustle up more than an omelet, Muller. Pot luck," he added.

He put down the receiver, remembering the apocryphal story he knew they told about him and the cannibals. He went to the window and looked out. Africa receded. The lights were the lights of the motorway leading to London and the office. He felt the approaching suicide of Melmotte—there was no other solution. He went to the drawing room: Mary was pouring out a cup of Earl Grey from the silver teapot which she had bought at a Christie sale. He said, "I'm sorry, Mary. We've got a guest for dinner."

"I was afraid of that. When he insisted on speaking to you . . . Who is it?"

"The man BOSS has sent over from Pretoria."

251

"Couldn't he wait till Monday?"

"He said it was too urgent."

"I don't like those apartheid buggers." Common English obscenities always sounded strange in her American accent.

"Nor do I, but we have to work with them. I suppose we can rustle up something to eat."

"There's some cold beef."

"That's better than the omelet I promised him."

It was a stiff meal because no business could be talked, though Lady Hargreaves did her best, with the help of the Beaujolais, to find a possible subject. She confessed herself completely ignorant of Afrikaaner art and literature, but it was an ignorance which Muller appeared to share. He admitted there were some poets and novelists around—and he mentioned the Hertzog Prize, but he added that he had read none of them. "They are unreliable," he said, "most of them."

"Unreliable?"

"They get mixed up in politics. There's a poet in prison now for helping terrorists." Hargreaves tried to change the subject, but he could think of nothing in connection with South Africa but gold and diamonds—they were mixed up with politics too, just as much as the writers. The word diamonds suggested Namibia and he remembered that Oppenheimer, the millionaire, supported the progressive party. His Africa had been the impoverished Africa of the bush, but politics lay like the detritus of a mine over the south. He was glad when they could be alone with a bottle of whisky and two easy chairs—it was easier to talk of hard things in an easy chair—it was difficult, he had always found, to get angry in an easy chair.

"You must forgive me," Hargreaves said, "for not having been in London to greet you. I had to go to Washington. One of those routine visits that one can't avoid. I hope my people have been looking after you properly."

"I had to go off too," Muller said, "to Bonn."

"But not exactly a routine visit there, I imagine? The Concorde has brought London so damnably close to Washington—they almost expect you to drop over for lunch. I hope all went satisfactorily in Bonn—within reason, of course. But I suppose you've been discussing all that with our friend Castle."

"Your friend, I think, more than mine."

"Yes, yes. I know there was a little trouble between you years ago. But that's ancient history surely."

"Is there such a thing, sir, as ancient history? The Irish don't think so, and what you call the Boer War is still very much our war, but we call it the war of independence. I'm worried about Castle. That's why I'm bothering you tonight. I've been indiscreet. I let him have some notes I made about the Bonn visit. Nothing very secret, of course, but all the same someone reading between the lines . . ."

"My dear fellow, you can trust Castle. I wouldn't have asked him to brief you if he wasn't the best man . . ."

"I went to have dinner with him at his home. I was surprised to find he was married to a black girl, the one who was the cause of what you call a little trouble. He even seems to have a child by her."

"We have no color bar here, Muller, and she was very thoroughly vetted, I can assure you."

"All the same, it was the Communists who organized her escape. Castle was a great friend of Carson. I suppose you know that."

"We know all about Carson—and the escape. It was Castle's job to have Communist contacts. Is Carson still a trouble to you?"

253

"No. Carson died in prison—from pneumonia. I could see how upset Castle was when I told him."

"Why not? If they were friends." Hargreaves looked with regret at his Trollope where it lay beyond the bottle of Cutty Sark. Muller got abruptly to his feet and walked across the room. He halted before the photograph of a black man wearing a soft black hat of the kind missionaries used to wear. One side of his face was disfigured by lupus and he smiled at whoever held the camera with one side of his mouth only.

"Poor fellow," Hargreaves said, "he was dying when I took that photograph. He knew it. He was a brave man like all the Krus. I wanted something to remember him by."

Muller said, "I haven't made a full confession, sir. I gave Castle the wrong notes by accident. I'd made one lot to show him and one to draw on for my reports and I confused them. It's true there's nothing very secret—I wouldn't have put anything very secret on paper over here—but there were some indiscreet phrases . . ."

"Really, you don't have to worry, Muller."

"I can't help worrying, sir. In this country you live in such a different atmosphere. You have so little to fear compared with us. That black in the photograph—you liked him?"

"He was a friend—a friend I loved."

"I can't say that of a single black," Muller replied. He turned. On the opposite side of the room, on the wall, hung an African mask.

"I don't trust Castle." He said, "I can't prove anything, but I have an intuition . . . I wish you had appointed someone else to brief me."

"There were only two men dealing with your material. Davis and Castle."

"Davis is the one who died?"

254

"Yes."

"You take things so lightly over here. I sometimes envy you. Things like a black child. You know, sir, in our experience there is no one more vulnerable than an officer in secret intelligence. We had a leak a few years back from BOSS—in the section which deals with the Communists. One of our most intelligent men. He too cultivated friendships—and the friendships took over. Carson was concerned in that case too. And there was another case— one of our officers was a brilliant chess player. Intelligence became to him just another game of chess. He was interested only when he was pitted against a really first-class player. In the end he grew dissatisfied. The games were too easy—so he took on his own side. I think he was very happy as long as the game lasted."

"What happened to him?"

"He's dead now."

Hargreaves thought again of Melmotte. People talked of courage as a primary virtue. What of the courage of a known swindler and bankrupt taking his place in the dining room of the House of Commons? Is courage a justification? Is courage in whatever cause a virtue? He said, "We are satisfied that Davis was the leak we had to close."

"A fortunate death?"

"Cirrhosis of the liver."

"I told you Carson died of pneumonia."

"Castle, I happen to know, doesn't play chess."

"There are other motives too. Love of money."

"That certainly doesn't apply to Castle."

"He loves his wife," Muller said, "and his child."

"What of that?"

"They are both black," Muller replied with simplicity, looking across the room at the photograph of the Kru chief upon the wall as though, thought Hargreaves, even I

255

am not beyond his suspicion, which, like some search-
light on the Cape, swept the unfriendly seas beyond in
search of enemy vessels.

Muller said, "I hope to God you are right and the leak
really was Davis. I don't believe it was."

Hargreaves watched Muller drive away through the
park in his black Mercedes. The lights slowed down and
became stationary; he must have reached the lodge,
where since the Irish bombings began, a man from the
Special Branch had been stationed. The park seemed no
longer to be an extension of the African bush—it was a
small parcel of the Home Counties which had never been
home to Hargreaves. It was nearly midnight. He went upstairs to his dressing room, but he didn't take off his
clothes further than his shirt. He wrapped a towel round
his neck and began to shave. He had shaved before dinner and it wasn't a necessary act, but he could always
think more clearly when he shaved. He tried to recall exactly the reasons Muller had given for suspecting Castle—
his relations with Carson—those meant nothing. A black
wife and child—Hargreaves remembered with sadness
and a sense of loss the black mistress whom he had
known many years ago before his marriage. She had died
of blackwater fever and when she died he had felt as
though a great part of his love for Africa had gone to the
grave with her. Muller had spoken of intuition—"I can't
prove anything, but I have an intuition . . ." Hargreaves
was the last man to laugh at intuition. In Africa he had
lived with intuition, he was accustomed to choose his
boys by intuition—not by the tattered notebooks they carried with illegible references. Once his life had been
saved by an intuition.

He dried his face, and he thought: I'll ring up Emmanuel. Doctor Percival was the only real friend he had
in the whole firm. He opened the bedroom door and
looked in. The room was in darkness and he thought his

256

wife was asleep until she spoke. "What's keeping you, dear?"

"I won't be long. I just want to ring up Emmanuel."

"Has that man Muller gone?"

"Yes."

"I don't like him."

"Nor do I."

Chapter III

1

Castle woke and looked at his watch, though he believed that he carried time in his head—he knew it would be a few minutes to eight, giving him just long enough to go to his study and turn on the news without waking Sarah. He was surprised to see that his watch marked eight five—the inner clock had never failed him before, and he doubted his watch, but by the time he reached his room the important news was over—there were only the little scraps of parochial interest which the reader used to fill the slot: a bad accident on the M4, a brief interview with Mrs. Whitehouse welcoming some new campaign against pornographic books, and perhaps as an illustration of her talk, a trivial fact, that an obscure bookseller called Holliday—"I'm sorry, *Halliday*"—had appeared before a magistrate in Newington Butts for selling a pornographic film to a boy of fourteen. He had been remanded for trial at the Central Criminal Court, and his bail had been set at two hundred pounds.

So he was at liberty, Castle thought, with the copy of Muller's notes in his pocket, presumably watched by the police. He might be afraid to pass them on at whatever drop they had given him, he might be afraid even to destroy them; what seemed his most likely choice was to keep them as a bargaining asset with the police. "I'm a more important man than you think: if this little affair can be arranged, I can show you things . . . let me talk to someone from the Special Branch." Castle could well imagine the kind of conversation which might be going on at that moment: the skeptical local police, Halliday exposing the first page of Muller's notes as an inducement.

Castle opened the door of the bedroom: Sarah was still asleep. He told himself that now the moment had arrived which he had always expected, when he must think clearly and act decisively. Hope was out of place just as much as despair. They were emotions which would confuse thought. He must assume Boris had gone, that the line was cut, and that he must act on his own.

He went down to the sitting room where Sarah wouldn't hear him dial and rang a second time the number he had been given to use only for a final emergency. He had no idea in what room it was ringing—the exchange was somewhere in Kensington: he dialed three times with an interval of ten seconds between and he had the impression that his SOS was ringing out to an empty room, but he couldn't tell. . . . There was no other appeal for help which he could make, nothing left for him to do but clear the home ground. He sat by the telephone and made his plans, or rather went over them and confirmed them, for he had made them long ago. There was nothing important left to be destroyed, he was almost sure of that, no books he had once used for coding . . . he was convinced there were no papers waiting to be burned . . . he could leave the house safely, locked and empty . . . you couldn't, of course, burn a dog . . . what was he to do with Buller? How absurd at this moment to be bothered by a dog, a dog he had never even liked, but his mother would never allow Sarah to introduce Buller into the Sussex house as a permanent lodger. He could leave him, he supposed, at a kennels, but he had no idea where . . . This was the one problem he had never worked out. He told himself that it was not an important one, as he went upstairs to wake Sarah.

Why this morning was she so deeply asleep? He remembered, as he looked at her, with the tenderness one can feel even for an enemy who sleeps, how after making love he had fallen into the deepest nullity he had known for months, simply because they had talked frankly, because they had ceased to have secrets. He kissed her and she opened her eyes and he could tell she knew at once there was no time to be lost; she couldn't, in her usual fashion, wake slowly, and stretch her arms and say, "I was dreaming . . ."

He told her, "You must ring my mother now. It will seem more natural for *you* to do it if we've had a quarrel. Ask if you can stay a few days with Sam. You can lie a little. All the better if she thinks you are lying. It will make it easier, when you are there, to let the story out slowly. You can say that I've done something unforgivable . . . We talked about it all last night."

"But you said we had time . . ."

"I was wrong."

"Something's happened?"

"Yes. You've got to get away with Sam right away."

"And you are staying here?"

260

"Either they'll help me to get out or the police will come for me. You mustn't be here if that happens."

"Then it's the end for us?"

"Of course it's not the end. As long as we are alive we'll come together again. Somehow. Somewhere."

They hardly spoke to each other, dressing rapidly, like strangers on a journey who have been forced to share the same *wagon lit*. Only as she turned at the door on her way to wake up Sam she asked, "What about the school? I don't suppose anyone will bother . . ."

"Don't worry now. Telephone on Monday and say he's ill. I want you both out of the house as quickly as possible. In case the police come."

She returned five minutes later and said, "I spoke to your mother. She wasn't exactly welcoming. She has someone for lunch. What about Buller?"

"I'll think of something."

At ten to nine she was ready to leave with Sam. A taxi was at the door. Castle felt a terrible sense of unreality. He said, "If nothing happens you can come back. We shall have made up our quarrel." Sam at least was happy. Castle watched him as he laughed with the driver.

"If . . ."

"You came to the Polana."

"Yes, but you said once things never happened twice the same way."

At the taxi they even forgot to kiss and then they clumsily remembered—a kiss which was meaningless, empty of everything except the sense that his going away couldn't be true—it was something they were dreaming. They had always exchanged dreams—those private codes more unbreakable than Enigma.

"Can I telephone?"

"Better not. If all's well, I'll telephone you in a few days from a call box."

When the taxi drove away, he couldn't even see the

last of her because of the tinted glass in the rear window. He went indoors and began to pack a small bag, suitable for a prison or an escape. Pajamas, washing things, a small towel—after hesitation he added his passport. Then he sat down and began to wait. He heard one neighbor drive away and then the silence of Saturday descended. He felt as though he were the only person left alive in King's Road, except for the police at the corner. The door was pushed open and Buller came waddling in. He settled on his haunches and fixed Castle with bulging and hypnotic eyes. "Buller," Castle whispered, "Buller, what a bloody nuisance you've always been, Buller." Buller went on staring—it was the way to get a walk.

Buller was still watching him a quarter of an hour later when the telephone rang. Castle let it ring. It rang over and over, like a child crying. This could not be the signal he hoped for—no control would have remained on the line so long—it was probably some friend of Sarah's, Castle thought. It would not, in any case, be for him. He had no friends.

2

Doctor Percival sat waiting in the hall of the Reform, near the great wide staircase, which looked as though it had been built to stand the heavy weight of old Liberal statesmen, those bearded or whiskered men of perpetual integrity. Only one other member was visible when Hargreaves came in and he was small and insignificant and short-sighted—he was having difficulty in reading the ticker tape. Hargreaves said, "I know it's my turn, Emmanuel, but the Travellers is closed. I hope you don't mind my asking Daintry to join us here."

"Well, he's not the gayest of companions," Doctor Percival said. "Security trouble?"

"Yes."

"I hoped you would have a little peace after Washington."

"One doesn't expect peace for long in this job. I don't suppose I'd enjoy it anyway, or why is it that I don't retire?"

"Don't talk of retirement, John. God knows what Foreign Office type they might foist on us. What's troubling you?"

"Let me have a drink first." They moved up the staircase and took their seats at a table on the landing outside the restaurant. Hargreaves drank his Cutty Sark neat. He said, "Suppose you killed the wrong man, Emmanuel?"

Doctor Percival's eyes showed no surprise. He examined carefully the color of his dry martini, smelled it, removed with a nail the nick of lemon peel as though he were making up his own prescription.

"I'm confident I didn't," he said.

"Muller doesn't share your confidence."

"Oh, Muller! What does Muller know about it?"

"He knows nothing. But he has an intuition."

"If that's all . . ."

"You've never been in Africa, Emmanuel. You get to trust an intuition in Africa."

"Daintry will expect a great deal more than intuition. He wasn't even satisfied with the facts about Davis."

"Facts?"

"That business of the Zoo and the dentist—to take only one example. And Porton. Porton was decisive. What are you going to tell Daintry?"

263

"My secretary tried to get Castle on the phone first thing this morning. There was no reply at all."

"He's probably gone away with his family for the weekend."

"Yes. But I've had his safe opened—Muller's notes aren't there. I know what you'll say. Anyone can be careless. But I thought if Daintry went down to Berkhamsted—well, if he found nobody there, it would be an opportunity to have the house looked over discreetly, and if he's in . . . he'll be surprised to see Daintry, and if he's guilty . . . he'd be a bit on edge . . ."

"Have you told 5?"

"Yes, I've spoken to Philips. He's having Castle's phone monitored again. I hope to God nothing comes of all this. It would mean Davis was innocent."

"You shouldn't worry so much about Davis. He's no loss to the firm, John. He should never have been recruited. He was inefficient and careless and drank too much. He'd have been a problem sooner or later anyway. But if Muller should be right, Castle will be a serious headache. Aflatoxin can't be used. Everyone knows he's not a heavy drinker. It will have to be the law courts, John, unless we can think of something else. Counsel for the defense. Evidence *in camera*. How the journalists hate that. Sensational headlines. I suppose Daintry will be satisfied if no one else is. He's a great stickler for doing things the legal way."

"And here he comes at last," Sir John Hargreaves said.

Daintry came up the great staircase toward them, slowly. Perhaps he wished to test every tread in turn as though it were a circumstantial piece of evidence.

"I wish I knew how to begin."

"Why not as you did with me—a little brutally?"

"Ah, but he hasn't your thick skin, Emmanuel."

3

The hours seemed very long. Castle tried to read, but
no book could relieve the tension. Between one para-
graph and another he would be haunted by the thought
that somewhere he had left in the house something which
would incriminate him. He had looked at every book on
every shelf—there was not one he had ever used for coding: *War and Peace* was safely destroyed. From his study
he had taken every sheet of used carbon paper—however
innocent—and burned them: the list of telephone numbers on his desk contained nothing more secret than the
butcher's and the doctor's, and yet he felt certain somewhere there must be a clue he had forgotten. He remembered the two men from Special Branch searching Davis's
flat; he remembered the lines which Davis had marked
with a "c" in his father's Browning. There would be no
traces of love in this house. He and Sarah had never exchanged love letters—love letters in South Africa would
have been the proof of a crime.

He had never spent so long and solitary a day. He
wasn't hungry, though only Sam had eaten any breakfast,
but he told himself one could not tell what might happen
before night or where he would eat his next meal. He sat
down in the kitchen before a plate of cold ham, but he
had only eaten one piece before he realized it was time to
listen to the one o'clock news. He listened to the end—
even to the last item of football news because one could
never be sure—there might be an urgent postscript.

But, of course, there was nothing which in the least
concerned him. Not even a reference to young Halliday.
It was unlikely there would be; his life from now on was

totally *in camera*. For a man who had dealt for many years with what was called secret information he felt oddly out of touch. He was tempted to make again his urgent SOS, but it had been imprudent to make it even the second time from home. He had no idea where his signal rang, but those who monitored his telephone might well be able to trace the calls. The conviction he had felt the evening before that the line had been cut, that he was abandoned, grew with every hour.

He gave what was left of the ham to Buller, who rewarded him with a string of spittle on his trousers. He should long before this have taken him out, but he was unwilling to leave the four walls of the house, even to go into the garden. If the police came he wanted to be arrested in his home, and not in the open air with the neighbors' wives peering through their windows. He had a revolver upstairs in a drawer beside his bed, a revolver which he had never admitted to Davis he possessed, a quite legal revolver dating from his days in South Africa. Nearly every white man there possessed a gun. At the time he bought it he had loaded one chamber, the second chamber to prevent a rash shot, and the charge had remained undisturbed for seven years. He thought: I could use it on myself if the police broke in, but he knew very well that suicide for him was out of the question. He had promised Sarah that one day they would be together again.

He read, he put on the television, he read again. A crazy notion struck him—to catch a train to London and go to Halliday's father and ask for news. But perhaps already they were watching his house and the station. At half-past four, between the dog and the wolf, as the gray evening gathered, the telephone rang a second time and this time illogically he answered the call. He half hoped to hear Boris's voice, though he knew well enough that Boris would never take the risk of calling him at home.

The stern voice of his mother came out at him as though she were in the same room. "Is that Maurice?"

"Yes."

"I'm glad you're there. Sarah seemed to think you might have gone away."

"No, I'm still here."

"What's all this nonsense between you?"

"It's not nonsense, Mother."

"I told her she ought to leave Sam with me and go straight back."

"She's not coming, is she?" he asked with fear. A second parting seemed an impossible thing to bear.

"She refuses to go. She says you wouldn't let her in. That's absurd, of course."

"It's not absurd at all. If she came I should leave."

"What on earth has happened between you?"

"You'll know one day."

"Are you thinking of a divorce? It would be very bad for Sam."

"At present it's only a question of a separation. Just let things rest for a while, Mother."

"I don't understand. I hate things I don't understand. Sam wants to know whether you've fed Buller."

"Tell him I have."

She rang off. He wondered whether a recorder somewhere was playing over their conversation. He needed a whisky, but the bottle was empty. He went down to what had once been a coal cellar where he kept his wine and spirits. The chute for the delivery of coal had been turned into a sort of slanting window. He looked up and saw on the pavement the reflected light of a street lamp and the legs of someone who must be standing below it.

The legs were not in uniform, but of course they might belong to a plain clothes officer from Special Branch. Whoever it was had placed himself rather crudely opposite the door, but of course the object of the watcher

267

might be to frighten him into some imprudent action. Buller had followed him down the stairs; he too noticed the legs above and began to bark. He looked dangerous, sitting back on his haunches with his muzzle raised, but if the legs had been near enough, he would not have bitten them, he would have dribbled on them. As the two of them watched, the legs moved out of sight, and Buller grunted with disappointment—he had lost an opportunity of making a new friend. Castle found a bottle of J & B (it occurred to him that the color of the whisky no longer had any importance) and went upstairs with it. He thought: If I hadn't got rid of *War and Peace* I might now have the time to read some chapters for pleasure.

Again restlessness drove him to the bedroom to rummage among Sarah's things for old letters, though he couldn't imagine how any letters he had ever written her could be incriminating, but then in the hands of Special Branch perhaps the most innocent reference could be twisted to prove her guilty knowledge. He didn't trust them not to want that—there is always in such cases the ugly desire for revenge. He found nothing—when you love and you are together old letters are apt to lose their value. Someone rang the front door bell. He stood and listened and heard it ring again and then a third time. He told himself that his visitor was not to be put off by silence and it was foolish not to open the door. If the line after all hadn't been cut there might be a message, an instruction . . . Without thinking why, he drew out of the drawer by his bed the revolver and put it with its single charge in his pocket.

In the hall he still hesitated. The stained glass above the door cast lozenges of yellow, green and blue upon the floor. It occurred to him that if he carried the revolver in his hand when he opened the door the police would have the right to shoot him down in self-defense—it would be an easy solution; nothing would ever be publicly proved against a dead man. Then he reproached himself with the thought that none of his actions must be dictated by despair any more than by hope. He left the gun in his pocket and opened the door.

"Daintry," he exclaimed. He hadn't expected a face he knew.

"Can I come in?" Daintry asked in a tone of shyness.

"Of course."

Buller suddenly emerged from his retirement. "He's not dangerous," Castle said as Daintry stepped back. He caught Buller by the collar, and Buller dropped his spittle between them like a fumbling bridegroom might drop the wedding ring. "What are you doing here, Daintry?"

"I happened to be driving through and I thought I'd look you up." The excuse was so palpably untrue that Castle felt sorry for Daintry. He wasn't like one of those smooth, friendly and fatal interrogators who were bred by MI5. He was a mere security officer who could be trusted to see that rules were not broken and to check briefcases.

"Will you have a drink?"

"I'd like one." Daintry's voice was hoarse. He said— it was as though he had to find an excuse for everything— "It's a cold wet night."

"I haven't been out all day."

"You haven't?"

Castle thought: That's a bad slip if the telephone call this morning was from the office. He added, "Except to take the dog into the garden."

Daintry took the glass of whisky and looked long at it and then round the sitting room, little quick snapshots like a press photographer. You could almost hear the eyelids click. He said, "I do hope I'm not disturbing you. Your wife . . ."

"She's not here. I'm quite alone. Except of course for Buller."

"Buller?"

"The dog."

The deep silence of the house was emphasized by the two voices. They broke it alternately, uttering unimportant phrases.

"I hope I haven't drowned your whisky," Castle said. Daintry still hadn't drunk. "I wasn't thinking . . ."

"No, no. It's just as I like it." Silence dropped again like the heavy safety curtain in a theater.

Castle began with a confidence, "As a matter of fact I'm in a bit of trouble." It seemed a useful moment to establish Sarah's innocence.

"Trouble?"

"My wife has left me. With my son. She's gone to my mother's."

"You mean you've quarreled?"

"Yes."

"I'm very sorry," Daintry said. "It's awful when these things happen." He seemed to be describing a situation which was as inevitable as death. He added, "Do you know the last time we met—at my daughter's wedding? It was very kind of you to come with me to my wife's afterward. I was very glad to have you with me. But then I broke one of her owls."

"Yes. I remember."

"I don't think I even thanked you properly for coming. It was a Saturday too. Like today. She was terribly angry. My wife, I mean, about the owl."

"We had to leave suddenly because of Davis."

"Yes, poor devil." Again the safety curtain dropped as though after an old-fashioned curtain line. The last act would soon begin. It was time to go to the bar. They both drank simultaneously.

"What do you think about his death?" Castle asked.

"I don't know what to think. To tell you the truth I try not to think."

"They believe he was guilty of a leak in my section, don't they?"

"They don't confide much in a security officer. What makes you think that?"

"It's not a normal routine to have Special Branch men in to search when one of us dies."

"No, I suppose not."

"You found the death odd too?"

"Why do you say that?"

Have we reversed our roles, Castle thought, am *I* interrogating *him*?

"You said just now you tried not to think about his death."

"Did I? I don't know what I meant. Perhaps it's your whisky. You didn't exactly drown it, you know."

"Davis never leaked anything to anyone," Castle said. He had the impression Daintry was looking at his pocket where it sagged on the cushion of the chair with the weight of the gun.

"You believe that?"

"I know it."

He couldn't have said anything which damned himself more completely. Perhaps after all Daintry was not so bad an interrogator; and the shyness and confusion and self-revelations he had been displaying might really be part of a new method which would put his training as a technician in a higher class than MI5's.

"You know it?"

"Yes."

He wondered what Daintry would do now. He hadn't the power of arrest. He would have to find a telephone and consult the office. The nearest telephone was at the police station at the bottom of King's Road—he would surely not have the nerve to ask if he might use Castle's?

And had he identified the weight in the pocket? Was he afraid? I would have time after he leaves to make a run for it, Castle thought, if there was anywhere to run to; but to run without a destination, simply to delay the moment of capture, was an act of panic. He preferred to wait where he was—that would have at least a certain dignity.

"I've always doubted it," Daintry said, "to tell the truth."

"So they did confide in you?"

"Only for the security checks. I had to arrange those."

"It was a bad day for you, wasn't it, first to break that owl and then to see Davis dead on his bed?"

"I didn't like what Doctor Percival said."   .

"What was that?"

"He said, 'I hadn't expected this to happen.' "

"Yes. I remember now."

"It opened my eyes," Daintry said. "I saw what they'd been up to."

"They jumped too quickly to conclusions. They didn't properly investigate the alternatives."

"You mean yourself?"

Castle thought, I'm not going to make it that easy for them, I'm not going to confess in so many words, however effective this new technique of theirs may be. He said, "Or Watson."

"Oh yes, I'd forgotten Watson."

"Everything in our section passes through his hands. And then, of course, there's 69300 in L.M. They can't properly check his accounts. Who knows if he hasn't a bank deposit in Rhodesia or South Africa?"

"True enough," Daintry said.

"And our secretaries. It's not only our personal secretaries who may be involved. They all belong to a pool. Don't tell me that a girl doesn't go sometimes to the loo without locking up the cable she's been decoding or the report she's been typing?"

272

"I realize that. I checked the pool myself. There has always been a good deal of carelessness."

"Carelessness can begin at the top too. Davis's death may have been an example of criminal carelessness."

"If he wasn't guilty it was murder," Daintry said. "He had no chance to defend himself, to employ counsel. They were afraid of the effect a trial might have upon the Americans. Doctor Percival talked to me about boxes . . ."

"Oh yes," Castle said. "I know that *spiel*. I've heard it often myself. Well, Davis is in a box all right now."

Castle was aware that Daintry's eyes were on his pocket. Was Daintry pretending to agree with him so as to escape safely back to his car? Daintry said, "You and I are making the same mistake—jumping to conclusions. Davis may have been guilty. What makes you so certain he wasn't?"

"You have to look for motives," Castle said. He had hesitated, he had evaded, but he had been strongly tempted to reply, "Because I am the leak." He felt sure by this time that the line was cut and he could expect no help, so what was the purpose of delaying? He liked Daintry, he had liked him ever since the day of his daughter's wedding. He had become suddenly human to him over the smashed owl, in the solitude of his smashed marriage. If anyone were to reap credit for his confession he would like it to be Daintry. Why therefore not give up and go quietly, as the police often put it? He wondered if he were prolonging the game only for the sake of company, to avoid the solitude of the house and the solitude of a cell.

"I suppose the motive for Davis would have been money," Daintry said.

"Davis didn't care much about money. All he needed was enough to bet a little on the horses and treat himself to a good port. You have to examine things a bit closer than that."

"What do you mean?"

"If our section was the one suspected the leaks could only have concerned Africa."

"Why?"

"There's plenty of other information that passes through my section—that we pass on—that must be of greater interest to the Russians, but if the leak was there, don't you see, the other sections would be suspect too? So the leak can only be about our particular share of Africa."

"Yes," Daintry agreed, "I see that."

"That seems to indicate—well, if not exactly an ideology—you don't need to look necessarily for a Communist—but a strong attachment to Africa—or to Africans. I doubt if Davis had ever known an African." He paused and then added with deliberation and a certain feeling of joy in the dangerous game, "Except, of course, my wife and my child." He was putting the dot on an i, but he wasn't going to cross the t's as well. He went on, "69300 has been a long time in L.M. No one knows what friendships he's made—he has his African agents, many of them Communist."

After so many years of concealment he was beginning to enjoy this snake-and-ladder game. "Just as I had in Pretoria," he continued. He smiled. "Even C, you know, has a certain love of Africa."

"Oh, there you are joking," Daintry said.

"Of course I'm joking. I only want to show how little they had against Davis compared with others, myself or 69300—and all those secretaries about whom we know nothing."

"They were all carefully vetted."

"Of course they were. We'll have the names of all their lovers on the files, lovers anyway of that particular year, but some girls change their lovers like they change their winter clothes."

Daintry said, "You've mentioned a lot of suspects, but

274

you are so sure about Davis." He added, unhappily, "You're lucky not to be a security officer. I nearly resigned after Davis's funeral. I wish I had."

"Why didn't you?"

"What would I have done to pass the time?"

"You could have collected car numbers. I did that once."

"Why did you quarrel with your wife?" Daintry asked. "Forgive me. That's no business of mine."

"She disapproved of what I'm doing."

"You mean for the firm?"

"Not exactly."

Castle could tell the game was nearly over. Daintry had surreptitiously looked at his wrist watch. He wondered whether it was a real watch or a disguised microphone. Perhaps he thought he had come to the end of his tape. Would he ask to go to the lavatory so that he could change it?

"Have another whisky."

"No, I'd better not. I have to drive home."

Castle went with him to the hall, and Buller too. Buller was sorry to see a new friend leave.

"Thanks for the drink," Daintry said.

"Thank you for the chance to talk about a lot of things."

"Don't come out. It's a beastly night." But Castle followed him into the cold drizzle. He noticed the tail lights of a car fifty yards down the road opposite the police station.

"Is that your car?"

"No. Mine's a little way up the road. I had to walk down because I couldn't see the numbers in this rain."

"Goodnight then."

"Goodnight. I hope things go all right—I mean with your wife."

Castle stood in the slow cold rain long enough to

wave to Daintry as he passed. His car didn't stop, he noticed, at the police station but turned right and took the London road. Of course he could always stop at the King's Arms or the Swan to use the telephone, but even in that case Castle doubted whether he would have a very clear report to make. They would probably want to hear his tape before making a decision—Castle felt sure now the watch was a microphone. Of course, the railway station might already be watched and the immigration officers warned at the airports. One fact had surely emerged from Daintry's visit. Young Halliday must have begun to talk or they would never have sent Daintry to see him.

At his door he looked up and down the road. There was no apparent watcher, but the lights of the car opposite the police station still shone through the rain. It didn't look like a police car. The police—he supposed even those of the Special Branch—had to put up with British makes, and this—he couldn't be sure but it looked like a Toyota. He remembered the Toyota on the road to Ashridge. He tried to make out the color, but the rain obscured it. Red and black were indistinguishable through the drizzle which was beginning to turn to sleet. He went indoors and for the first time he dared to hope.

He took the glasses to the kitchen and washed them carefully. It was as though he were removing the fingerprints of his despair. Then he laid two more glasses in the sitting room, and for the first time he encouraged hope to grow. It was a tender plant and it needed a great deal of encouragement, but he told himself that the car was certainly a Toyota. He wouldn't let himself think how many Toyotas there were in the region but waited in patience for the bell to ring. He wondered who it was who would come and stand in Daintry's place on the threshold. It wouldn't be Boris—he was sure of that—and neither would it be young Halliday, who was only out of custody on sufferance and was probably deeply engaged now with men from the Special Branch.

He went back to the kitchen and gave Buller a plate of biscuits—perhaps it would be a long time before he would be able to eat again. The clock in the kitchen had a noisy tick which seemed to make time go more slowly. If there was really a friend in the Toyota he was taking a long time to appear.

4

Colonel Daintry pulled into the yard of the King's Arms. There was only one car in the yard, and he sat for a while at the wheel, wondering whether to telephone now and what to say if he did. He had been shaken with a secret anger during his lunch at the Reform with C and Doctor Percival. There were moments when he had wanted to push his plate of smoked trout aside and say, "I resign. I don't want to have any more to do with your bloody firm." He was tired to death of secrecy and of errors which had to be covered up and not admitted. A man came across the yard from the outside lavatory whistling a tuneless tune, buttoning his fly in the security of the dark, and went on into the bar. Daintry thought: They killed my marriage with their secrets. During the war there had been a simple cause—much simpler than the one his father knew. The Kaiser had not been a Hitler, but in the cold war they were now fighting it was possible, as in the Kaiser's war, to argue right and wrong. There was nothing clear enough in the cause to justify murder by mistake. Again he found himself in the bleak house of his childhood, crossing the hall, entering the room where his father and his mother sat hand in hand. "God knows best," his father said, remembering Jutland and Admiral Jellicoe. His mother said, "My dear, at your age, it's difficult to find another job." He turned off his lights and moved through the slow heavy rainfall into the bar. He thought: My wife has enough money, my daughter is married, I could live—somehow—on my pension.

On this cold wet night there was only one man in the bar—he was drinking a pint of bitter. He said, "Good evening, sir," as though they were well acquainted.

"Good evening. A double whisky," Daintry ordered.

"If you can call it that," the man said as the barman turned away to hold a glass below a bottle of Johnnie Walker.

"Call what?"

"The evening, I meant, sir. Though this weather's only to be expected, I suppose, in November."

"Can I use your telephone?" Daintry asked the barman.

The barman pushed the whisky across with an air of rejection. He nodded in the direction of a box. He was clearly a man of few words: he was here to listen to what customers chose to say but not to communicate himself more than was strictly necessary, until—no doubt with pleasure—he would pronounce the phrase, "Time, Gentlemen."

Daintry dialled Doctor Percival's number and while he listened to the engaged tone, he tried to rehearse the words he wished to use. "I've seen Castle . . . He's alone in the house . . . He's had a quarrel with his wife . . . There's nothing more to report . . ." He would slam down the receiver as he slammed it down now—then he went

278

back to the bar and his whisky and the man who insisted on talking.

"Uh," the barman said, "uh" and once, "That's right."

The customer turned to Daintry and included him in his conversation. "They don't even teach simple arithmetic these days. I said to my nephew—he's nine—what's four times seven, and do you think he could tell me?"

Daintry drank his whisky with his eye on the telephone box, still trying to make up his mind what words to use.

"I can see you agree with me," the man said to Daintry. "And you?" he asked the barman. "Your business would go to pot, wouldn't it, if you couldn't say what four times seven was?"

The barman wiped some spilled beer off the bar and said, "Uh."

"Now you, sir, I can guess very easily what profession you follow. Don't ask me how. It's a hunch I have. Comes from studying faces, I suppose, and human nature. That's how I came to be talking about arithmetic while you were on the telephone. That's a subject, I said to Mr. Barker here, about which the gentleman will have strong opinions. Weren't those my very words?"

"Uh," Mr. Barker said.

"I'll have another pint if you don't mind."

Mr. Barker filled his glass.

"My friends sometimes ask me for an exhibition. They even have a little bet on it now and then. He's a schoolmaster, I say, about someone in the tube, or he's a chemist, and then I inquire politely—they don't take offense when I explain to them—and nine times out of ten, I'm right. Mr. Barker has seen me at it in here, haven't you, Mr. Barker?"

"Uh."

"Now you, sir, if you'll excuse me playing my little

279

game just to amuse Mr. Barker here on a cold wet evening—you are in Government service. Am I right, sir?"

"Yes," Daintry said. He finished his whisky and put down his glass. It was time to try the telephone again.

"So we're getting warm, eh?" The customer fixed him with beady eyes. "A sort of confidential position. You know a lot more about things than the rest of us."

"I have to telephone," Daintry said.

"Just a moment, sir. I just want to show Mr. Barker . . ." He wiped a little beer from his mouth with a handkerchief and thrust his face close to Daintry's. "You deal in figures," he said. "You are in the Inland Revenue."

Daintry moved to the telephone box.

"You see," the customer said, "touchy fellow. They don't like to be recognized. An inspector probably."

This time Daintry got the ringing tone and soon he heard Doctor Percival's voice, bland and reassuring as though he had kept his bedside manner long after he had abandoned bedsides. "Yes? Doctor Percival here. Who is that?"

"Daintry."

"Good evening, my dear fellow. Any news? Where are you?"

"I'm at Berkhamsted. I've seen Castle."

"Yes. What's your impression?"

Anger took the words he meant to speak and tore them in pieces like a letter one decides not to send. "My impression is that you've murdered the wrong man."

"Not murdered," Doctor Percival said gently, "an error in the prescription. The stuff hadn't been tried before on a human being. But what makes you think that Castle . . .?"

"Because he's certain that Davis was innocent."

"He said that—in so many words?"

"Yes."

"What's he up to?"

"He's waiting."

"Waiting for what?"

"Something to happen. His wife's left him, taking the child. He says they've quarreled."

"We've already circulated a warning," Doctor Percival said, "to the airports—and the sea ports too of course. If he makes a run for it, we'll have *prima facie* evidence—but we'll still need the hard stuff."

"You didn't wait for the hard stuff with Davis."

"C insists on it this time. What are you doing now?"

"Going home."

"You asked him about Muller's notes?"

"No."

"Why?"

"It wasn't necessary."

"You've done an excellent job, Daintry. But why do you suppose he came clean like that to you?"

Daintry put the receiver down without answering and left the box. The customer said, "I was right, wasn't I? You are an inspector of the Inland Revenue."

"Yes."

"You see, Mr. Barker. I've scored again."

Colonel Daintry went slowly out to his car. For a while he sat in it with the engine running and watched the drops of rain pursue each other down the windscreen. Then he drove out of the yard and turned in the direction of Boxmoor and London and the flat in St. James's Street where yesterday's Camembert was awaiting him. He drove slowly. The November drizzle had turned into real rain and there was a hint of hail. He thought: Well, I did what they would call my duty, but though he was on the road toward home and the table where he would sit beside the Camembert to write his letter, he was in no hurry to arrive. In his mind the act of resignation had already been accomplished. He told himself he was a free man,

281

that he had no duties any longer and no obligations, but he had never felt such an extreme solitude as he felt now.

5

The bell rang. Castle had been waiting for it a long time and yet he hesitated to go to the door; it seemed to him now that he had been absurdly optimistic. By this time young Halliday would surely have talked, the Toyota was one of a thousand Toyotas, the Special Branch had probably been waiting for him to be alone, and he knew how absurdly indiscreet he had been with Daintry. A second time the bell rang and then a third; there was nothing he could do but open. He went to the door with his hand on the revolver in his pocket, but it was of no more value than a rabbit's foot. He couldn't shoot his way out of an island. Buller gave him a spurious support, growling heavily, but he knew, when the door opened, Buller would fawn on whoever was there. He couldn't see through the stained glass which ran with the rain. Even when he opened the door he saw nothing distinctly—only a hunched figure.

"It's a shocking night," a voice he recognized complained to him out of the dark.

"Mr. Halliday—I wasn't expecting you."

Castle thought: He's come to ask me to help his son, but what can I do?

"Good boy. Good boy," the almost invisible Mr. Halliday said nervously to Buller.

"Come in," Castle assured him. "He's quite harmless."

"I can see he's a very fine dog."

Mr. Halliday entered cautiously, hugging the wall, and Buller wagged what he had of a tail and dribbled.

"You can see, Mr. Halliday, he's a friend of all the world. Take off your coat. Come and have a whisky."

"I'm not much of a drinking man, but I won't say No."

"I was sorry to hear on the radio about your son. You must be very anxious."

Mr. Halliday followed Castle into the living room. He said, "He had it coming to him, sir, perhaps it will teach him a lesson. The police have been carting a lot of stuff out of his shop. The inspector showed me one or two of the things and really disgusting they were. But as I said to the inspector I don't suppose he read the stuff himself."

"I hope the police have not been bothering you?"

"Oh no. As I told you, sir, I think they feel quite sorry for me. They know I keep a very different kind of shop."

"Did you have a chance to give him my letter?"

"Ah, there, sir, I thought it wiser not. Under the circumstances. But don't you worry. I passed the message on where it truly belongs."

He raised a book which Castle had been trying to read and looked at the title.

"What on earth do you mean?"

"Well, sir, you've always been, I think, under a bit of a misunderstanding. My son never concerned himself with things in your way of business. But *they* thought it just as well—in case of trouble—that *you* believed . . ." He bent and warmed his hands in front of the gas fire, and his eyes looked up with a sly amusement. "Well, sir, things being as they are, we've got to get you out of here pretty quick."

It came as a shock to Castle to realize how little he

had been trusted even by those who had the most reason to trust.

"If you'll forgive my asking, sir, where exactly are your wife and your boy? I've orders . . ."

"This morning, when I heard the news about your son, I sent them away. To my mother. She believes we've had a quarrel."

"Ah, that's one difficulty out of the way."

Old Mr. Halliday, after warming his hands sufficiently, began to move around the room: he cast his eye over the bookshelves. He said, "I'll give as good a price for those as any other bookseller. Twenty-five pounds down—it's all you are allowed to take out of the country. I've got the notes on me. They fit my stock. All these World's Classics and Everyman's. They are not reprinted as they should be, and when they do reprint, what a price!"

"I thought," Castle said, "we were in a bit of a hurry."

"There's one thing I've learned," Mr. Halliday said, "in the last fifty years is to take things easy. Once start being hurried and you are sure to make mistakes. If you've got half an hour to spare always pretend to yourself you've got three hours. You did say something, sir, about a whisky?"

"If we can spare the time . . ." Castle poured out two glasses.

"We've got the time. I expect you have a bag packed with all the needful?"

"Yes."

"What are you going to do about the dog?"

"Leave him behind, I suppose. I hadn't thought . . . Perhaps you could take him to a vet."

"Not wise, sir. A connection between you and me—it wouldn't do—if they went searching for him. All the same we've got to keep him quiet for the next few hours. Is he a barker when he's left alone?"

"I don't know. He's not used to being alone."

"What I have in mind is the neighbors complaining. One of them could easily ring the police, and we don't want them finding an empty house."

"They'll find one soon enough anyway."

"It won't matter when you're safe abroad. It's a pity your wife didn't take the dog with her."

"She couldn't. My mother has a cat. Buller kills cats at sight."

"Yes, they're naughty ones, those boxers, where cats are concerned. I have a cat myself." Mr. Halliday pulled at Buller's ears and Buller fawned on him. "It's what I said. If you are in a hurry you forget things. Like the dog. Have you a cellar?"

"Not a soundproof one. If you mean to shut him up there."

"I notice, sir, that in your right pocket you seem to have a gun—or am I mistaken?"

"I thought if the police came . . . There's only one charge in it."

"The counsel of despair, sir?"

"I hadn't made up my mind to use it."

"I would rather you let me have it, sir. If we were stopped, at least I have a license, with all this shoplifting we have nowadays. What's his name, sir? I mean the dog."

"Buller."

"Come here, Buller, come here. There's a good dog." Buller laid his muzzle on Mr. Halliday's knee. "Good dog, Buller. Good dog. You don't want to cause any trouble, do you, not to a good master like you have." Buller wagged his stump. "They think they know when you like them," Mr. Halliday said. He scratched Buller behind the ears and Buller showed his appreciation. "Now, sir, if you wouldn't mind giving me the gun . . . Ah, you kill cats, eh . . . Ah, the wicked one."

"They'll hear the shot," Castle said.

"We'll take a little walk down to the cellar. One

285

shot—nobody pays any attention. They think it's a backfire."

"He won't go with you."

"Let's see. Come on, Buller, my lad. Come for a walk. A walk, Buller."

"You see. He won't go."

"It's time to be off, sir. You'd better come down with me. I wanted to spare you."

"I don't want to be spared."

Castle led the way down the stairs to the cellar. Buller followed him and Mr. Halliday tailed Buller.

"I wouldn't put on the light, sir, a shot and a light going out. *That* might arouse curiosity."

Castle closed what had once been the coal chute.

"Now, sir, if you'll give me the gun . . ."

"No, I'll do this." He held the gun out, pointing it at Buller, and Buller, ready for a game and probably taking the muzzle for a rubber bone, fastened his jaws around it and pulled. Castle pressed the trigger twice because of the empty chamber. He felt nausea.

"I'll have another whisky," he said, "before we go."

"You deserve one, sir. It's odd how fond one can get of a dumb animal. My cat . . ."

"I disliked Buller intensely. It's only . . . well, I've never killed anything before."

6

"It's hard driving in this rain," Mr. Halliday said, breaking a very long silence. The death of Buller had clogged their tongues.

"Where are we going? Heathrow? The immigration officers will be on the look-out by this time."

"I'm taking you to a hotel. If you open the glove compartment, sir, you'll find a key. Room 423. All you have to do is take the lift straight up. Don't go to the desk. Wait in the room until someone comes for you."

"Suppose a maid . . ."

"Hang a Don't Disturb notice on the door."

"And after that . . ."

"I wouldn't know, sir. Those were all the instructions I have."

Castle wondered how the news of Buller's death would reach Sam. He knew that he would never be forgiven. He asked, "How did you get mixed up in this?"

"Not mixed up, sir. I've been a member of the Party, on the quiet as you might say, since I was a boy. I was in the army at seventeen—volunteered. Gave my age wrong. Thought I was going to France, but it was Archangel they sent me to. I was a prisoner for four years. I saw a lot and learned a lot in those four years."

"How did they treat you?"

"It was hard, but a boy can stand a lot, and there was always someone who was friendly. I learned a bit of Russian, enough to interpret for them, and they gave me books to read when they couldn't give me food."

"Communist books?"

"Of course, sir. A missionary hands out the Bible, doesn't he?"

"So you are one of the faithful."

"It's been a lonely life, I have to admit that. You see, I could never go to meetings or walk in marches. Even my boy doesn't know. They use me when they can in little ways—like in your case, sir. I've picked up from your drop many a time. Oh, it was a happy day for me when you walked into my shop. I felt less alone."

"Have you never wavered a bit, Halliday? I mean—Stalin, Hungary, Czechoslovakia?"

"I saw enough in Russia when I was a boy—and in England too with the Depression when I came home—to inoculate me against little things like that."

"Little?"

"If you will forgive me saying so, sir, your conscience is rather selective. I could say to you—Hamburg, Dresden, Hiroshima. Didn't they shake your faith a bit in what you call democracy? Perhaps they did or you wouldn't be with me now."

"That was war."

"My people have been at war since 1917."

Castle peered into the wet night between the sweeps of the wipers. "You *are* taking me to Heathrow."

"Not exactly." Mr. Halliday laid a hand light as an autumn Ashridge leaf on Castle's knee. "Don't you worry, sir. *They* are looking after you. I envy you. You'll be seeing Moscow I shouldn't wonder."

"Have you never been there?"

"Never. The nearest I ever came to it was the prison camp near Archangel. Did you ever see *The Three Sisters*? I saw it only once, but I always remember what one of them said and I say it to myself when I can't sleep at night—'To sell the house, to make an end of everything here, and off to Moscow . . .'"

"You'd find a rather different Moscow to Chekhov's."

"There's another thing one of those sisters said, 'Happy people don't notice if it's winter or summer. If I lived in Moscow I wouldn't mind what the weather was like.' Oh well, I tell myself when I'm feeling low, Marx never knew Moscow either, and I look across Old Compton Street and I think, London is still Marx's London. Soho's Marx's Soho. This was where the *Communist Manifesto* was first printed." A lorry came suddenly out of the rain and swerved and nearly hit them and went on

288

indifferently into the night. "Shocking drivers there are," Mr. Halliday said, "they know nothing's going to hurt *them* in those juggernauts. We ought to have bigger penalties for dangerous driving. You know, sir, that's what was really wrong in Hungary and Czechoslovakia—dangerous driving. Dubcek was a dangerous driver—it's as simple as that."

"Not to me it isn't. I've never wanted to end up in Moscow."

"I suppose it will seem a bit strange—you not being one of us, but you shouldn't worry. I don't know what you've done for us, but it must be important, and they'll look after you, you can be sure of that. Why, I wouldn't be surprised if they didn't give you the Order of Lenin or put you on a postage stamp like Sorge."

"Sorge was a Communist."

"And it makes me proud to think you are on the road to Moscow in this old car of mine."

"If we drove for a century, Halliday, you wouldn't convert me."

"I wonder. After all, you've done a lot to help us."

"I've helped you over Africa, that's all."

"Exactly, sir. You are on the road. Africa's the thesis, Hegel would say. You belong to the antithesis—but you are an active part of the antithesis—you are one of those who will belong to the synthesis yet."

"That's all jargon to me. I'm no philosopher."

"A militant doesn't have to be, and you are a militant."

"Not for Communism. I'm only a casualty now."

"They'll cure you in Moscow."

"In a psychiatric ward?"

That phrase silenced Mr. Halliday. Had he found a small crack in the dialectic of Hegel, or was it the silence of pain and doubt? He would never know, for the hotel was ahead of them, the lights smudging through the rain. "Get out here," Mr. Halliday said. "I'd better not be seen." Cars passed them when they halted, in a long illuminated chain, the headlamps of one car lighting the rear lamps of another. A Boeing 707 slanted noisily down on London Airport. Mr. Halliday scrabbled in the back of the car. "There's something I've forgotten." He pulled out a plastic bag which might once have contained duty free goods. He said, "Put the things out of your case into this. They might notice you at the desk if you go to the lift carrying a suitcase."

"There's not enough room in it."

"Then leave what you can't get in."

Castle obeyed. Even after all those years of secrecy he realized that in an emergency the young recruit of Archangel was the real expert. He abandoned with reluctance his pajamas—thinking, a prison will provide them—his sweater. If I get so far, they will have to give me something warm.

Mr. Halliday said, "I have a little present. A copy of that Trollope you asked for. You won't need a second copy now. It's a long book, but there'll be a lot of waiting. There always is in war. It's called *The Way We Live Now*."

"The book recommended by your son?"

"Oh, I deceived you a little there. It's me that reads Trollope, not him. His favorite author is a man called Robbins. You must forgive me my little deception—I wanted you to think a bit better of him in spite of that shop. He's not a bad boy."

Castle shook Mr. Halliday's hand. "I'm sure he's not. I hope all goes well with him."

"Remember. Go straight to room 423, and wait."

Castle walked away toward the light of the hotel carrying the plastic bag. He felt as though he had already lost contact with everything he had known in England— Sarah and Sam were out of reach in the house of his mother which had never been his home. He thought: I was more at home in Pretoria. I had work to do there. But now there's no work left for me to do. A voice called after him through the rain, "Good luck, sir. The best of luck," and he heard the car drive away.

7

He was bewildered—when he walked through the door of the hotel he walked straight into the Caribbean. There was no rain. There were palm trees around a pool, and the sky shone with innumerable pinpoint stars; he smelled the warm stuffy wet air which he remembered from a distant holiday he had taken soon after the war: he was surrounded—that was inevitable in the Caribbean— by American voices. There was no danger of his being remarked by anyone at the long desk—they were far too busy with an influx of American passengers, just deposited from what airport, Kingston? Bridgetown? A black waiter went by carrying two rum punches toward a young couple sitting by the pool. The lift was there, beside him, waiting with open doors, and yet he hung back amazed . . . The young couple began to drink their punch through straws under the stars. He put out a hand to convince himself that there was no rain and someone close behind him said, "Why, if it isn't Maurice? What are you doing in this joint?" He stopped his hand halfway to his pocket and looked round. He was glad he no longer had his revolver.

The speaker was someone called Blit who had been his contact a few years back in the American Embassy until Blit was transferred to Mexico—perhaps because he could speak no Spanish. "Blit!" he exclaimed with false enthusiasm. It had always been that way. Blit had called him Maurice from their first meeting, but he had never got further than "Blit."

"Where are you off to?" Blit asked, but didn't wait for an answer. He had always preferred to talk about himself. "Off to New York," Blit said. "Non-arrival of incoming plane. Spending the night here. Smart idea, this joint. Just like the Virgin Islands. I'd put on my Bermuda shorts if I had them."

"I thought you were in Mexico."

"That's old history. I'm on the European desk again now. You still on darkest Africa?"

"Yes."

"You delayed here too?"

"I've got to wait around," Castle said, hoping his ambiguity would not be questioned.

"What about a Planter's Punch? They do them OK here, so I'm told."

"I'll meet you in half an hour," Castle said.

"OK. OK. By the pool then."

"By the pool."

Castle got into the lift and Blit followed him. "Going up? So am I. Which floor?"

"Fourth."

"Me too. I'll give you a free ride."

Was it possible that the Americans too might be watching him? In these circumstances it seemed unsafe to put down anything to coincidence.

"Eating here?" Blit asked.

"I'm not sure. You see, it depends . . ."

"You sure are security minded," Blit said. "Good old Maurice." They walked together down the corridor. Room 423 came first, and Castle fumbled with his key long enough to see that Blit went on without a pause to 427—

292

no, 429. Castle felt safer when his door was locked and the Don't Disturb notice was hanging outside.

The dial of the central heating stood at 75°. It was hot enough for the Caribbean. He went to the window and looked out. Below was the round bar and above the artificial sky. A stout woman with blue hair weaved her way along the edge of the pool: she must have had too many rum punches. He examined the room carefully in case it contained some hint of the future, as he had examined his own house for any hint of the past. Two double beds, an armchair, a wardrobe, a chest of drawers, a desk which was bare except for a blotting pad, a television set, a door that led to the bathroom. The lavatory seat had a strip of paper pasted across it assuring him that it was hygienic: the toothglasses were swathed in plastic. He went back into the bedroom and opened the blotting pad and learned from the printed notepaper that he was in the Starflight Hotel. A card listed the restaurants and the bars—in one restaurant there was music and dancing—it was called the Pizarro. The grill room by contrast was called the Dickens, and there was a third, self-service, which was called the Oliver Twist. "You help yourself to more." Another card informed him that there were buses every half-hour to Heathrow airport.

He discovered under the television set a refrigerator containing miniature bottles of whisky and gin and brandy, tonic water and soda, two kinds of beer and quarter bottles of champagne. He chose a J & B from habit and sat down to wait. "There'll be a lot of waiting," Mr. Halliday had said, when he gave him the Trollope, and he began to read for want of anything else to do: "Let the reader be introduced to Lady Carbury, upon whose character and doings much will depend of whatever interest these pages may have, as she sits at her writing table in her own room in her own house in Welbeck Street." He found it was not a book which could distract him from the way he lived now.

He went to the window. The black waiter passed below him, and then he saw Blit come out and gaze around. Surely half an hour couldn't possibly have gone by: he reassured himself—ten minutes. Blit would not have really missed him yet. He turned the lights out in his room, so that Blit, if he looked up, would not see him. Blit sat himself down by the circular bar: he gave his order. Yes, it was a Planter's Punch. The waiter was putting in the slice of orange and the cherry. Blit had taken off his jacket and he was wearing a shirt with short sleeves, which added to the illusion of the palm trees and the pool and the starry night. Castle watched him use the telephone in the bar and he rang a number. Was it only in Castle's imagination that Blit seemed to raise his eyes toward the window of room 423 while he talked? Reporting what? To whom?

He heard the door open behind him and the lights went on. Turning quickly, he saw an image flash across the looking-glass of the wardrobe door like someone who didn't want to be seen—the image of a small man with a black moustache wearing a dark suit carrying a black attaché case. "I was delayed by the circulation," the man said in precise but rather incorrect English.

"You've come for me?"

"Time is a little lacking for us. There is a necessity for you to catch the next autobus to the airport." He began to unpack the attaché case on the desk: first an air ticket, then a passport, a bottle which looked as if it might contain gum, a bulging plastic bag, a hairbrush and comb, a razor.

"I have with me everything I need," Castle said, catching the precise tone.

The man ignored him. He said, "You will find your

294

ticket is to Paris only. That is something I will explain to you."

"Surely they'll be watching all the planes wherever they go."

"They will be watching in particular the one to Prague which is due to leave at the same time as the one to Moscow which has been delayed due to trouble with the engines. An unusual occurrence. Perhaps Aeroflot await an important passenger. The police will be very attentive to Prague and Moscow."

"The watch will be set earlier—at the immigration desks. They won't wait at the gates."

"That will be taken care of. You must approach the desks—let me see your watch—in about fifty minutes. The bus will leave in thirty minutes. This is your passport."

"What do I do in Paris if I get that far?"

"You will be met as you leave the airport, and you will be given another ticket. You will have just time to catch another plane."

"Where to?"

"I have no idea. You will learn all that in Paris."

"Interpol will have warned the police there by this time."

"No. Interpol never act in a political case. It is against the rules."

Castle opened the passport. "Partridge," he said, "you've chosen a good name. The shooting season isn't over." Then he looked at the photograph. "But this photo will never do. It's not like me."

"That is true. But now we shall make you more like the photograph."

He carried the tools of his trade into the bathroom. Between the toothglasses he propped an enlarged photograph of the one in the passport.

"Sit on this chair, please." He began to trim Castle's eyebrows and then began on his hair—the man of the passport had a crewcut. Castle watched the scissors move in the mirror—he was surprised to see how a crewcut changed the whole face, enlarging the forehead; it seemed to change even the expression of the eyes. "You've taken ten years off my age," Castle said.

"Sit still, please."

The man then began to attach the hairs of a thin moustache—the moustache of a timid man who lacked confidence. He said, "A beard or a heavy moustache is always an object of suspicion." It was a stranger who looked back at Castle from the mirror. "There. Finished. I think it is good enough." He went to his briefcase and took from it a white rod which he telescoped into a walking stick. He said, "You are blind. An object of sympathy, Mr. Partridge. An Air France hostess has been asked to meet the autobus from the hotel and she will lead you through immigration to your plane. In Paris at Rossy when you depart from the airport you will be driven to Orly—another plane there with engine trouble. Perhaps you will no longer be Mr. Partridge, another make-up in the car, another passport. The human visage is infinitely adaptable. That is a good argument against the importance of heredity. We are born with much the same face— think of a baby—but environment changes it."

"It seems easy," Castle said, "but will it work?"

"We think it will work," the little man said as he packed his case. "Go out now, and remember to use your stick. Please do not move your eyes, move your whole head if someone speaks to you. Try to keep the eyes blank."

Without thinking Castle picked up *The Way We Live Now*.

"No, no, Mr. Partridge. A blind man is not likely to possess a book. And you must leave that sack behind."

296

"It only holds a spare shirt, a razor . . ."

"A spare shirt has the mark of a laundry."

"Won't it seem odd if I have no luggage?"

"That is not known to the immigration officer unless he asks to see your ticket."

"He probably will."

"Never mind, you are only going home. You live in Paris. The address is in your passport."

"What profession am I?"

"Retired."

"That at least is true," Castle said.

He came out of the lift and began to tap his way toward the entrance where the bus waited. As he passed the doors which led to the bar and the pool he saw Blit. Blit was looking at his watch with an air of impatience. An elderly woman took Castle's arm and said, "Are you catching the bus?"

"Yes."

"I am too. Let me help you."

He heard a voice calling after him. "Maurice!" He had to walk slowly because the woman walked slowly. "Hi! Maurice."

"I think someone's calling you," the woman said.

"A mistake."

He heard footsteps behind them. He took his arm away from the woman and turned his head as he had been instructed to do and stared blankly a little to the side of Blit. Blit looked at him with surprise. He said, "I'm sorry. I thought . . ."

The woman said, "The driver's signaling to us. We must hurry."

When they were seated together in the bus she looked through the window. She said, "You sure must be very like his friend. He's still standing there staring."

"Everybody in the world, so they say, has a double," Castle replied.

297

Part Six

Chapter I

1

She had turned to look back through the window of the taxi and seen nothing through the smoke-gray glass: it was as though Maurice had deliberately drowned himself, without so much as a cry, in the waters of a steely lake. She was robbed, without hope of recovery, of the only sight and sound she wanted, and she resented all that was charitably thrust on her like the poor substitute a butcher offers for the good cut which he has kept for a better customer.

Lunch in the house among the laurels was an ordeal. Her mother-in-law had a guest she couldn't cancel—a clergyman with the unattractive name of Bottomley—she called him Ezra—who had come home from a mission field in Africa. Sarah felt like an exhibit at one of the lantern lectures he probably gave. Mrs. Castle didn't introduce her. She simply said, "This is Sarah," as though she had come out of an orphanage, as indeed she had. Mr. Bottomley was unbearably kind to Sam and treated her like a member of his colored congregation with calculated interest. Tinker Bell, who had fled at the first sight of them, fearing Buller, was now too friendly and scratched at her skirts.

"Tell me what it's really like in a place like Soweto," Mr. Bottomley said. "My field, you know, was Rhodesia. The English papers exaggerated there too. We are not as black as we are painted," he added and then blushed at his mistake. Mrs. Castle poured him another glass of water. "I mean," he said, "can you bring up a little fellow properly there?" and his bright gaze picked Sam out like a spotlight in a night club.

"How would Sarah know, Ezra?" Mrs. Castle said. She explained with reluctance, "Sarah is my daughter-in-law."

Mr. Bottomley's blush increased. "Ah, then you are over here on a visit?" he asked.

"Sarah is living with me," Mrs. Castle said. "For the time being. My son has never lived in Soweto. He was in the Embassy."

"It must be nice for the boy," Mr. Bottomley said, "to come and see Granny."

Sarah thought: Is this what life is to be from now on?

After Mr. Bottomley had departed Mrs. Castle told her that they must have a serious conversation. "I rang up Maurice," she said, "he was in a most unreasonable mood." She turned to Sam. "Go into the garden, dear, and have a game."

"It's raining," Sam said.

302

"I'd forgotten, dear. Go upstairs and play with Tinker Bell."

"I'll go upstairs," Sam said, "but I won't play with your cat. Buller is my friend. He knows what to do with cats."

When they were alone Mrs. Castle said, "Maurice told me if you returned home he would leave the house. What *have* you done, Sarah?"

"I'd rather not talk about it. Maurice told me to come here, so I've come."

"Which of you is—well, what they call the guilty party?"

"Does there always have to be a guilty party?"

"I'm going to ring him again."

"I can't stop you, but it won't be any use."

Mrs. Castle dialed the number, and Sarah prayed to God whom she didn't believe in that she might at least hear Maurice's voice, but "There's no reply," Mrs. Castle said.

"He's probably at the office."

"On a Saturday afternoon?"

"Times are irregular in his job."

"I thought the Foreign Office was better organized."

Sarah waited until the evening, after she had put Sam to bed, then walked down into the town. She went to the Crown and gave herself a J & B. She made it a double in memory of Maurice and then went to the telephone box. She knew Maurice had told her not to contact him. If he were still at home, and his telephone was tapped, he would have to pretend anger, continue a quarrel which didn't exist, but at least she would know he was there in the house and not in a police cell or on his way across a Europe she had never seen. She let the telephone ring a long time before she put down the receiver—she was aware she was making it easy for Them to trace the call, but she didn't care. If They came to see her at least she would have news of him. She left the box and drank her J & B at the bar and walked back to Mrs. Castle's house. Mrs. Castle said, "Sam's been calling for you." She went upstairs.

"What is it, Sam?"

"Do you think Buller's all right?"

"Of course he's all right. What could be wrong?"

"I had a dream."

"What did you dream?"

"I don't remember. Buller will miss me. I wish we could have him here."

"We can't. You know that. Sooner or later he'd be sure to kill Tinker Bell."

"I wouldn't mind that."

She went reluctantly downstairs. Mrs. Castle was watching television.

"Anything interesting on the news?" Sarah asked.

"I seldom listen to the news," Mrs. Castle said. "I like to read the news in *The Times*." But next morning there was no news which could possibly interest her in the Sunday papers. Sunday—he never had to work on Sunday. At midday she went back to the Crown and rang the house again, and again she held on for a long while— he might be in the garden with Buller, but at last she had to give up even that hope. She comforted herself with the thought that he *had* escaped, but then she reminded herself that They had the power to hold him—wasn't it for three days?—without a charge.

Mrs. Castle had lunch—a joint of roast beef—served very punctually at one. "Shall we listen to the news?" Sarah asked.

"Don't play with your napkin ring, Sam dear," Mrs. Castle said. "Just take out your napkin and put the ring down by your plate." Sarah found Radio 3. Mrs. Castle said, "There's never news worth listening to on Sundays," and she was right, of course.

Never had a Sunday passed more slowly. The rain stopped and the feeble sun tried to find a gap through the clouds. Sarah took Sam for a walk across what was called—she didn't know why—a forest. There were no trees—only low bushes and scrub (one area had been cleared for a golf course). Sam said, "I like Ashridge better," and a little later, "A walk's not a walk without Buller." Sarah wondered: How long will life be like this? They cut across a corner of the golf course to get home and a golfer who had obviously had too good a lunch shouted to them to get off the fairway. When Sarah didn't respond quickly enough he called, "Hi! You! I'm talking to you, Topsy!" Sarah seemed to remember that Topsy had been a black girl in some book the Methodists had given her to read when she was a child.

That night Mrs. Castle said, "It's time we had a serious talk, dear."

"What about?"

"You ask me what about? Really, Sarah! About you and my grandson of course—and Maurice. Neither of you will tell me what this quarrel is all about. Have you or has Maurice grounds for a divorce?"

"Perhaps. Desertion counts, doesn't it?"

"Who has deserted whom? To come to your mother-in-law's house is hardly desertion. And Maurice—he hasn't deserted you if he's still at home."

"He isn't."

"Then where is he?"

"I don't know, I don't know, Mrs. Castle. Can't you just wait awhile and not talk?"

"This is *my* home, Sarah. It would be convenient to know just how long you plan to stay. Sam should be at school. There's a law about that."

"I promise if you'll just let us stay for a week . . ."

"I'm not driving you away, dear, I'm trying to get you to behave like an adult person. I think you should see a lawyer and talk to him if you won't talk to me. I can telephone Mr. Bury tomorrow. He looks after my will."

"Just give me a week, Mrs. Castle." (There had been a time when Mrs. Castle had suggested Sarah should call her "mother," but she had been obviously relieved when Sarah continued to call her Mrs. Castle.)

On Monday morning she took Sam into the town and left him in a toyshop while she went to the Crown. There she telephoned to the office—it was a senseless thing to do, for if Maurice were still in London at liberty he would surely have telephoned her. In South Africa, long ago when she had worked for him, she would never have been so imprudent, but in this peaceful country town which had never known a racial riot or a midnight knock at the door the thought of danger seemed too fantastic to be true. She asked to speak to Mr. Castle's secretary, and, when a woman's voice answered, she said, "Is that Cynthia?" (she knew her by that name, though they had never met or talked to each other). There was a long pause— a pause long enough for someone to be asked to listen in —but she wouldn't believe it in this small place of retired people as she watched two lorry drivers finish their bitter. Then the dry thin voice said, "Cynthia isn't in today."

"When will she be in?"

"I'm afraid I can't say."

"Mr. Castle then?"

"Who is that speaking, please?"

She thought: I was nearly betraying Maurice and she put down the receiver. She felt she had betrayed her own past too—the secret meetings, the coded messages, the care which Maurice had taken in Johannesburg to instruct her and to keep them both out of the reach of BOSS. And, after all that, Muller was here in England—he had sat at table with her.

When she got back to the house she noticed a strange car in the laurel drive, and Mrs. Castle met her in the hall. She said, "There's someone to see you, Sarah. I've put him in the study."

"Who is it?"

Mrs. Castle lowered her voice and said in a tone of distaste, "I think it's a policeman."

The man had a large fair moustache which he stroked nervously. He was definitely not the kind of policeman that Sarah had known in her youth and she wondered how Mrs. Castle had detected his profession—she would have taken him for a small tradesman who had dealt with local families over the years. He looked just as snug and friendly as Doctor Castle's study, which had been left unchanged after the doctor's death: the pipe rack still over the desk, the Chinese bowl for ashes, the swivel armchair in which the stranger had been too ill at ease to seat himself. He stood by the bookcase partly blocking from view with his burly form the scarlet volumes of the Loeb classics and the green leather *Encyclopaedia Britannica*, 11th edition. He asked, "Mrs. Castle?" and she nearly answered, "No. That's my mother-in-law," so much a stranger did she feel in this house.

"Yes," she said. "Why?"

"I'm Inspector Butler."

"Yes?"

"I've had a telephone call from London. They asked me to come and have a word with you—that is, if you were here."

"Why?"

"They thought perhaps you could tell us how to get in touch with your husband."

She felt an immense relief—he wasn't after all in prison—till the thought came to her that this might be a

307

trap—even the kindness and shyness and patent honesty of Inspector Butler might be a trap, the kind of trap BOSS were likely to lay. But this wasn't the country of BOSS. She said, "No. I can't. I don't know. Why?"

"Well, Mrs. Castle, it's partly to do with a dog."

"Buller?" she exclaimed.

"Well . . . if that's his name."

"It is his name. Please tell me what this is all about."

"You have a house in King's Road, Berkhamsted. That's right, isn't it?"

"Yes." She gave a laugh of relief. "Has Buller been killing a cat again? But I'm here. I'm innocent. You must see my husband, not me."

"We've tried to, Mrs. Castle, but we can't reach him. His office says he's not been in. He seems to have gone away and left the dog, although . . ."

"Was it a very valuable cat?"

"It's not a cat we are concerned about, Mrs. Castle. The neighbors complained about the noise—a sort of whining—and someone telephoned the police station. You see there've been burglars recently at Boxmoor. Well, the police sent a man to see—and he found a scullery window open—he didn't have to break any glass . . . and the dog . . ."

"He wasn't bitten? I've never known Buller bite a *person*."

"The poor dog couldn't do any biting: not in the state he was in. He'd been shot. Whoever had done it made a messy job. I'm afraid, Mrs. Castle, they had to finish your dog off."

"Oh God, what will Sam say?"

"Sam?"

"My son. He loved Buller."

"I'm fond of animals myself." The two-minute silence that followed seemed very long, like the two-minute tribute to the dead on Armistice Day. "I'm sorry to bring bad news," Inspector Butler said at last and the wheeled and pedestrian traffic of life started up again.

"I'm wondering what I'll say to Sam."

"Tell him the dog was run over and killed right away."

"Yes. I suppose that's best. I don't like lying to a child."

"There are white lies and black lies," Inspector Butler said. She wondered whether the lies he would force her to tell were black or white. She looked at the thick fair moustache and into the kindly eyes and wondered what on earth had made him into a policeman. It would be a little like lying to a child.

"Won't you sit down, Inspector?"

"You sit down, Mrs. Castle, if you'll excuse me. I've been sitting down all the morning." He looked at the row of pipes in the pipe rack with concentration: it might have been a valuable picture of which, as a connoisseur, he could appreciate the value.

"Thank you for coming yourself and not just telling me over the telephone."

"Well, Mrs. Castle, I had to come because there are some other questions. The police at Berkhamsted think there may have been a robbery. There was a scullery window open and the burglar may have shot the dog. Nothing seems to have been disturbed, but only you or your husband can tell, and they don't seem able to get in touch with your husband. Did he have any enemies? There's no sign of a struggle, but then there wouldn't be if the other man had a gun."

"I don't know of any enemies."

"A neighbor said he had an idea he worked in the Foreign Office. This morning they had quite a difficulty trying to find the right department and then it seemed they hadn't seen him since Friday. He should have been in, they said. When did you last see him, Mrs. Castle?"

"Saturday morning."

"You came here Saturday?"

"Yes."

"He stayed behind?"

"Yes. You see, we had decided to separate. For good."

"A quarrel?"

"A decision, Inspector. We've been married for seven years. You don't flare up after seven years."

"Did he own a revolver, Mrs. Castle?"

"Not that I know of. It's possible."

"Was he very upset—by the decision?"

"We were neither of us happy if that's what you mean."

"Would you be willing to go to Berkhamsted and look at the house?"

"I don't want to, but I suppose they could make me, couldn't they?"

"There's no question of making you. But, you see, they can't rule out a robbery . . . There might have been something valuable which they couldn't tell was missing. A piece of jewelry?"

"I've never gone in for jewelry. We weren't rich people, Inspector."

"Or a picture?"

"No."

"Then it makes us wonder if he might have done something foolish or rash. If he was unhappy and it was his gun." He picked up the Chinese bowl and examined the pattern, then turned to examine her in turn. She realized those kindly eyes were not after all the eyes of a child. "You don't seem worried about *that* possibility, Mrs. Castle."

"I'm not. It isn't the kind of thing he'd do."

"Yes, yes. Of course you know him better than anyone else and I'm sure you're right. So you'll let us know at once, won't you, if he gets in touch with you, I mean?"

"Of course."

"Under strain people sometimes do odd things. Even lose their memory." He took a last long look at the pipe rack as if he were unwilling to part from it. "I'll ring up Berkhamsted, Mrs. Castle. I hope you won't have to be troubled. And I'll let you know if I get any news."

When they were at the door she asked him, "How did you know I was here?"

"Neighbors with children get to know more than you'd allow for, Mrs. Castle."

She watched him until he was safely in his car and then she went back into the house. She thought: I shan't tell Sam yet. Let him get used to life without Buller first. The other Mrs. Castle, the true Mrs. Castle, met her outside the sitting room. She said, "Lunch is getting cold. It *was* a policeman, wasn't it?"

"Yes,"

"What did he want?"

"Maurice's address."

"Why?"

"How would I know?"

"Did you give it to him?"

"He's not at home. How should I know where he is?"

"I hope that man won't come back."

"I wouldn't be surprised if he does."

2

But the days passed without Inspector Butler and without news. She made no further telephone calls to London. There was no point to it now. Once when she telephoned to the butcher on her mother-in-law's behalf to order some lamb cutlets she had an impression the line was tapped. It was probably imagination. Monitoring had become too fine an art for an amateur to detect. Under pressure from Mrs. Castle she had an interview at the local school and she arranged for Sam to attend it; from this meeting she returned in deep depression—it was as though she had just finalized the new life, stamped it like a document with a wax seal, nothing would ever change it now. On her way home she called at the greengrocer's, at the library, at the druggist's—Mrs. Castle had provided her with a list: a tin of green peas, a novel of Georgette Heyer's, a bottle of aspirin for the headaches of which Sarah felt sure that she and Sam were the cause. For no reason she could put a name to she thought of the great gray-green pyramids of earth which surrounded Johannesburg—even Muller had spoken of their color in the evening, and she felt closer to Muller, the enemy, the racialist, than to Mrs. Castle. She would have exchanged this Sussex town with its liberal inhabitants who treated her with such kindly courtesy even for Soweto. Courtesy could be a barrier more than a blow. It wasn't courtesy one wanted to live with—it was love. She loved Maurice, she loved the smell of the dust and degradation of her country—now she was without Maurice and without a country. Perhaps that was why she welcomed even the voice of an enemy on the telephone. She knew at once it was an enemy's voice although it introduced itself as "a friend and colleague of your husband."

"I hope I'm not ringing you up at a bad time, Mrs. Castle."

"No, but I didn't hear your name."

"Doctor Percival."

It was vaguely familiar. "Yes. I think Maurice has spoken of you."

"We had a memorable night out once in London."

"Oh yes, I remember now. With Davis."

"Yes. Poor Davis." There was a pause. "I was wondering, Mrs. Castle, if we could have a talk."

"We are having one now, aren't we?"

"Well, a rather closer talk than a telephone provides."

"I'm a long way from London."

"We could send a car for you if it would help."

"We," she thought, "we." It was a mistake on his part to speak like an organization. "We" and "they" were uncomfortable terms. They were a warning, they put you on your guard.

The voice said, "I thought if you were free for lunch one day this week . . ."

"I don't know if I can manage."

"I wanted to talk to you about your husband."

"Yes. I guessed that."

"We are all rather anxious about Maurice." She felt a quick elation. "We" hadn't got him in some secret spot unknown to Inspector Butler. He was well away—all Europe was between them. It was as though she too, as well as Maurice, had escaped—she was already on her way home, that home which was where Maurice was. She had to be very careful just the same, as in the old days in Johannesburg. She said, "Maurice doesn't concern me any more. We've separated."

"All the same, I expect, you'd like some news of him?"

So they *had* news. It was as when Carson told her, "He's safe in L.M. waiting for you. Now we've only got to get you there." If he were free, they would soon be together. She realized she was smiling at the telephone—thank God, they hadn't yet invented a visual telephone, but all the same she wiped the smile off her face. She said, "I'm afraid I don't much care where he is. Couldn't you write? I have a child to look after."

"Well no, Mrs. Castle, there are things one can't write. If we could send a car for you tomorrow . . ."

"Tomorrow's impossible."

"Thursday then."

She hesitated as long as she dared. "Well . . ."

"We could send a car for you at eleven."

"But I don't need a car. There's a good train at 11:15."

"Well then, if you could meet me at a restaurant, Brummell's—close to Victoria."

"What street?"

"There you have me. Walton—Wilton—never mind, any taxi driver will know Brummell's. It's very quiet there," he added soothingly as though he were recommending with professional knowledge a good nursing home, and Sarah had a quick mental picture of the speaker—a very self-assured Wimpole Street type, with a dangling eyeglass which he would only use when it came to writing out the prescription, the signal, like royalty rising, that it was time for the patient to depart.

"Until Thursday," he said. She didn't even reply. She put down the receiver and went to find Mrs. Castle—she was late again for lunch and she didn't care. She was humming a tune of praise the Methodist missionaries had taught her, and Mrs. Castle looked at her in astonishment. "What's the matter? Is something wrong? Was it that policeman again?"

"No. It was only a doctor. A friend of Maurice. Nothing's wrong. Would you mind just for once if I went up to town on Thursday? I'll take Sam to school in the morning and he can find his own way back."

"I don't *mind*, of course, but I was thinking of having Mr. Bottomley for lunch again."

"Oh, Sam and Mr. Bottomley will get on very well together."

"Will you go and see a solicitor when you are in town?"

"I might." A half-lie was a small price to pay in return for her new happiness.

314

"Where will you have lunch?"

"Oh, I expect I'll pick up a sandwich somewhere."

"It's such a pity you've chosen Thursday. I've ordered a joint. However"—Mrs. Castle sought for a silver lining—"if you had lunch at Harrods there are one or two things you could bring me back."

She lay in bed that night unable to sleep. It was as if she had procured a calendar and could now begin to mark off the days of term. The man she had spoken to was an enemy—she was convinced of that—but he wasn't the Security Police, he wasn't BOSS, she wouldn't lose her teeth or the sight of an eye in Brummell's: she had no reason to fear.

3

Nonetheless she felt a little let down when she identified him where he waited for her at the end of a long glassy glittering room at Brummell's. He wasn't, after all, a Wimpole Street specialist: he was more like an old-fashioned family doctor with his silver-rimmed spectacles and a small rounded paunch which seemed to prop itself on the edge of the table when he rose to greet her. He was holding an outsize menu in his hand in place of a prescription. He said, "I'm so glad you had the courage to come here."

"Why courage?"

"Well, this is one of the places the Irish like to bomb. They've thrown a small one already, but unlike the blitz their bombs are quite liable to hit the same place twice."

He gave her a menu to read: a whole page was given up she saw to what were called Starters. The whole menu, which bore the title Bill of Fare above a portrait, seemed almost as long as Mrs. Castle's local telephone directory. Doctor Percival said helpfully, "I'd advise you against the smoked trout—it's always a bit dry here."

"I haven't got much appetite."

"Let's wake it up, then, while we consider matters. A glass of sherry?"

"I'd rather have a whisky if you don't mind." When asked to choose, she said, "J & B."

"You order for me," she implored Doctor Percival. The sooner all these preliminaries were over, the sooner she would have the news she waited for with a hunger she hadn't got for food. While he made his decision she looked around her. There was a dubious and glossy portrait on the wall labeled George Bryan Brummell—it was the same portrait as on the menu—and the furnishing was in impeccable and tiring good taste—you felt no possible expense had been spared and no criticism would be sanctioned: the few customers were all men and they all looked alike as though they had come out of the chorus of an old-fashioned musical comedy: black hair, neither too long nor too short, dark suits and waistcoats. Their tables were set discreetly apart and the two tables nearest to Doctor Percival's were empty—she wondered whether this was by design or chance. She noticed for the first time how all the windows were wired.

"In a place like this," Doctor Percival said, "it's best to go English and I would suggest the Lancashire hot pot."

"Anything you say." But for a long time he said nothing except some words to the waiter about the wine. At last he turned his attention and his silver-rimmed glasses toward her with a long sigh. "Well, the hard work's done. It's up to them now," and he took a sip of his sherry. "You

must have been having a very anxious time, Mrs. Castle."
He put out a hand and touched her arm as though he
really were her family doctor.

"Anxious?"

"Not knowing from day to day . . ."

"If you mean Maurice . . ."

"We were all very fond of Maurice."

"You speak as though he were dead. In the past
tense."

"I didn't mean to. Of course we are still fond of him—
but he's taken a different road and I'm afraid a very dangerous one. We all hope you won't get involved."

"How can I? We're separated."

"Oh yes, yes. It was the obvious thing to do. It would
have been a little conspicuous to have gone away together. I don't think Immigration would have been quite
so foolish as all that. You are a very attractive woman and
then your color . . ." He said, "Of course we know he
hasn't telephoned you at home, but there are so many
ways of sending messages—a public telephone box, an intermediary—we couldn't monitor all his friends, even if
we knew them all." He pushed aside his sherry and made
room for the hot pot. She began to feel more at ease now
that the subject was laid plainly there on the table before
them—like the hot pot. She said, "You think I'm a traitor
too?"

"Oh, in the firm, you know, we don't use a word like
traitor. That's for the newspapers. You are African—I
don't say *South* African—and so is your child. Maurice
must have been a good deal influenced by that. Let's
say—he chose a different loyalty." He took a taste of the
hot pot. "Be careful."

"Careful?"

"I mean the carrots are very hot." If this was really an
interrogation it was a very different method to that prac-

317

ticed by the Security Police in Johannesburg or Pretoria. "My dear," he said, "what do you intend to do—when he *does* communicate?"

She gave up caution. As long as she was cautious she would learn nothing. She said, "I shall do what he tells me to do."

Doctor Percival said, "I'm so glad you've said that. It means we can be frank with each other. Of course we know, and I expect you know, that he's arrived safely in Moscow."

"Thank God."

"Well, I'm not sure about God, but you can certainly thank the KGB. (One mustn't be dogmatic—they may be on the same side, of course.) I imagine that sooner or later he'll ask you to join him there."

"And I'll go."

"With your child?"

"Of course."

Doctor Percival plunged again into his hot pot. He was obviously a man who enjoyed his food. She became more reckless in her relief at knowing that Maurice was safe. She said, "You can't stop me going."

"Oh, don't be so sure of that. You know, at the office we have quite a file on you. You were very friendly in South Africa with a man called Carson. A Communist agent."

"Of course I was. I was helping Maurice—for your service, though I didn't know it then. He told me it was for a book on apartheid he was writing."

"And Maurice perhaps was even then helping Carson. And Maurice is now in Moscow. It's not strictly speaking our business, of course, but MI5 might well feel you ought to be investigated—in depth. If you'll let an old man advise you—an old man who was a friend of Maurice . . ."

A memory flashed into her mind of a shambling figure in a teddy-bear coat playing hide-and-seek with Sam among the wintry trees. "And of Davis," she said, "you were a friend of Davis too, weren't you?"

A spoonful of gravy was stopped on the way to Doctor Percival's mouth.

"Yes. Poor Davis. It was a sad death for a man still young."

"I don't drink port," Sarah said.

"My dear girl, how irrelevant can you be? Let's wait to decide about port until we get to the cheese—they have excellent Wensleydale. All I was going to say was do be reasonable. Stay quietly in the country with your mother-in-law and your child . . ."

"Maurice's child."

"Perhaps."

"What do you mean, perhaps?"

"You've met this man Cornelius Muller, a rather unsympathetic type from BOSS. And what a name! He's under the impression that the real father—my dear, you must forgive a little plain speaking—I don't want you to make the sort of mistake Maurice has made—"

"You aren't being very plain."

"Muller believes that the father was one of your own people."

"Oh, I know the one he means—even if it was true he's dead."

"He isn't dead."

"Of course he's dead. He was killed in a riot."

"Did you see his body?"

"No, but . . ."

"Muller says he's safely under lock and key. He's a lifer—so Muller says."

"I don't believe it."

"Muller says this fellow is prepared to claim paternity."

"Muller's lying."

319

"Yes, yes. That's quite possible. The man may well be a stooge. I haven't been into the legal aspects yet myself, but I doubt if he could prove anything in our courts. Is the child on your passport?"

"No."

"Has he a passport?"

"No."

"Then you'd have to apply for a passport to take him out of this country. That means a lot of bureaucratic rigmarole. The passport people can sometimes be very, very slow."

"What bastards you are. You killed Carson. You killed Davis. And now . . ."

"Carson died of pneumonia. Poor Davis—that was cirrhosis."

"Muller says it was pneumonia. You say it was cirrhosis, and now you are threatening me and Sam."

"Not threatening, my dear, advising."

"Your advice . . ."

She had to break off. The waiter had come to clear their plates. Doctor Percival's was clean enough, but most of her portion had remained uneaten.

"What about an old English apple pie with cloves and a bit of cheese?" Doctor Percival asked, leaning seductively forward and speaking in a low voice as though he were naming the price he was prepared to pay for certain favors.

"No. Nothing. I don't want any more."

"Oh dear, the bill then," Doctor Percival told the waiter with disappointment, and when the waiter had gone he reproached her, "Mrs. Castle, you mustn't get angry. There's nothing personal in all this. If you get angry you are sure to make the wrong decision. It's just an affair of boxes," he began to elaborate, and then broke off as though for once he was finding that metaphor inapplicable.

320

"Sam is *my* child and I shall take him wherever I want. To Moscow, to Timbuctoo, to . . ."

"You can't take Sam until he has a passport, and I'm anxious to keep MI5 from taking any preventive action against you. If they learned you were applying for a passport . . . and they would learn . . ."

She walked out, she walked out on everything, leaving Doctor Percival to wait behind for the bill. If she had stayed a moment longer she wasn't sure that she could have trusted herself with the knife which remained by her plate for the cheese. She had once seen a white man just as well fed as Doctor Percival stabbed in a public garden in Johannesburg. It had looked such a very easy thing to do. From the door she looked back at him. The wire grill over the window behind made him appear to be sitting at a desk in a police station. Obviously he had followed her with his eyes, and now he raised an index finger and shook it gently to and fro in her direction. It could be taken for an admonition or a warning. She didn't care which.

Chapter II

1

From the window on the twelfth floor of the great gray building Castle could see the red star over the University. There was a certain beauty in the view as there is in all cities at night. Only the daylight was drab. They had made it clear to him, particularly Ivan, who had met his plane in Prague and accompanied him to a debriefing in some place near Irkutsk with an unpronounceable name, that he was extraordinarily lucky in his apartment. It had belonged, both rooms of it with a kitchen and a private shower, to a comrade recently dead who had nearly succeeded before his death in furnishing it completely. An empty apartment as a rule contained only a stove—everything else even to the toilet had to be bought. That was not easy and wasted a great deal of time and energy. Castle wondered sometimes if that was why the comrade had died, worn out by his long hunt for the green wicker armchair, the brown sofa hard as a board, without cushions, the table which looked as though it had been stained a nearly even color by the application of gravy. The television set, the latest black and white model, was a gift of the government. Ivan had carefully explained that when they first visited the apartment. In his manner he hinted his personal doubt whether it had been truly earned. Ivan seemed to Castle no more likable here than he had been in London. Perhaps he resented his recall and blamed it on Castle.

The most valuable object in the apartment seemed to be the telephone. It was covered with dust and disconnected, but all the same it had a symbolic value. One day, perhaps soon, it could be put to use. He would speak through it to Sarah—to hear her voice meant everything to him, whatever comedy they would have to play for the listeners, and there certainly would be listeners. To hear her would make the long wait bearable. Once he broached the matter to Ivan. He had noticed Ivan preferred to talk out of doors even on the coldest day, and as it was Ivan's job to show him around the city he took an opportunity outside the great GUM department store (a place where he felt almost at home because it reminded him of photographs he had seen of the Crystal Palace). He asked, "Is it possible, do you think, to have my telephone connected?" They had gone to GUM to find Castle a fur-lined overcoat—the temperature was twenty-three degrees.

"I'll ask," Ivan said, "but for the moment I suppose they want to keep you under wrappers."

"Is that a long process?"

"It was in the case of Bellamy, but you're not such

323

an important case. We can't get much publicity out of you."

"Who's Bellamy?"

"You must remember Bellamy. A most important man in your British Council. In West Berlin. That was always a cover, wasn't it, like the Peace Corps?"

Castle didn't bother to deny it—it was none of his business.

"Oh yes, I think I remember now." It had happened at the time of his greatest anxiety, while he waited for news of Sarah in Lourenço Marques, and he couldn't recall the details of Bellamy's defection. Why did one defect from the British Council and what value or harm would such a defection have to anyone? He asked, "Is he still alive?" It all seemed such a long time ago.

"Why not?"

"What does he do?"

"He lives on our gratitude." Ivan added, "As you do. Oh, we invented a job for him. He advises our publications division. He has a *dacha* in the country. It's a better life than he would have had at home with a pension. I suppose they will do the same for you."

"Reading books in a *dacha* in the country?"

"Yes."

"Are there many of us—I mean living like that on your gratitude?"

"I know at least six. There was Cruickshank and Bates—you'll remember them—they were from your service. You'll run into them I expect in the Aragvi, our Georgian restaurant—they say the wine's good there—I can't afford it—and you will see them at the Bolshoi, when they take the wrappers off."

They passed the Lenin Library—"You'll find them there too." He added with venom, "Reading the English papers."

Ivan had found him a large stout middle-aged woman

324

as a daily who would also help him to learn a little Russian. She gave a Russian name to everything in the flat, pointing a blunt finger at everything in turn, and she was very fussy about pronunciation. Although she was several years younger than Castle she treated him as though he were a child, with an admonitory sternness which slowly melted into a sort of maternal affection as he became more house-trained. When Ivan was otherwise occupied she would enlarge the scope of her lessons, taking him with her in search of food at the Central Market and down into the Metro. (She wrote figures on a scrap of paper to explain the prices and the fares.) After a while she began to show him photographs of her family—her husband a young man in uniform, taken somewhere in a public park with a cardboard outline of the Kremlin behind his head. He wore his uniform in an untidy way (you could see he wasn't used to it), and he smiled at the camera with a look of great tenderness—perhaps she had been standing behind the photographer. He had been killed, she conveyed to him, at Stalingrad. In return he produced for her a snapshot of Sarah and Sam which he hadn't confessed to Mr. Halliday that he had secreted in his shoe. She showed surprise that they were black, and for a little while afterward her manner to him seemed more distant—she was not so much shocked as lost, he had broken her sense of order. In that she resembled his mother. After a few days all was well again, but during those few days he felt an exile inside his exile and his longing for Sarah was intensified.

He had been in Moscow now for two weeks, and he had bought with the money Ivan had given him a few extras for the flat. He had even found school editions in English of Shakespeare's plays, two novels of Dickens, *Oliver Twist* and *Hard Times, Tom Jones* and *Robinson Crusoe*. The snow was ankle deep in the side streets and he had less and less inclination to go sightseeing with

Ivan or even on an educational tour with Anna—she was called Anna. In the evening he would warm some soup and sit huddled near the stove, with the dusty disconnected telephone at his elbow, and read *Robinson Crusoe*. Sometimes he could hear Crusoe speaking, as though on a tape recorder, with his own voice: "I drew up the state of my affairs in writing; not so much to leave them to any that were to come after me, for I was like to have but few heirs, as to deliver my thoughts from daily poring upon them, and afflicting my mind."

Crusoe divided the comforts and miseries of his situation into Good and Evil and under the heading Evil he wrote: "I have no soul to speak to, or relieve me." Under the opposing Good he counted "so many necessary things" which he had obtained from the wreck "as will either supply my wants, or enable me to supply myself even as long as I live." Well, he had the green wicker armchair, the gravy-stained table, the uncomfortable sofa, and the stove which warmed him now. They would have been sufficient if Sarah had been there—she was used to far worse conditions and he remembered some of the grim rooms in which they had been forced to meet and make love in dubious hotels without a color bar in the poorer quarters of Johannesburg. He remembered one room in particular without furniture of any kind where they had been happy enough on the floor. Next day when Ivan made his snide references to "gratitude" he broke furiously out: "You call this gratitude."

"Not so many people who live alone possess a kitchen and shower all to themselves . . . and two rooms."

"I'm not complaining of that. But they promised me I wouldn't be alone. They promised me that my wife and child would follow."

The intensity of his anger disquieted Ivan. Ivan said, "It takes time."

"I don't even have any work. I'm a man on the dole. Is that your bloody socialism?"

"Quiet, quiet," Ivan said. "Wait awhile. When they take the wrappers off . . ."

Castle nearly struck Ivan and he saw that Ivan knew it. Ivan mumbled something and backed away down the cement stairs.

2

Was it perhaps a microphone that conveyed this scene to a higher authority or had Ivan reported it? Castle would never know, but all the same his anger had worked the trick. It had swept away the wrappers, swept away, as he realized later, even Ivan. Just as when Ivan was removed from London because they must have decided he had the wrong temperament to be the right control for Castle, so now he put in only one more appearance—a rather subdued appearance—and then disappeared forever. Perhaps they had a pool of controls, just as in London there had been a pool of secretaries, and Ivan had sunk back into the pool. No one in this sort of service was ever likely to be sacked, for fear of revelations.

Ivan made his swan song as an interpreter in a building not far from the Lubianka prison, which he had pointed proudly out to Castle on one of their walks. Castle asked him that morning where they were going and he answered evasively, "They have decided on your work."

The room where they waited was lined with books in

ugly economy bindings. Castle read the names of Stalin, Lenin, Marx in Russian script—it pleased him to think he was beginning to make out the script. There was a big desk with a luxurious leather blotting pad and a nine-teenth-century bronze of a man on horseback too large and heavy to use as a paperweight—it could only be there for decorative purposes. From a doorway behind the desk emerged a stout elderly man with a shock of gray hair and an old-fashioned moustache yellowed by cigarette smoke. He was followed by a young man dressed very correctly who carried a file. He was like an acolyte attending a priest of his faith, and in spite of the heavy moustache there *was* something priestly about the old man, about his kindly smile and the hand he extended like a blessing. A lot of conversation—questions and answers—went on among the three of them, and then Ivan took the floor as translator. He said, "The comrade wants you to know how highly your work has been appreciated. He wants you to understand that the very importance of your work has pre-sented us with problems which had to be solved at a high level. That is why you have been kept apart during these two weeks. The comrade is anxious that you should not think it was through any lack of trust. It was hoped that your presence here would only become known to the Western Press at the right moment."

Castle said, "They must know I am here by now. Where else would I be?" Ivan translated and the old man replied, and the young acolyte smiled at the reply with his eyes cast down.

"The comrade says, 'Knowing is not the same as pub-lishing.' The Press can only publish when you are offi-cially here. The censorship would see to that. A press conference is going to be arranged very soon and then we will let you know what you should say to the journalists. Perhaps we will rehearse it all a little first."

"Tell the comrade," Castle said, "that I want to earn my keep here."

"The comrade says you have earned it many times over already."

"In that case I expect him to keep the promise they made me in London."

"What was that?"

"I was told my wife and son would follow me here. Tell him, Ivan, that I'm damned lonely. Tell him I want the use of my telephone. I want to telephone my wife, that's all, not the British Embassy or a journalist. If the wrappers are off, then let me speak to her."

The translation took a lot of time. A translation, he knew, always turned out longer than the original text, but this was inordinately longer. Even the acolyte seemed to be adding more than a sentence or two. The important comrade hardly bothered to speak—he continued to look as benign as a bishop.

Ivan turned back to Castle at last. He had a sour expression which the others couldn't see. He said, "They are very anxious to have your cooperation in the publishing section which deals with Africa." He nodded in the direction of the acolyte, who permitted himself an encouraging smile which might have been a plaster cast of his superior's. "The comrade says he would like you to act as their chief adviser on African literature. He says there are a great number of African novelists and they would like to choose the most valuable for translation, and of course the best of the novelists (selected by you) would be invited to pay us a visit by the Writer's Union. This is a very important position and they are happy to offer it to you."

The old man made a gesture with his hand toward the bookshelves as though he were inviting Stalin, Lenin and Marx—yes, and there was Engels too—to welcome the novelists whom he would pick for them.

329

Castle said, "They haven't answered me. I want my wife and son here with me. They promised that. Boris promised it."

Ivan said, "I do not want to translate what you are saying. All that business concerns quite a different department. It would be a big mistake to confuse matters. They are offering you . . ."

"Tell him I won't discuss anything until I've spoken to my wife."

Ivan shrugged his shoulders and spoke. This time the translation was no longer than the text—an abrupt angry sentence. It was the commentary by the old comrade which took up all the space, like the footnotes of an over-edited book. To show the finality of his decision Castle turned away and looked out of the window into a narrow ditch of a street between walls of concrete of which he couldn't see the top through the snow which poured down into the ditch as though from some huge inexhaustible bucket up above. This was not the snow he remembered from childhood and associated with snowballs and fairy stories and games with toboggans. This was a merciless, interminable, annihilating snow, a snow in which one could expect the world to end.

Ivan said angrily, "We will go away now."

"What do they say?"

"I do not understand the way they are treating you. I know from London the sort of rubbish you sent us. Come away." The old comrade held out a courteous hand: the young one looked a bit perturbed. Outside the silence of the snow-drowned street was so extreme that Castle hesitated to break it. The two of them walked rapidly like secret enemies who are seeking the right spot to settle their differences in a final fashion. At last, when he could bear the uncertainty no longer, Castle said, "Well, what was the result of all that talk?"

Ivan said, "They told me that I was handling you

wrongly. Just the same as they told me when they brought me back from London. 'More psychology is needed, comrade, more psychology.' I would be much better off if I was a traitor like you." Luck brought them a taxi and in it he leaped into a wounded silence. (Castle had already noticed that one never talked in a taxi.) In the doorway of the apartment block Ivan gave grudgingly the information Castle demanded.

"Oh, the job will wait for you. You have nothing to fear. The comrade is very sympathetic. He will speak to others about your telephone and your wife. He begs you—begs, that was the word he used himself—to be patient a little longer. You will have news, he says, very soon. He understands—understands, mark you—your anxiety. *I* do not understand a thing. My psychology is obviously bad."

He left Castle standing in the entry and strode away into the snow and was lost to Castle's eyes forever.

3

The next night, while Castle was reading *Robinson Crusoe* by the stove, someone knocked at his door (the bell was out of order). A sense of distrust had grown in him through so many years that he called out automatically before he opened, "Who is it?"

"The name is Bellamy," a high-pitched voice answered, and Castle unlocked the door. A small gray man in a gray fur coat and a gray astrakhan hat entered with an air of shyness and timidity. He was like a comedian playing a mouse in a pantomime and expecting the applause of little hands. He said, "I live so near here, so I thought I'd take up my courage and call." He looked at the book in Castle's hand. "Oh dear, I've interrupted your reading."

"Only *Robinson Crusoe*. I've plenty of time for that."

"Ah ha, the great Daniel. He was one of us."

"One of us?"

"Well, Defoe perhaps was more an MI5 type." He peeled off gray fur gloves and warmed himself at the stove and looked around. He said, "I can see you're still at the bare stage. We've all passed through it. I never knew where to find things myself till Cruickshank showed me. And then later, well, I showed Bates. You haven't met them yet?"

"No."

"I wonder they haven't called. You've been unwrapped, and I hear you're having a press conference any day now."

"How do you know?"

"From a Russian friend," Bellamy said with a little nervous giggle. He produced a half bottle of whisky from the depths of his fur coat. "A little *cadeau*," he said, "for the new member."

"It's very kind of you. Do sit down. The chair is more comfortable than the sofa."

"I'll unwrap myself first if I may. Unwrap—it's a good expression." The unwrapping took some time—there were a lot of buttons. When he was settled in the green wicker chair he giggled again. "How is *your* Russian friend?"

"Not very friendly."

"Get rid of him then. Have no nonsense. They *want* us to be happy."

"How do I get rid of him?"

"You just show them that he's not your type. An indiscreet word to be caught by one of those little gadgets

332

we are probably talking into now. Do you know, when I came here first, they entrusted me to—you'll never guess—to a middle-aged lady from the Union of Writers? That was because I had been British Council, I suppose. Well, I soon learned how to deal with *that* situation. Whenever Cruickshank and I were together I used to refer to her scornfully as 'my governess' and she didn't last very long. She was gone before Bates arrived and—it's very wrong of me to laugh—Bates married her."

"I don't understand how it was—I mean why it was they wanted you here. I was out of England when it all happened. I didn't see the newspaper reports."

"My dear, the newspapers—they were quite awful. They *grilled* me. I read them in the Lenin Library afterward. You would really have thought I was a sort of Mata Hari."

"But what value were you to them—in the British Council?"

"Well, you see I had a German friend and it seems he was running a lot of agents in the East. It never occurred to him that little me was watching him and making my notes—then the silly boy went and got seduced by a quite awful woman. He deserved to be punished. He was safe enough, I would never have done anything to endanger *him,* but his agents . . . of course he guessed who had given him away. Well, I admit I didn't make it difficult for him to guess. But I had to get away very quickly because he went to the Embassy about me. How glad I was when I put Checkpoint Charlie behind me."

"And you are happy here?"

"Yes, I am. Happiness always seems to me a matter of persons not of places, and I have a very nice friend. It's against the law, of course, but they do make exceptions in the service, and he's an officer in the KGB. Of course, poor boy, he has to be unfaithful sometimes in the course of duty, but that's quite different from my German

333

friend—it isn't *love*. We even have a little laugh about it sometimes. If you're lonely, he knows a lot of girls . . ."

"I'm not lonely. As long as my books last."

"I'll show you a little place where you can pick up English language paperbacks under the counter."

It was midnight before they had finished the half bottle of whisky and then Bellamy took his leave. He spent a long time getting back into his furs, and he chattered all the while. "You must meet Cruickshank one day—I'll tell him I've seen you—and Bates too, of course, but that means meeting Mrs. Union-of-Writers Bates." He warmed his hands well before pulling on his gloves. He had an air of being quite at home, although "I was a bit unhappy at first," he admitted. "I felt rather lost until I had my friend—like in that chorus of Swinburne's, 'the foreign faces, the tongueless vigil and'—how does it go?—'all the pain.' I used to lecture on Swinburne—an underrated poet." At the door he said, "You must come out and see my *dacha* when the spring comes . . ."

4

Castle found that after a few days he even missed Ivan. He missed having someone to dislike—he couldn't in justice dislike Anna, who seemed to realize that now he was more alone than ever. She stayed a little longer in the morning and pressed even more Russian names on his attention with her pointing finger. She became even more exigent too over his pronunciation: she began to add verbs to his vocabulary, beginning with the word for

334

"run," when she made motions of running, raising her elbows and each knee. She must have been receiving wages from some source for he paid her none; indeed the little store of rubles Ivan had given him on his arrival had been much diminished.

It was a painful part of his isolation that he earned nothing. He began even to long for a desk at which he could sit and study lists of African writers—they might take his mind for a little from what had happened to Sarah. Why hadn't she followed him with Sam? What were they doing to fulfill their promise?

At nine thirty-two one evening he came to the end of Robinson Crusoe's ordeal—in noting the time he was behaving a little like Crusoe. "And thus I left the island, the nineteenth of December, and I found by the ship's account, in the year 1686, after I had been upon it eight and twenty years, two months and nineteen days . . ." He went to the window: the snow for the moment was not falling and he could see clearly the red star over the University. Even at that hour women were at work sweeping the snow: from above they looked like enormous turtles. Somebody was ringing at the door—let him, he wouldn't open, it was probably only Bellamy or perhaps someone even more unwelcome, the unknown Cruickshank or the unknown Bates—but surely, he remembered, the bell was out of order. He turned and stared at the telephone with amazement. It was the telephone which was ringing.

He lifted the receiver and a voice spoke to him in Russian. He couldn't understand a word. There was nothing more—only the high-pitched dialing sound—but he kept the receiver to his ear, stupidly waiting. Perhaps the operator had told him to hold on. Or had he told him— "Replace the receiver. We will ring you back"? Perhaps a call was coming from England. Unwillingly he put the receiver back and sat on beside the telephone waiting for it to ring again. He had been "unwrapped" and now it

335

seemed he had been "connected." He would have been "in touch" if only he had been able to learn the right phrases from Anna—he didn't even know how to ring the operator. There was no telephone book in the flat—he had checked that two weeks ago.

But the operator must have been telling him something. At any moment he was sure the telephone would call to him. He fell asleep beside it and dreamt, as he had not dreamt for a dozen years, of his first wife. In his dream they quarreled as they had never done in life.

Anna found him in the morning asleep in the green wicker chair. When she woke him he said to her, "Anna, the telephone's connected," and because she didn't understand, he waved toward it and said "Ting-a-ling-a-ling," and they both laughed with pleasure at the absurdity of such a childish sound in the mouth of an elderly man. He took out the photograph of Sarah and pointed at the telephone and she nodded her head and smiled to encourage him, and he thought, she'll get on with Sarah, she will show her where to shop, she will teach her Russian words, she will like Sam.

5

When later that day the telephone rang he felt certain it would be Sarah—someone in London must have conveyed the number to her, perhaps Boris. His mouth was dry when he answered and he could hardly bring out the words "Who is that?"

"Boris."

"Where are you?"

"Here in Moscow."

"Have you seen Sarah?"

"I have talked to her."

"Is she all right?"

"Yes, yes, she is all right."

"And Sam?"

"He is all right too."

"When will they be here?"

"That is what I want to speak to you about. Stay in, please. Do not go out. I am coming to the apartment now."

"But when will I see them?"

"That is something we have to discuss. There are difficulties."

"What difficulties?"

"Wait till I see you."

He couldn't stay still: he picked up a book and put it down; he went into the kitchen, where Anna was making soup. She said, "Ting-a-ling-a-ling," but it wasn't funny any more. He walked back to the window—snow again. When the knock came on the door he felt that hours had passed.

Boris held out a duty-free plastic sack. He said, "Sarah told me to get you J & B. One bottle from her and one from Sam."

Castle said, "What are the difficulties?"

"Give me time to get my coat off."

"Did you really see her?"

"I spoke to her on the telephone. At a call box. She's in the country with your mother."

"I know."

"I would have looked a little conspicuous visiting her there."

"Then how do you know she's well?"

"She told me so."

"Did she sound well?"

"Yes, yes, Maurice. I am sure . . ."

"What are the difficulties? You got *me* out."

"That was a very simple affair. A false passport, the blind man dodge, and that little trouble we arranged at the immigration while you were led through by the Air France hostess. A man rather like you. Bound for Prague. His passport wasn't quite in order . . ."

"You haven't told me what difficulties."

"We always assumed, when you were safely here, they couldn't stop Sarah joining you."

"They can't."

"Sam has no passport. You should have put him on his mother's. Apparently it *can* take a lot of time to arrange. And another thing—your people have hinted that if Sarah tries to leave she can be arrested for complicity. She was a friend of Carson, she was your agent in Johannesburg . . . My dear Maurice, things are not simple at all, I'm afraid."

"You promised."

"I know we promised. In good faith. It might still be possible to smuggle her out if she left the child behind, but she says she won't do that. He's not happy at school. He's not happy with your mother."

The duty free plastic bag waited on the table. There was always whisky—the medicine against despair. Castle said, "Why did you fetch me out? I wasn't in immediate danger. I thought I was, but you must have known . . ."

"You sent the emergency signal. We answered it."

Castle tore the plastic, opened the whisky, the label J & B hurt him like a sad memory. He poured out two large measures. "I have no soda."

"Never mind."

Castle said, "Take the chair. The sofa's as hard as a school bench." He took a drink. Even the flavor of J & B hurt him. If only Boris had brought him a different whisky—Haig, White Horse, Vat 69, Grant's—he recited to himself the names of the whiskies which meant nothing to him, to keep his mind blank and his despair at bay until the J & B began to work—Johnnie Walker, Queen Anne, Teacher's. Boris misunderstood his silence. He said, "You do not have to worry about microphones. Here in Moscow, you might say we are safe at the center of the cyclone." He added, "It was very important for us to get you out."

"Why? Muller's notes were safe with old Halliday."

"You have never been given the real picture, have you? Those bits of economic information you sent us had no value in themselves at all."

"Then why . . .?"

"I know I am not very clear. I am not used to whisky. Let me try to explain. Your people imagined they had an agent in place, here in Moscow. But it was we who had planted him on them. What you gave us he passed back to them. Your reports authenticated him in the eyes of your service, they could check them, and all the time he was passing them other information which we wanted them to believe. That was the real value of your reports. A nice piece of deception. But then came the Muller affair and Uncle Remus. We decided the best way to counter Uncle Remus was publicity—we couldn't do that and leave you in London. You had to be our source—you brought Muller's notes with you."

"They'll know I brought news of the leak too."

"Exactly. We couldn't carry on a game like that much longer. Their agent in Moscow will disappear into a great silence. Perhaps in a few months rumors will come to your people of a secret trial. It will make them all the more certain that all the information he gave them was true."

"I thought I was only helping Sarah's people."

"You were doing much more than that. And tomorrow you meet the Press."

339

"Suppose I refuse to talk unless you bring Sarah . . ."

"We'll do without you, but you couldn't expect us then to solve the Sarah problem. We are grateful to you, Maurice, but gratitude like love needs to be renewed daily or it's liable to die away."

"You are talking as Ivan used to talk."

"No, not like Ivan. I am your friend. I want to stay your friend. One needs a friend badly to make a new life in a new country."

Now the offer of friendship had the sound of a menace or a warning. The night in Watford came back to him when he searched in vain for the shabby tutorial flat with the Berlitz picture on the wall. It seemed to him that all his life after he joined the service in his twenties he had been unable to speak. Like a Trappist he had chosen the profession of silence, and now he recognized too late that it had been a mistaken vocation.

"Take another drink, Maurice. Things are not so bad. You just have to be patient, that's all."

Castle took the drink.

Chapter III

1

The doctor confirmed Sarah's fears for Sam, but it was Mrs. Castle who had been the first to recognize the nature of his cough. The old don't need medical training—they seem to accumulate diagnoses through a lifetime of experience instead of through six years of intensive training. The doctor was no more than a kind of legal requirement—to put his signature at the end of *her* prescription. He was a young man who treated Mrs. Castle with great respect as though she were an eminent specialist from whom he could learn a lot. He asked Sarah, "Do you have much whooping cough—I mean at home?" By home he obviously meant to indicate Africa.

"I don't know. Is it dangerous?" she asked.

"Not dangerous." He added, "But a rather long quarantine"—a sentence which was not reassuring. Without Maurice it proved more difficult to disguise her anxiety because it wasn't shared. Mrs. Castle was quite calm—if a little irritated at the break in routine. If there had not been that stupid quarrel, she obviously thought, Sam could have had his sickness well away in Berkhamsted, and she could have conveyed the necessary advice over the telephone. She left the two of them, throwing a kiss in Sam's direction with an old leaflike hand, and went downstairs to watch the television.

"Can't I be ill at home?" Sam asked.

"No. You must stay in."

"I wish Buller were here to talk to." He missed Buller more than Maurice.

"Shall I read to you?"

"Yes, please."

"Then you must go to sleep."

She had packed a few books at random in the hurry of departure, among them what Sam always called the Garden book. He liked it a great deal better than she did—her memories of childhood contained no garden: the hard light had struck off roofs of corrugated iron onto a playground of baked clay. Even with the Methodists there had been no grass. She opened the book. The television voice muttered on below in the sitting room. It couldn't be mistaken even at a distance for a living voice—it was a voice like a tin of sardines. Packaged.

Before she even opened the book Sam was already asleep with one arm flung out of the bed, as his habit was, for Buller to lick. She thought: Oh yes, I love him, of course I love him, but he's like the handcuffs of the Security Police around my wrists. It would be weeks before she was released, and even then . . . She was back at Brummell's staring down the glittering restaurant papered

342

with expense accounts to where Doctor Percival raised his warning finger. She thought: Could they even have arranged this?

She closed the door softly and went downstairs. The tinned voice had been cut off and Mrs. Castle stood waiting for her at the bottom of the stairs.

"I missed the news," Sarah said. "He wanted me to read to him, but he's asleep now." Mrs. Castle glared past her as though at a horror only she could see.

"Maurice is in Moscow," Mrs. Castle said.

"Yes. I know."

"There he was on the screen with a lot of journalists. Justifying himself. He had the nerve, the effrontery . . . Was that why you quarreled with him? Oh, you did right to leave him."

"That wasn't the reason," Sarah said. "We only pretended to quarrel. He didn't want me involved."

"Were you involved?"

"No."

"Thank God for that. I wouldn't want to turn you out of the house with the child ill."

"Would you have turned Maurice out if you had known?"

"No. I'd have kept him just long enough to call the police." She turned and walked back into the sitting room—she walked all the way across it until she stumbled against the television set like a blind woman. She was as good as blind, Sarah saw—her eyes were closed. She put a hand on Mrs. Castle's arm.

"Sit down. It's been a shock."

Mrs. Castle opened her eyes. Sarah had expected to see them wet with tears, but they were dry, dry and merciless. "Maurice is a traitor," Mrs. Castle said.

"Try to understand, Mrs. Castle. It's my fault. Not Maurice's."

"You said you were not involved."

343

"He was trying to help my people. If he hadn't loved me and Sam . . . It was the price he paid to save us. You can't imagine here in England the kind of horrors he saved us from."

"A traitor!"

She lost control at the reiteration. "All right—a traitor then. A traitor to whom? To Muller and his friends? To the Security Police?"

"I have no idea who Muller is. He's a traitor to his country."

"Oh, his country," she said in despair at all the easy clichés which go to form a judgment. "He said once I was his country—and Sam."

"I'm glad his father's dead."

It was yet another cliché. In a crisis perhaps it is old clichés one clings to, like a child to a parent.

"Perhaps his father would have understood better than you."

It was a senseless quarrel like the one she had that last evening with Maurice. She said, "I'm sorry. I didn't mean to say that." She was ready to surrender anything for a little peace. "I'll leave as soon as Sam is better."

"Where to?"

"To Moscow. If they'll let me."

"You won't take Sam. Sam is my grandson. I'm his guardian," Mrs. Castle said.

"Only if Maurice and I are dead."

"Sam is a British subject. I'll have him made a Ward in Chancery. I'll see my lawyer tomorrow."

Sarah hadn't the faintest notion what a Ward in Chancery was. It was, she supposed, one more obstacle which even the voice that had spoken to her over the telephone of a public call box had not taken into account. The voice had apologized: the voice claimed, just as Doctor Percival had done, to be a friend of Maurice, but she trusted it more, even with its caution and its ambiguity and its trace of something foreign in the tone.

The voice apologized for the fact that she was not already on the way to join her husband. It could be arranged almost at once if she would go alone—the child made it almost impossible for her to pass unscrutinized, however effective any passport they arranged might seem to be.

She had told him in the flat voice of despair, "I can't leave Sam alone," and the voice assured her that "in time," a way would be found for Sam. If she would trust him . . . The man began to give guarded indications of how and when they could meet, just some hand-luggage—a warm coat—everything she lacked could be bought at the other end—but "No," she said. "No. I can't go without Sam" and she dropped the receiver. Now there was his sickness and there was the mysterious phrase which haunted her all the way to the bedroom, "a Ward in Chancery." It sounded like a room in a hospital. Could a child be forced into a hospital as he could be forced into a school?

2

There was nobody to ask. In all England she knew no one except Mrs. Castle, the butcher, the greengrocer, the librarian, the school-mistress—and of course Mr. Bottomley, who had been constantly cropping up, on the doorstep, in the High Street, even on the telephone. He had lived so long on his African mission that perhaps he felt really at home only with her. He was very kind and very inquisitive and he dropped little pious platitudes. She wondered what he would say if she asked him for help to escape from England.

On the morning after the press conference Doctor Percival telephoned for what seemed an odd reason. Apparently some money was due to Maurice and they wanted the number of his bank account so that they might pay it in: they seemed to be scrupulously honest in small things, though she wondered afterward if they were afraid that money difficulties might drive her to some desperate course. It might be a sort of bribe to keep her in place. Doctor Percival said to her, still in the family doctor voice, "I'm so glad you are being sensible, my dear. Go on being sensible," rather as he might have advised "Go on with the antibiotics."

And then at seven in the evening when Sam was asleep and Mrs. Castle was in her room, "tidying" as she called it, for dinner, the telephone rang. It was a likely hour for Mr. Bottomley, but it was Maurice. The line was so clear that he might have been speaking from the next room. She said with astonishment, "Maurice, where are you?"

"You know where I am. I love you, Sarah."

"I love you, Maurice."

He explained, "We must talk quickly, one never knows when they may cut the line. How's Sam?"

"Not well. Nothing serious."

"Boris said he was well."

"I didn't tell him. It was only one more difficulty. There are an awful lot of difficulties."

"Yes. I know. Give Sam my love."

"Of course I will."

"We needn't go on pretending any more. They'll always be listening."

There was a pause. She thought he had gone away or that the line had been cut. Then he said, "I miss you terribly, Sarah."

"Oh, so do I. So do I, but I can't leave Sam behind."

"Of course you can't. I can understand that."

She said on an impulse she immediately regretted, "When he's a little older . . ." It sounded like the promise of a distant future when they would both be old. "Be patient."

"Yes—Boris says the same. I'll be patient. How's Mother?"

"I'd rather not talk about *her*. Talk about us. Tell me how you are."

"Oh, everyone is very kind. They have given me a sort of job. They are grateful to me. For a lot more than I ever intended to do." He said something she didn't understand because of a crackle on the line—something about a fountain pen and a bun which had a bar of chocolate in it. "My mother wasn't far wrong."

She asked, "Have you friends?"

"Oh yes, I'm not alone, don't worry, Sarah. There's an Englishman who used to be in the British Council. He's invited me to his *dacha* in the country when the spring comes. When the spring comes," he repeated in a voice which she hardly recognized—it was the voice of an old man who couldn't count with certainty on any spring to come.

She said, "Maurice, Maurice, please go on hoping," but in the long unbroken silence which followed she realized that the line to Moscow was dead.